The Research Data

Book II

Sarah Fawcett

To my husband Rob
I lost my jobs and you're still sticking around!
It's not about the money, money, money.
Thank you for letting me do my thing.
Ain't about the uh cha-ching cha-ching.
I'm one lucky woman.
Forget about the price tag.

Acknowledgements

To my amazing friend, lil Sarah, who never ceases to amaze me. Through tears and laughter, I will always treasure our friendship. Everything's all right when we get together.

To Sarah T, whose advice is always golden, support is unfailing and being the type of friend who is there, even when I don't see you.

To Monique, for being my cheerleader when I was supposed to be yours. Thanks for making me get off my butt. You'll never know how much I needed it.

To my dear friend, Cathrine Marshall and her beautiful spirit for the yoga assistance. She was always my favourite yogi.

To S.J. for the solid guidance about cop lingo, laws and lawbreakers.

The Research Data
Book II

1.

I could never understand how some people take long showers. You get in. You do your thing. You get out. Why waste precious time and water? I'm only doing it now to kill time, hoping that Jack won't be patient enough to wait for me. At first, I linger with anxiety, but then, I actually begin to enjoy the indulgence.

Facing the shower head, I look down and slowly rotate my head from side to side, so that the pulse of the spray hits my neck. I turn the handle to increase the heat and close my eyes, feeling the water run down my back. I brace the walls, to enjoy the soothing warmth and I can feel the stress leaving my body.

Jack was so adamant about staying and comforting me. It had made me so angry. I clench my teeth together and adjust my stance. Can't he trust that I'll be all right? I sigh deeply and try to relax again. When he had his warm, strong arms around me, it made me feel so safe…so comforted… But I don't need him to help me!

My eyes flash open and I slap at the faucet, turning it off. Enough! I towel off quickly and use my hand to clear the steamed up mirror, staring at myself. What now?

Would Jack still be downstairs anyway? There's no way any man would have that much patience. I'm relieved with that thought, but I feel guilty. I told him straight out that I wanted him to leave and I was pretty harsh about it. I could've given the guy a break for rescuing me. He did go out of his way to follow me to Windsor and risked his life fighting Mr. Baker. I barely gave him any credit for his heroism. Why did I have to be so nasty and self-absorbed?

Is that the door closing? I pull the towel tightly around me and sit carefully on the edge of my bed, trying to hear anything coming from downstairs. There's nothing. I'll just lie back and stay here a few minutes to make sure that Jack's gone.

For a short while, I stare at the cracks on my ceiling, inspect my nail beds and pause to look at my bare ring finger. I frown. I'll never get my wedding ring back. That's one thing Mr. Baker took from me that I'll always remember with anger. I'm sure the traumatic memories and nightmares will ease up and eventually disappear, but I'll never forget Mr. Baker's pure spite or even, selfishness, for stealing my ring. It'll replay in my mind endlessly and I won't ever forgive myself for letting it all happen.

When I can't lie down any longer, I pull on some tights and a hoodie and tiptoe down the stairs. From the bottom step, I see that the dirty dishes are away, the pizza box is out of sight, and the money I left Jack for the pizza remains on the counter. Jerk. He was supposed to take the money. But he's gone. The only memory of him is the folded up blankets on the couch.

My insides start to twist and ache. I caress the blankets and stare out the living room window. I wanted to be alone. That's what I told Jack. Now I am, so why aren't I happy? What is it that I'm feeling? What is this ache? Is it loneliness? I have that fluttery feeling in my chest, too. The same feeling I get when I'm trying to be somewhere on time. Is that anxiousness? Or stress? Why am I in such turmoil? I knock the blankets onto the ground and stuff my hands into my sweatshirt pocket.

In the kitchen, I plug in the kettle for tea. I'm still full from the waffles that Jack made me for breakfast, so I don't know if I can even drink a cup of tea, but it's the only thing that may bring me comfort. Sometimes, it's just the process of making it and the smell of the tea leaves that soothes me, even if I don't drink the tea. I don't know what else to do.

The kettle starts making noises, preparing to boil and I fondle my new house keys that were left on the counter. I gave Jack such a hard time and he was only trying to help, but I don't need anyone to baby me and make decisions for me. I could've called a locksmith. I have connections too! And Jack didn't need to sleepover. He's not my babysitter. I would've been fine on my own. I toss the keys across the counter.

The kettle clicks off and I pour the boiling water over the tea bags in my aunt's teapot. I place the teapot and my mug on a tray, and move into the living room. Jack even placed the television remote back in the basket on the coffee table. I pick it up, turn on the television and cuddle under one of the blankets that Jack used. It smells like him.

At 10:00 a.m., the majority of channels are broadcasting talk shows or news. I flip through more channels and find a romantic comedy that I've seen before, but decide it's worth viewing again, since there's nothing else on. I settle in with my tea and watch the last half of the movie.

The plot involves a beautiful woman, who is in love with a man, who is hard to get, so she enlists a male friend to help her woo him. The man she likes is a womanizer and treats her badly. Of course, the male

6

friend is gorgeous, with a great job and a good head on his shoulders. Like a true fairy tale ending, the male friend and the woman fall in love. I know the movie, but I still can't help crying at the ending. When he says 'I love you' to the woman, I'm a mess of tears.

The final kiss at the end, reminds me of Steve. The actors are making out in bleachers, watching a basketball game and I remember when Steve and I kissed in some bleachers, during the men's basketball finals in university. The movie is mocking me. I'm already at my worst. I've been through hell and back, and now I have to be reminded of my failed marriage?

I shut off the television and shuffle to my office, with the blanket still around me. I use the corner of the blanket to wipe away my tears. I need to get my mind in a better place. Logic. Intellect. I need to use my brain.

A pile of unread psychology journals lie on my desk and I sit down to search through them to find an article about traumatic experiences. I easily find one. I mean, that's the extent of my job, right? If there was no trauma, I wouldn't be employed.

Now, I have to help myself. I sit in my yellow, leather chair and start reading. *Following a traumatic event, people react in different ways, experiencing a wide-range of physical and emotional reactions. There is no 'right' or 'wrong way to think, feel, or respond to trauma, so don't judge your own reactions or those of other people.*

This is no news to me. I feel anger, irritability, guilt, self-blame, hopelessness, fear, anxiety, withdrawal from others… I check 'yes' to everything.

Many people feel a lot of guilt or shame about a traumatic experience because we're often told that we should just get over difficult experiences. Others may feel embarrassed talking with others. Some people even feel like it's somehow their own fault. Trauma is hurtful. If you experience problems in your life related to trauma, it's important to take your feelings seriously and talk to a health care professional.

I'm angry that the article undermines how I want to handle myself. I understand and know it would be easier if I turned to someone for support, but I'm not ready to talk about it yet. I know I shouldn't isolate myself and ignore the situation. It's in the hundreds of books I've read and it's what I've learned throughout school, but I'm above this. I *am* a psychologist. I can easily analyze my own needs and if I need help, I'll talk to someone. I make that promise to myself.

I put the journal down, but a title catches my eye: *The Psychology of Kidnapping and Abducting.* I open up to the article and begin to read.

Strong emotion and mental defect also play a large part in the overall number of kidnappings. The kidnapping of a child by a non-custodial parent is usually based upon emotional turmoil created when the kidnapper feels that he/she is losing the child. Non-custodial parent kidnappings also occur out of spite or revenge.

I'm not as educated about this topic, but I do know that this profile fits Mr. Baker. He lost custody of Connie and felt he needed to take her away from everyone. He was desperate. I wonder if he had a pre-existing mental defect. An anti-social personality or drug use could've really heightened his aggression. Oh! The flask! Maybe he's an alcoholic!

The article lists tips about how to avoid being kidnapped, which in my situation, wouldn't have helped. The first tip states to keep a full tank of gas, so that one doesn't end up at the side of the road and thus, get abducted. First of all, I was abducted in my office, not at the side of the road. And secondly, it didn't matter how big or small my gas tank was, Mr. Baker had it covered.

Another tip is to own a GPS-aware mobile phone, so that one's whereabouts could be tracked. Again, it doesn't help. Mr. Baker made me leave my phone in my office.

Finally, the article states guidelines about fighting off your attacker. *Fight your abductor and make as much of a commotion for as long as you are able. An attacker may give up if the attacker feels he might be hurt or caught during the process. The longer you can drag out the instance of being abducted, the better your odds become of avoiding the eventuality of the attacker's success.*

I feel like I've been slapped in the face. I didn't do anything and I let it happen. I didn't fight or make any noise. The article makes complete sense. How could I have been so stupid? I throw the journal onto the floor. I should've done something. I'm fucking useless. I rip the blanket off my shoulders and storm up the stairs. I'm going back to bed.

2.

It's completely dark and I'm sitting straight up in bed, with my heart beating furiously. The tights and sweater I'm wearing are drenched in sweat. It was a dream. The same dream that I keep having every time I close my eyes. I can't shake Mr. Baker's dark, beady eyes. They're etched in my mind. Am I still sleeping?

I look around my room and can't tell whether it's morning or night. I pulled down the black-out blind on the window, when I came up to take a nap. I look at the clock on my bedside table and see that it's 10:00 a.m. How long ago was that?

I'm still rattled by the dream. The comforter scratches my chin, but I hold it tight against me and take deep, calming breaths. I'm so confused. It's 10:00 a.m.? I was watching TV at 10:00 a.m.... Is today Thursday or Friday? I rack my brain trying to figure it out. Wow. Today is Friday. I slept for almost twenty-two hours. I must've needed it. Margie was right. She told me to take the rest of the week off and I shushed her, thinking I'd come in today and catch up on recordings. There's no way I'm doing that today, but I hate it when Margie's right.

In the shower, I notice that my routine is slower. The heat and the water seem to be a new comfort for me. I've always suggested to patients, to try a warm bath to help with relaxation and stress. I know that the physiological process of warming up the blood causes the blood vessels to dilate, which lessens the resistance to blood flow and thus, lowers blood pressure. Scientifically, it's sound, but I've never had this much stress before, to actually try it. I must say that it works incredibly well. I stay under the spray for a while and reluctantly, dry off and throw on some comfy sweats again. I still have guilt about the wastefulness of water.

As soon as I sit on the couch and cover myself with the blanket, I'm annoyed. Even though I've only been home a few days, I'm tired of the monotony. The television sickens me with the same channels and I rifle through them, without even seeing them. There's nothing on. One more talk show and I'm going to scream. I turn it off and throw the controller onto the cluttered coffee table.

The mess of dirty dishes in front of me catches my attention. My teapot still sits on the tray and I see a splash of milk on the coffee table. It'll probably stain. The fact that my mug isn't on a coaster doesn't even bother me. I push it forward with my toe and I can see a ring on the surface of the table. I shrug. I can also see a thin film of dust on my fireplace and the plants haven't been watered for a couple of days. Who the fuck cares anymore? I just want to swipe the plates off the table and watch them crash to the floor. I want to push over the large calla lily planter, by the window, and see the dirt spill onto the carpet.

I stand up and a pillow falls to the ground. I pick it up and pitch it across the room. It hits the curtains and lands in the planter, but does no damage. It frustrates me. I need to get out of here and do something.

Just then, the doorbell rings. "Fuck!" I growl. I don't want to see anyone.

I creep around the corner and recognize Christine's blonde hair through the crack of the curtain. My stomach sinks. I've already ignored a number of her calls and the messages she's left are filled with worry and pity. I can't handle her drama and I don't feel like regurgitating the whole sordid story again. I duck down a little and stay away from the door.

"I know you're in there, Ci-Ci. Open up." She bangs on the door loudly.

I release the breath I've been holding and skulk toward the door. I guess I have to tell her eventually. I open the door with a large, fake smile on my face. "What are you doing here? Shouldn't you be at work?"

"Take that bogus smile off your face." She grabs me and hugs me tightly. "I'm on an extended lunch. Listen, I know everything. Margie told me." She steps back and looks at me. "Are you ok?"

I nod and see that she is deeply concerned. Her forehead and eyebrows are scrunched up in a scowl and her blue eyes are tipped down at the corners. She's gorgeous, even when she's worried.

She takes my hand and leads me to the couch. "I need to see that you're dealing with everything properly. I'm glad you're taking some time off work, but I know you, Ci-Ci. You'll bottle it all up and try to deal with it yourself. You can't do that this time." She takes off her black suede coat and I see that she's wearing a brown, chevron-patterned skirt and a beautiful beige sweater.

"You look great." Swerve and avoid.

"Ci-Ci," she grumbles. "I'm here to talk about *you*. How can I help?"

Shoot. "Can we go out? I'm sick of being inside." Another avoidance tactic.

"That's a great idea. Yes, I'll take you out for lunch, but you need to change first."

I look down in frustration. I like my sweatpants. They're so comfortable. "Do I have to?"

"I'm sure that the restaurants around here don't let in hobos. Go!"

"Fine." I stomp up the stairs and forcefully pull out a pair of jeans from my shelf. The pile of jeans falls to the floor. I step over them to reach for a bulky knit sweater. I start to check my hair and face, but stop. There's no one to impress.

"Much better," she says when she sees me. She tries to pat down my hair, but I dodge her hand.

"Let's go."

Outside, I panic for a quick second because I don't see my car in the driveway, but I remember that I don't have a car anymore. Back in Windsor, I told the police that they could give it away to a family in need. I never want to see that car again. Maybe my next car will be a sports utility vehicle. Something big. I picture a Hummer, outfitted to defend a zombie apocalypse. I smile.

"What are you smiling at?" Christine asks.

"Oh, nothing. It's just a nice day. I haven't been outside in a while."

She takes my arm and we walk to down the street toward the block of small restaurants, a couple of streets away. The fresh air feels good and I breathe it in slowly. Out of the corner of my eye, I see Christine staring at me and I know she's dying to know the details.

I take another deep breath and slowly tell Christine about the night that I was abducted. She immediately tightens her grasp on my arm, so I promptly shorten the version, to avoid more drama. If Margie told Christine already, I don't need to tell her too much more. She already seems so affected by it and I really don't want to relive it all over again. I get enough of that in my dreams.

Christine squeezes my hand when I tell her that Jack busted into the hotel room and knocked out Mr. Baker.

"Oh my God! I can't believe that this all happened to you. You must've been so scared!"

"Mr. Baker wouldn't hurt me." It's such a bold-faced lie, but I need to relieve her worry. "He just wanted his daughter back."

"But he had a knife!"

"He wasn't going to use it." I don't even believe that.

She stops in the middle of the sidewalk and faces me. "How are you dealing with it? Are you going to see your old therapist?"

"Christine, I'm getting over it." I avoid her eyes. "Of course, it will take time, but I'm just going to take it day by day." These are words that I repeat to my patients.

"You've always been a strong woman, Ci-Ci, but this is going to test how strong you really are." We start walking again.

I take a deep breath and try to ignore her comment, but it angers me. I want to yell and tell her that I'm a coward. A useless weakling. She should know the real me, the person who cowered to Mr. Baker and let him take me and poor Connie. I start to shake. She needs to know.

I'm about to explode, but I notice that she stops at the door to Pat's Diner. I'm only a few steps away. I can't fly into a rage here, where everyone can see.

"Did you want to eat here?"

I nod and open the door for Christine, but don't look at her. I'm too embarrassed about what I almost admitted in front of an entire restaurant and to my best friend. I have to calm down.

Pat's Diner is packed and I let Christine talk to the hostess. The home-style restaurant is busy for good reason. Many people love Pat's cooking. She's a little old lady who both owns and cooks at the restaurant. She makes comfort foods like stew, macaroni and cheese and meat loaf. It's one of my favourite places to eat, but I'm not very hungry today. My stomach churns at the smell of cabbage rolls.

In our corner booth, Christine starts in on me again, "What happened after the police station in Windsor?"

"We were there for a couple of hours and then, Jack drove me home. That's it. End of story." I hope she gets the hint.

"I have to meet Jack to thank him for saving you."

My blood pressure rises again and I open my mouth to tell her that he's been thanked enough, but the waitress comes over with menus. I shut my mouth and try to listen to the daily specials, but I don't hear her.

When the waitress walks away, I open the menu and try to look engrossed in it. I don't know what I was thinking before. I can't get angry or emotional in front of Christine. If I do, she won't leave me alone. My eyes are blurry and I can't read the menu. I hold it higher, so Christine can't see the tears in my eyes.

The waitress comes back and Christine orders a chicken pot pie and salad. I stumble over my words and order a tea and the soup of the day. I hope the soup is a kind that I like.

"That's all you're going to eat?"

Here we go. "I'm not very hungry."

"You're definitely not yourself. What can I do to help?"

For fuck sakes. "Christine, I don't want to dwell on it, ok?" I look at her and fake another smile. "What's new in your life? How's work?"

She grunts quietly, "Everything is good, Ci-Ci." She glowers at me, but starts telling me about her boss and how he keeps hitting on her and scheduling late night work meetings. Christine's very animated and reveals how relentless he is, but she describes how she's been able to elude him.

We talk about sexual harassment and joke about neutering her boss. It's fun. This is how I want to get over the trauma. I want to live my life in the present and forget about Mr. Baker. We laugh just like old times and I start to feel normal again.

On the way back home, Christine picks up where she left off, becoming motherly and over-bearing. "You barely ate your minestrone, Ci-Ci. I'm still so worried about you."

"Minestrone's not my favourite. I'll eat a bagel later."

"Are you sure you're going to be ok tonight? I can come back after I finish work and we could go out for dinner or just hang out, if you want."

The door to my house is now open and I'm standing in the threshold, with my hand on the doorknob. I want her to leave. I've had enough. I tilt my head to the side and sigh. "I'm going to watch more television, maybe read a book and then go to bed."

"Please don't be angry with me for trying to help you."

"I don't need help, Christine. I'm glad we went out for lunch. It was great catching up and we need to do it again soon," I say it harsher than I wanted. "I just don't want to dwell on the bad stuff anymore."

Christine just looks at me.

I turn to look into the kitchen. "It's only two o'clock. I have the whole afternoon to myself and I'm going to relax, I promise. I'm fine." I turn back to her. How many times can I say that?

"I guess I'll just have to trust you. If you need anything, please call me." She hugs me tightly. "I love you, Ci-Ci. I couldn't bear it if anything ever happened to you."

I feel the tears well up in my eyes, but I try to stifle them. If I cry now, she'll never leave. Deep breath. "I love you too, Christine." I gently push her away. "Now leave before we start being too mushy."

"Nothing wrong with a little mush, girl." She looks at me and smiles.

"Thanks for lunch."

"Call me anytime."

I nod and close the door softly, locking the new dead bolt. Leaning against the door, I look around at my house. Now what?

3.

This time, I know it's a dream, but I can't wake myself up. Mr. Baker looms over me in a monstrous form. I think he's going to hit me, but he ties up my hands and he slaps a piece of duct tape over my mouth. I see Connie in the corner of the hotel room. She's crying and yelling for her mommy. I try to run to her, but trip over the couch and fall to the ground. Mr. Baker's sadistic laugh resonates in my ears and makes my body tremor with fear. I can feel him standing over me and I cringe when I feel his hands on my body. It's difficult to breathe with the tape on my mouth. I'm going to hyperventilate.

He easily picks me up and pushes me roughly towards the bedroom. I stumble backwards and my legs hit the bed. He watches me slyly and an ominous feeling washes over me. This is not about Connie anymore. He wants to hurt me.

Mr. Baker lumbers at me and his eyes blacken completely. I can't back up anymore, so I try to go around the bed, to get away from him. He catches me and shoves me onto the bed, crawling on top of me. My scream is muffled by the tape. This mood is different. It's threatening, but more sexual. I know what he wants and I'm horrified. I hope Connie's closing her eyes.

Both of my hands are tightly in his grasp above my head. He has me pinned to the bed. I thrash my body and kick both of my legs, but his weight crushes me. I can't get away. I'm tired from the exertion, but I don't give up.

His hand travels up my body, over my stomach and grabs at my breast. I freeze and suddenly, feel so sick. He's never been sexual in my dreams. I'm disgusted. Millions of bugs crawl under my skin. I use all my strength and try to buck him off of me, but he doesn't move.

He rips the tape off of my mouth and kisses me hard. I try to keep my lips tightly sealed, but he forces my mouth open with his tongue. I can smell the alcohol on his hot breath. I think I'm going to vomit.

I'm unable to wake up and sweat accumulates at the nape of my neck and between my breasts. I cry out over and over again, wishing that Jack was here to wake me up again.

The dream makes an abrupt change. I feel gentle kisses on my neck and on my cheek. It tickles and feels sensual. I breathe a sigh of relief and I'm instantly turned on. All of the weight has lifted off of me and when I'm kissed on the mouth again, it's gentle and alluring. I open my eyes, but can't see who's kissing me. I know it's not Mr. Baker, but the man's eyes are closed and it's dark in the room. It might be Steve. I hope that it's Steve. The kiss deepens and I let my eyes close, melting into the sensations.

When Steve starts kissing my breasts, I realize that I'm naked. He tugs at one nipple with his mouth and twists the other nipple with his thumb and forefinger. My back arches and an incredible bolt of electricity travels down to my sex. It pulses with anticipation. It's been a long time, Steve.

I pull and twist his hair in my fingers, pushing his head down. He licks my stomach and each hip bone slowly, lowering further down my body, between my legs. I push my hips up and I finally feel his mouth on my sex. Steve's never done that before.

His tongue dives into me and I gasp with surprise and need. I'm already wet with intense desire. I feel his teeth nibble on my lips and his tongue toy with my clitoris. He licks my sex with a soft, flat tongue, over and over. He's slow and meticulous and it's bringing me to the brink of an orgasm. I'm moaning loudly and I've lifted my hips as high as I can. I want him to fully devour me. I'm almost there.

Steve stops suddenly and my eyes flash open, but I can't see him. He flips me around and I'm on my hands and knees on the bed. Wow. Steve is really trying new things with me. I feel his hands softly caressing my hips and his hardness pushing at my entrance. He's teasing me. I push back at him. He laughs. Does Steve laugh like that? I push back at him again. He laughs again. That doesn't sound like Steve.

I start to pull away and turn around to get a better look, but he drives his hardness into me. I clutch the bed and groan brashly. He pumps his hips firmly into my backside. He fills my sex completely and then pulls out almost entirely. The feeling is immensely satisfying.

His fingers are at my clitoris, lightly tapping and flicking at it, and that's when I topple over the edge. I burst and shatter at my innermost core. The sensation travels to every extremity of my body and lingers there, making me shudder tirelessly.

He continues to plunge faster into me, quickening his pace, and then, I feel him explode. He muffles his moans, somewhat grunting, and pushing against me in short, quick bursts.

We collapse on the bed and he pulls out of me. I catch my breath and casually get up on one elbow. I need to know who it is. My gut is telling me that it's Steve, but I'm not sure. It would be amazing if it was him. Who else would it be? I still can't see his face. His body looks like Steve's... I think.

He sluggishly turns toward me. I can't speed up my dream. Who is it?

"Am I everything you want in a hero?"
Jack?

4.

I wake up immediately and angrily throw my pillow against the wall. I know enough about dreams and my consciousness to be thoroughly angered. I knew I was dreaming and what I was dreaming about, and with that kind of lucidity, I should've been having sex with Steve. That's what I truly want, so why did it end up being Jack? What does my dream mean?

Sigmund Freud is not my favourite thinker in the world of psychology because he was sexist, fraudulent and mostly just plain wrong, but he revolutionized the study of dreams. I wrote one of my papers about his dream analysis in relation to personality and I'm sure it'd help me decipher this dream. God, this dream and my messed up thoughts are definitely not normal. I run downstairs to my office.

The essay's in my filing cabinet, in a folder marked *Year IV Papers*. I pull it out and skim through it.

Freud believes that nothing occurs by chance. Every action and thought is motivated by the unconscious at some level. In order to live in a civilized society, one has to hold back urges and repress impulses. However, these urges and impulses must be released in some way and have a way of coming to the surface in disguised forms.

I remember all of this. The desires of the id are suppressed by the superego. Where's the part about dreams? I scan it further.

Freud theorized that dreams serve as wish fulfillment. Dreams are fabricated from background information which has transpired in our lives, such as from past experiences and motivations. As a result, the content of our dreams is largely determined by what we fear, hope for, and expect.

This is what I wanted to read, but I don't want to believe it. I know that I don't desire Jack in any way. I haven't harboured any sexual feelings about him. I mean, he's kissed me a few times, but I haven't reciprocated the feelings. I shake my head. No, I haven't! I don't feel that way about him! No, I'm not repressing my feelings… It must be that he's just been in my life in a different way lately. I'm dreaming of him because he saved me, not because I want him.

I re-familiarize myself with Freud, and how he believed that dreams allow the subconscious mind to run wild and express its most hidden desires. I become sicker and sicker. Not only has this whole situation with Mr. Baker made me feel incompetent and worthless, I now have a repressed desire to sleep with my hypothetical guardian. The man who saved me. My saviour. This is bullshit.

The paper crumples in my hands and I let it drop to the floor, purposely stepping on it, as I leave my office. These thoughts and dreams are ridiculous. I have to stop napping during the day and do something constructive with my time.

I stomp into the living room and look around. No more TV. I stomp into the kitchen and pick up a dirty plate from the sink. I start to wash it, but drop it back into the sink and dry my hands. Housework is pointless. I stomp back to my office and think about checking my email. No! I need to get out of here! It's only 6:00 p.m. I throw on my puffy winter coat, grab a twenty dollar bill and head out the door.

The cold air takes my breath away. It was much warmer at lunchtime. I take a few steps and think about grabbing some mittens or to just stay home, but change my mind. I can't stay in the house right now. I can handle the weather. I pull the zipper all the way up, stuff my hands in my pockets and head toward the coffee shop, a couple of blocks away. Leaves crunch under my feet and I quietly scoff at the thought of snow and ice. I'm not looking forward to winter.

I stop walking and slap my head. I still have that vacation booked. My anniversary vacation to Mexico. I roll my eyes and start walking again. I'm not fucking going. Why would I go? I reserved a honeymoon suite, with a hot tub and all of the amenities for a couple in love. Flowers, chocolate covered strawberries and champagne will be there upon arrival. It's supposed to be a romantic getaway. If I went alone, it would be a horrible reminder of my failures. I'd probably cry about how much I miss Steve and how much my life sucks. There's no way that I'm going. I wonder if I can get my money back.

In an angry motion, I throw open the door of the coffee shop and continue stomping toward the counter to order. I don't look at anyone, while standing in line. I keep my chin tucked in my coat and look at the floor, until I order.

When I receive my steeped tea, I sit down near a window, but slump down in my seat. I hold my tea, trying to warm up my hands on the outside of the cup and start to people-watch.

The older men beside me are speaking loudly in Italian, I think. I listen to them carefully. *Bella ragazza*. Yes, it's Italian. I know I've seen them here before. Steve and I would often walk to this place after dinner and sometimes on Saturday mornings for breakfast. It's cute how they use their hands to talk, but I remember that Steve would make fun of them. The one with a thick mustache, nods at me, so I give him a small smile and quickly look in another direction.

Further away, two older women hold their pinkies up, while they drink coffee. I see their napkins neatly folded in their lap and their legs crossed daintily. They aren't speaking and don't even look at each other. They just dab the napkins at the corners of their mouths after each sip. Very fancy. Perhaps that will be Christine and me when we get older. I smirk. No more strip clubs at that age, I hope.

A young child runs by, followed by a mother and that's when I notice how many children are around me. Most of them are eating donuts and hot chocolate, and their parents try to keep up with wiping the crumbs and dribbles from their faces, but the kids don't care. The boy that ran by drops a sprinkle donut onto the floor and looks at his mom. His mom warns him not to pick it up, but he does anyway and takes a big bite. Her screech echoes throughout the store.

I notice how calm I am right now. Life feels normal, just like this afternoon when Christine was talking about her horny boss. Why do I get so angry? And so easily? Christine's my best friend and I got annoyed by her constant prodding, but she just cares about me and my well-being. I should apologize. And Jack... he saved me, but I pushed him away. Why can't I accept help?

Christine suggested that I see a therapist. Should I? I shake my head and take a sip of tea. It seems pretty useless to make an appointment when I've already analyzed my own dreams, found information about traumatic experiences and read about abduction. I have the knowledge I need to figure things out. It's just going to take time to heal.

Perhaps I'm ready to go back to work? Ugh. That though deflates me. Why? Helping other people is not my idea of healing. I need to work on me first and stop dwelling. What can I do to take my mind off everything? Where can I focus my energy?

Suddenly, a swarm of boisterous people walk into the coffee shop carrying yoga mats. The talking and laughing is so loud that I can hear them order their pretentious green teas and soy lattes. They end up sitting beside me, as a large group and the smell of patchouli fills my nostrils. I scrunch up my nose in distaste.

"Is anyone sitting here?" A very handsome man in loose-fitting yoga pants stands before me, pointing at the chair across from me.

I sit up straighter and pull my shoulders back. "No, not at all."

"Could I take this chair?"

"Yes, of course." I thought he wanted to sit with me. "Where do you go to yoga?"

"*Breathe Yoga*," he points to the right. "It's about a block down that way. You should try it." He winks at me and takes the chair over to his friends.

"Thanks." Maybe I will. I look out the window and wonder if I would like yoga. I certainly don't feel like I have the energy to run, any time soon, but I need to do something. Yoga may be it.

Then my heart stops. Was that Mr. Baker? For a quick second, I thought I saw him staring at me from across the street. I frantically scan the street, with my heart beating as fast as the movement of my eyes. My body feels a million degrees warmer. I feel perspiration form on my upper lip.

I put my tea down and stand up, backing away from the window. Where did he go? I run to open the café door and look up and down the street. He's not there now. I feel light-headed. Was it him?

I sit back down and almost knock over my tea. The entire table of yogis is staring at me. I'm embarrassed and look down at the table. Yes, this girl needs yoga. When I look up again, they've already turned back around, talking to each other. Nope, don't pay attention to me. I'm crazy.

My hands are trembling as I bring my cup to my lips, so I put it back down, to avoid spilling it. I shake my head. Mr. Baker wouldn't come back to Toronto, would he? No, the police are looking for him. He wouldn't be that stupid. My eyes must be playing tricks on me.

Why am I being so silly? I take a sip of my tea and look out the window. I feel calmer and laugh at myself. *Come on, Colleen.* There's no way he'd be here. What would he want from me anyway? It's Connie who he wants, not me. My dream's in the back of my mind and it's warning me that Mr. Baker wants revenge. I shake my head. No, it's over. He's gone. *Get over it, Colleen.*

By the time I finish my tea, I've talked myself into being composed and appearing strong, so I walk down the street to check out the prices at the yoga studio.

5.

    The next evening, I grab my newly-purchased yoga mat and walk to *Breathe Yoga*. I picked up the schedule last night and committed to unlimited classes for three months. The price was reasonable, especially if I decide I hate it and only go once. I won't go bankrupt or regret the cost.
    Saturday night's easy class is *Yoga Basics*. The lady at the front desk assured me that all beginners start there. I know I could probably handle more, but this was the first class of the evening and I slept through all of the early classes this morning. I was angry that I overslept and missed them, but on the other hand, I was happy that I didn't have any bad dreams. I actually had a good night's sleep. It was really difficult waiting all day for the next class, though. There's only so much television that can be watched in a day. I hope yoga helps to calm me and my negativity. I'm on a mission.
    Inside the studio, I immediately notice the pile of shoes by the front door and respectfully take off my own. I also hang up my bulky sweatshirt, but carry my purse and mat with me. My yoga pants and long tank top help me to fit in with the rest of the crowd, but I'm still somewhat nervous.
    Class starts in another five minutes, so I wander around the front entrance where they have yoga clothing on display. I notice that the yoga mats are crazy expensive. I scrutinize the one I bought today from Walmart. It seems fine, but the ones they're selling are thicker. I squeeze one of them between my fingers. It's spongier, too. I don't care. My mat's adequate. I don't need to spend that much money on a stupid mat. I'm not even sure I like yoga yet.
    "Don't you find the prices insane?"
    I look up, and a man with longer hair and a goatee, is staring at me. He's cute, if you like a hairy face. He must be one of those hippie-vegan-yoga types that I've heard about. Look at me, stereotyping these people.

"Are you talking to me?"

"Yes." He smiles. "I borrowed this mat from a friend of mine and looking at these prices, I don't intend on buying my own mat anytime soon. My friend's not getting this mat back."

I notice he has a diamond earring in his left ear. It's probably cubic zirconia. "You can buy the mats cheaper anywhere, but these seem to be really good quality." I rub my hand along one and he does the same.

"Are you going to buy one?"

"Oh no." I pull my hand away. "I don't even know if I like yoga."

"Are you doing the basic class tonight?"

I nod. "I have to start somewhere."

"I've been doing the same class for a couple of months and I've been afraid to try the next level. This one has been hard enough."

"You're making me more nervous."

"Don't be. From what I see in class, you'll be fine. I'm the minority here. Men are not meant to be flexible. It's painful."

"Then why do you do it?"

Suddenly, the studio door opens and the previous class files out. The participants coming out are all glistening with sweat and I get a whiff of incense and body odour. There really isn't a specific yoga participant. I see a couple of males, mixed in with many females, but they're all different ages, sizes and shapes. I feel a bit better.

"I thought this was the first class of the evening," I say to my new friend.

"The schedule changed last week. You might have an old schedule."

Great. I feel my body tense up at my mistake.

The other people, who have been waiting outside with us, start walking into the room and I see them quickly rolling out their mats.

Goatee man says, "We can go in now."

He allows me to go first and I scan the room for a spot. I see lit candles everywhere and incense is burning at the front of the room. I'm about to put my mat down when a woman beats me to it. She smiles, somewhat smartly at me and rolls out her mat. I'm surprised at her response. I shake my head and turn around to look for another spot. It's getting tight.

"Over here."

Goatee man is gesturing to me, in an open area. I step over the bodies splayed out on their mats, but a large-breasted blonde rushes past me and smiles at him, thanking him. It figures. He wasn't talking to me.

She's about to roll out her mat where he's standing, when I hear him say, "Sorry, this spot is taken." He's looking at me.

Oh. I walk over to him and the blonde gives me a dirty look. She walks to the back of the room and squeezes in between another man and the back wall.

"Thank you." I start rolling out my mat. "These people are vicious."

"One thing about yogis is that they never seem to take enough yoga classes."

"What do you mean?"

"Yoga is supposed to calm you, right? People do it to de-stress and to get those happy endorphins. Well, the people who come to these classes are high-strung and... They're bitchy. "

I laugh. "Good to know."

"I'm Mark."

"I'm Colleen. It's nice to meet you."

The lights dim and a quiet voice says, "Could everyone please start in savasana?"

I look around and can't tell who said it. Almost everyone is now lying on their backs, legs slightly apart and eyes closed. I look at Mark. He winks and lies down. I do the same.

"My name is Marisol and welcome to basic yoga," the voice is slow and deliberate, "I hope you've left your egos at the door. This class is about what you can do. Don't compare yourself to the person beside you. This is your own yoga practice." An ambient, tribal sound fills the studio.

As we start moving around, I finally catch a glimpse of Marisol. She's very cute and athletic. She calls out poses in a vinyasa style of teaching. One pose leads into the next, with either an inhale or an exhale. The poses themselves aren't hard, as I've always been pretty flexible, but I do have a hard time with what she's actually saying. She says the name of a pose, but I don't know what she means, so I have to look around at everybody else, just to see where to position my legs and arms.

Marisol walks around the room over and over again. She's very dynamic and powerful. I watch her stride by, while I'm in triangle pose, and I hear her anklet jingle as she walks.

During the next forty minutes, I'm doing poses like downward dog and cobra. Some of the names of the positions sound a little strange and they're mostly animal references. I do like something called chaturanga. Not the movement itself, but the name of it. Marisol has a Latin accent and she rolls her tongue when she says it. *Chaturrrrrrranga*. There are so many poses and everything is named. I think someone just picked names out of a hat or asked a two-year-old what to name some of them. I get happy baby, but what's with pigeon? Even the position with my legs crossed is called sukhasana. I thought it was just called criss-cross applesauce.

I can't help noticing Mark during the standing poses. He does have trouble getting his long torso into certain positions and he really needs to work on his balance. He seems to be concentrating really hard, too. Sweat's dripping down his forehead, into his eyes and his t-shirt is drenched. Poor guy. But he's definitely buff. He has sculpted biceps and his legs are rippling under the stress of holding the poses. His beard isn't that bad either. Maybe hippies are hot.

Mark was right, though. The women don't seem to be having any trouble at all. I mean, their form isn't perfect, but they aren't struggling to keep it together. Even the women, who I thought would be bad at yoga, are excelling. I'll leave my ego at the door next time.

Marisol tells us to lie down on our backs again in savasana. She tells us that it means corpse pose. The name fits. I think we're almost done. The music suddenly changes and I recognize the twangy, exotic sound of the sitar. When the Indian vocals are added, it's hard not to think of anything else.

Then I hear Marisol's voice, "As your muscles relax, the nerve impulses traveling to and from them decrease, and the brain calms down. A message of relaxation should spread throughout your entire nervous system." I hear the light patter of her feet by my head. "Gradually the tensions that have crept into your body and mind will release. You'll begin to notice that distracting or stressful thoughts are increasingly unimportant and fall away. You'll be more alert to the mental processes that disturb your relaxation. As you recognize how these thought patterns affect your body, you'll enable yourself to change—and to empower your body's natural healing properties."

She slowly lists every single part of our body, explaining how to relax each one, from our feet to the top of our head, even our tongues.

"Feel the weight of your body settling effortlessly into the earth underneath you. Let your body melt into the earth, so that you, and the world around you, blur and become less distinct. Enjoy the spaciousness inside you and around you. Feel the infinite connection you have right now to the world around you.

All of a sudden, I feel like crying. I take a deep breath in, to try to contain it, but I can't. I feel a tear run down the side of my face. What the hell? Why am I so emotional?

Then I hear someone at my head. My eyes flutter open and I see Marisol rubbing her hands back and forth, like she's trying to stay warm. What is she doing? She crouches down low and softly places her thumbs in between my eyebrows. I close my eyes, unsure of what to expect. She then lowers the heels of her hands to my forehead. Her fingers are soft on the side of my face. She holds it there for a few moments.

I feel the emotions well up inside me again. I want to curl up in a ball and hide from everyone. Another tear falls toward my ear. *Get it together, Colleen!* I want to run out of the studio, but that would call more attention to me. I scrunch my eyes together and try to disappear into the floor.

Her hands leave my head and I quickly feel her palms on the front of my shoulders. I open my eyes again, panicking. She can see me crying! Marisol smiles at me and gently wipes away my tears with her hand. I close my eyes quickly. She squeezes my shoulders and then adds more pressure with the heels of her palms. My arms involuntarily spread out on the floor a little further and my upper back stretches out on my mat. The pressure feels nice. Her palms keep pushing, but slide softly off my shoulders, toward the floor. And then she is gone.

I peek out through my lashes and see that Marisol is doing the same thing to each participant. Everyone else is just lying there with their eyes closed. Does this happen in every class? Marisol should've warned us or maybe I should've done some research. How do you opt out of the touching part, when you're not supposed to talk? I guess it was nice, her hands were gentle, but I'm embarrassed that I was crying. Running doesn't make me cry! I'm getting stressed out again, so I breathe and try to remain motionless, with my eyes closed.

What's going on with me? I can't control my emotions at all. I don't like the touching. I like the touching. *Figure it out, Colleen!* Yoga isn't supposed to cause stress, it's supposed to be relaxing and calming. I feel stupid for crying and I can't believe I let a stranger see how weak I am. How can I ever come back here and face Marisol? Did anyone else see me cry?

We wiggle our hands and feet and turn over on our side just before we sit up. Criss-cross applesauce again, but this time we put our hands in prayer position at our heart. I open one eye and watch Marisol.

"As you go back out into your world, may you be filled with ease, loving, kindness, compassion and peace... for yourself and all beings. Know that you are being held in the arms of a loving, supportive and compassionate Universe."

I am about to lose it again. It would be comforting to have someone lovingly watch over me. I bite the inside of my cheek to stop the tears.

"The light in me, humbly honours the light in each of you. Namaste."

Marisol and the entire class bends forward at the waist, so I do too. Then I hear people say, "Namaste." I want to sit up, but everyone is still bowing, so I stay there. I finally see Marisol sit up straight and smile at everyone. Some people clap, some say thank you and others start rolling up their mats.

"How was that?"

I wipe away the tears and stay crouched down to roll up my mat. I don't look at Mark. "It was good."

"You looked like you were rocking the poses. I think it was pretty easy for you."

I nod and smile. Sure, it was easy, but it was extremely difficult to keep my mood intact. I was all over the place.

There must be a class afterwards because people are already coming in and unrolling their mats. I quickly roll up my mat and head towards the door with Mark. I feel a hand on my arm. It's Marisol.

"Can I speak to you for a minute?" She asks.

I look at Mark and back to Marisol. "Sure."

"See you around," Mark says, as he smiles and walks away.

"Are you ok?" Marisol asks.

"Sure." I look down, "Oh, you mean the tears..."

"Listen, I haven't seen you before and I don't want to overwhelm you at all. Are you new to yoga?"

"Yes."

"I want you to know that crying in yoga is very normal. Don't let it freak you out. Yoga allows you to strip away all of your layers and leads you to a state of overwhelming emotional connectedness. Think about it. You just stepped out of the world's chaos and into a dimly lit studio after a long day of being who the world expects you to be. Most likely you were just releasing something that you needed to get out."

This hits too close to home. "I guess it makes sense." I look around to make sure no one is listening to our conversation.

"Your tears could be considered a cleansing. Your body just eliminated a bunch of toxins. It flushed out the emotions you carried into class and now, you can welcome the fresh, new emotions you absorbed while you were on your mat."

She seems very passionate about this, but it's a little implausible to me. I've never really believed in or experienced the mind-body connection. "That's an interesting thought."

"Isn't it?" She smiles. "Have a good night."

"Thank you. You too."

I put my sweatshirt on and try to find my shoes amongst the pile. They are buried under some black rubber boots. Outside, I start to walk home, but a voice stops me.

"Colleen!"

I turn to find Mark standing against the wall of the studio. "Hey there. Are you waiting for me?"

"Don't be afraid," he laughs. "I'm not a stalker. There's a coffee house down the street where a lot of us go after yoga. Would you like to join me?"

"Sure." I really don't want to go home yet.

6.

We end up at a dimly lit pub across the street from the studio. Neither of us wanted coffee and beer sounded more satisfying. There are no yoga mats in sight and we're slightly undressed, but no one seems to care. I'm still sweaty and the cool air from outside has chilled me, so I keep my sweatshirt on. Mark takes his jacket off and I notice that he changed from his sweaty t-shirt into a long-sleeve jersey, and he now has jogging pants on, too. I wish I brought a change of clothes.

The crowd is a mixed age group drinking draft beer and mingling with friends. Thankfully, it's not a couples' scene. It's pretty casual and I instantly don't care that I'm wearing spandex or smell like sweat.

"I'm glad you don't wear that patchouli scent. It's not a good smell for a man."

"Is that what that smell is? Patchouli? It's a cross between my grandma's house and a spice drawer. It's not a good fragrance for a woman, either. A pot of stew, maybe..." He makes a face.

I laugh. "I think it's too woodsy and it bothers my nose. I guess we're not the typical yogis."

"I'm good with that. I'd rather smell like a man and have beer." He notices the pub tent card on the table and picks it up. He nods his head. "Yes, I'd rather be manly and have beer and beef nachos any day."

I laugh again. He's not vegan, but he still may be a hippie.

"You have a great laugh." He sits back in his stool and eyes me carefully.

I know that look. "Thanks." I look away. Is this a date now? I look around the pub, trying to think.

"Do you want to play darts?"

"I'm not really sure how to play."

"You throw a pointy thing at a big corkboard. It's not difficult." He smiles.

"Ok."

We order two pints and a plate of nachos and we walk over to an empty dart board. Mark pulls out three darts and hands them to me, but doesn't let go. I look at him, confused.

"These are tungsten darts. Professionals use them, but these ones are old." He places them into my hands. "They'll have to do."

"Oh no. You know darts. How can I compete?"

"We'll just have a friendly game."

"Why don't I believe that?" I shake my head, smiling. "I'll play, but if I'm going to get my butt whooped, I want the darts with the blue and white wing things." I point to another dart board, where I see them. "I don't like green."

He chuckles and pulls them out, giving them to me. He puts the ones that I didn't want on a ledge. "You're cute. The blue and white wing things are called flights. See the dimpled surface on them? It will help slow down and stabilize your dart."

"Who cares?" I laugh. "Can I start throwing now?" I take a swig of beer and put it on the table.

"Go ahead."

I pull off my sweatshirt and start aiming, but I'm startled by Mark's hands seizing my waist. I stiffen up and suck in my breath. He's pulling me backward. What's he doing? I look at him over my shoulder.

"Sorry. You're way too close to the board." He taps his shoe on the floor and I look down to see him toeing a line of tape. "Stand behind this line."

I relax a little, but his hands linger a little too long. It feels nice and I don't want to push him away, but I wasn't expecting this to happen. I wait until he releases and walks away, before I begin to aim again. I take a second to collect my thoughts. Am I here for a friendly game of darts or more than that? Would I want more? I close one eye, stare at the board and throw and release the dart. It lands one foot to the left and three feet below the dart board.

"Wow. I suck."

Mark walks up to me again and touches my shoulder. Even though I saw him sweat at yoga, he still smells nice. Like a man. "Your shoulder is the only point in the whole process that doesn't change its position. Don't move your body when throwing. The only throwing action comes from your arm." He demonstrates, but doesn't release the dart.

"Ok," I say. He squeezes my shoulder before he walks away. I like this attention. I release my next dart and it lands an inch below the board.

Mark stands in front of me. "That's better, but finally, you need to remember your follow-through." He gently pushes away a curl away from my eyes and comes to stand on my right. He places his left hand on the small of my back. "You're letting your arm fall down after the release. Try to end up with your hand aiming at the board." He now has my right hand in his right and he's showing me a follow-through, keeping my arm up in the air.

He's very hands-on. I hope he can't feel the goose bumps on my arms.

"Got it." He walks away and I rub my arms, trying to compose myself. I take a deep breath, aim and release. My last dart lands in the number twenty. I jump up and down slightly with excitement and turn around to smile at Mark.

He hands me my beer and clinks my glass with his. "Good job."

"Thank you. You're a good coach." I take a couple of gulps and try not to notice that he's watching me while he's drinking. I don't know if I feel awkward or thrilled. I'm happy that he finds me attractive, but is this something I need right now?

"My turn." He puts his beer on the ledge and stands at the tape line. He rifles off his darts quickly, barely even aiming, and hits the twenty each time.

"Really? Don't even try to hide that you're a pro or anything. Go for those twenties each time," I chide.

"I actually got triple twenties. They're worth sixty points each."

I look carefully at the board and notice the thin red and green segments. He has all three darts in the middle red segment of the twenty. "You just got one hundred and eighty points?" I'm shocked and impressed.

He nods.

"Why didn't you just go for the bulls-eye?"

"I didn't want to show off." He smiles, boyishly.

I raise my glass. "Here's to the dart pro and his modesty."

"Cheers to that."

We finish our beer and Mark orders another two pints. We keep throwing darts and I'm completely inconsistent. Sometimes I hit the board, most times I don't. Darts are definitely not my thing and drinking doesn't help my aim. More pints are ordered and I eat a few nachos to soak up the beer.

"Let's play a game called, around the board. You get three throws each turn, to hit the numbers in order from one to twenty."

"But you're way better than me. I can't even hit the board, let alone aim for a certain number." I feel like I'm stumbling through my words. I may have to stop drinking.

"I'll take one throw to your three."

"Sure. Whatever. Let's play." I need to keep moving.

I go first and hit number one on my first try. "Woohoo!" I do a little dance. Yes, I'm drunk. I glance at Mark and he's laughing.

"Keep going, sharp shooter."

My second throw misses the number two, but my third one lands it, but then falls out. "Hey! That was in! You saw it!"

"You're right. It was in. I'll let you take it."

"You'll let me?" I walk up towards him, trying to look tough, and he looks down at me. He's tall. I'm feeling very relaxed and a bit giddy.

"You think you can take me, little girl?" He's smiling and puffing out his chest.

I shake my head and quickly walk away, laughing.

"I thought so." He stands up to the line and as he's about to throw, I tiptoe up behind him and nudge his elbow.

He pauses to look at me seriously. "Is this how you're going to play?"

I try to look innocent, but I'm not sure if he's mad. I don't do it again. He hits number one easily and sits down without looking at me.

I think he's upset. I grab my three darts and start to aim. I'm troubled by his response. I thought we were joking around.

Just before I release my dart, I feel something hit the back of my knee and my leg buckles. I turn around and it was Mark. He's smiling innocently now.

"That's not fair."

"Why? Are we betting on something?" He bumps my hip with his.

"I don't know. What should we bet?"

He eyes me, daringly. "I've got a good idea."

Oh. I think I know what he wants, but I want to see if he can admit it. "What's your idea?"

"If I win, I get to kiss you."

That's pretty tame. "And if I win?"

"What do you want?"

I smile. "I'll figure it out when the time comes."

7.

After a few more horrible throws, I excuse myself to visit the ladies room. I know I'm going to lose the game. The idea of Mark kissing me doesn't bother me. He's funny and nice, but are those reasons to kiss a random guy? Why else would I bother? I haven't even thought about my Sex Project lately. Obviously, other things have been on my mind. I still want to reconcile with Steve, but I know I need to get out of my funk before I proceed with anything. Would hooking up with Mark be a part of my Sex Project? Or is it just something to do? I do love the attention and he doesn't know anything about me. He likes me for me and he's not trying to help me get over my so-called trauma.

I look in the mirror and shrug my shoulders. I take the elastic out of my hair and try to finger curl the strands. It's a bit messy, but it'll do. I splash water on my face and dry off. I look all right. I don't look like an abductee or a victim. Mark seems to like what he sees. Let's see where tonight takes me. I pull my shoulders back and head out the door.

I walk out of the washroom and see Mark standing there

"Hi."

He doesn't say anything. He steps close to me and starts kissing me. I kiss him back. I don't know what comes over me. I'm not being gentle. I force my tongue in his mouth and he responds with equal enthusiasm. I grab the back of his neck and pull him closer to me and he caresses my bottom with both of his hands.

"Get a room!" Someone calls out.

I break away from him and see two younger women eyeing us, as they walk into the washroom. They giggle as the door closes.

"You didn't even win the game! You cheated," I tease.

"Oh, we both know that I was going to cream you."

"I might have won."

"You weren't going to win," he states bluntly, with a smile.

I pout, thinking I'm cute.

He pokes at my lip. "You're adorable, but I have to tell you that I won the Canadian Open for darts last year. You had no chance."

"That's not surprising." I shrug my shoulders and go on my tiptoes for another kiss. The beer has definitely gone to my head. Mark doesn't seem to mind and we kiss for a few minutes, until he pulls away.

"Do you want to go to my place?" Mark asks. "It's just a few blocks away."

I nod. I need some loving.

We gather up our coats and mats and Mark throws some money on the table. He takes my hand and leads me out of the pub.

"Come on!" He starts jogging and I follow.

I'm a little foggy from the beer, but it has also made me relax and feel comfortable. I realize that I'm not using my brain and that my libido is controlling me. Oh well. He's a great kisser, I enjoy his company and I don't have anywhere to go. I don't have to think. I'm a grown woman. I just want to get fucked. Ooh, I'm a bad girl. Whether this is right or wrong, it's what I need right now.

The street that Mark turns onto is one that Steve and I frequently drove down, to see his mother Sylvia. It's quite a hike away from where we are, but I'm confident that it's the same street. Hopefully, we don't have to walk that far.

When I met Steve, he'd leave me on Sunday morning, after spending the night, and go to Sylvia's house for brunch. He felt he needed to continue with that ritual, as his dad passed away months before I met him, so I started going with him. I didn't mind the visits, the food was always amazing and I always ate too much, but my relationship with her was strained, even after we got married.

Sylvia always offered me unsolicited advice on any and all problems, even things that she has had no experience with at all. She thought she knew more than me and sure, she's been around the block, but she was very old fashioned. She had years of experience coping with the problems that a married couple face, like settling money issues, furnishing a home, and allocating responsibilities fairly. Her main difficulty with me was my lifestyle, or specifically, my job. She didn't like that I worked and she wanted grandchildren yesterday. I quickly learned to be quiet about issues and pinched Steve when he would start to bring up our life together.

Months before our separation, Steve started going alone to his mom's, every Sunday. He said that she needed his help with things around the house and he didn't want to make me wait around for him. I didn't mind, I'd go for a run and get the house cleaning done instead. I'm not sure what kind of help she needed, but he was always there until dinner and sometimes he even missed dinner, coming home late. It put a slight strain on our marriage, as Sunday was a day off for both of us. I expected to spend the day with him, but I never bitched or said anything. I wanted to be a good wife. Perhaps that was another reason for our failing marriage. I start kicking myself mentally.

We don't walk very far, just two blocks, and he leads me to an old two-storey house. Mark takes a key from under a stone urn and unlocks the door. Thinking about Steve, I'm not sure if I want to be here with Mark anymore. How do I get out of this?

He replaces the key and when I step inside, an odour invades my nostrils. I think its mothballs, but I've never smelled them before. It's a bad smell. The house is a living museum of the sixties era, complete with an old fashioned rotary phone and floral print couches and wallpaper. The shag carpet under my feet is bright blue and the wood staircase and baseboards are old and worn. Yeah, he's a hippie.

"Before you say anything, I just inherited this house from my grandmother. I haven't been able to fix a thing or get rid of that smell."

I laugh and touch his arm. "I was hoping that this wasn't your style."

"I promise she's not decomposing upstairs."

"Mark! That's not nice." I hit him lightly on the arm.

He catches my hand and pulls me to him. He takes my mat out of my hands and places it on a chair by the door. Then he lifts the bottom of my sweatshirt and lifts it over my head, putting it with my mat. We start kissing tentatively, but the attraction is still there.

His hands roam my body cautiously. They come up my ribcage on both sides and he cups my breasts through the yoga top. I lose my breath and my sex tingles. Ok, change of plan. I definitely want to be here. I push my hips towards his and reach up to place my hands behind his head, pulling his long hair. His hands travel down and go underneath my shirt to rub my skin. He starts to pull my tank top up slowly and I don't stop him. I stand back slightly and put my hands in the air. He pulls it right over my head. I still have a fitness bra on.

He takes me by the hand and leads me upstairs. In the hallway, I pull down my spandex leggings, revealing my black thong. I think he'll like that view. I drop the pants on the floor and smile. Mark takes his shorts off and stands in his black boxer briefs, smiling back. He's very fit and lean. I want to touch his abdominal muscles. I step forward and place my hands on his stomach.

The first time I saw Steve's abs, I licked them. At that time, I had never been with a man before and I didn't know what came over me. I was just so turned on. This isn't Steve, though.

"Stop. Stop. Wait." I back away slowly.

"What's wrong?"

"Nothing. Just give me a minute."

"Did I do something wrong?"
"No. I'm just... Where's your bathroom?"
He points. "Right there. Are you ok?"
Here comes my favourite word again, "Yes, I'm fine." Am I fine? I walk down the hall, looking for the bathroom, without another word.

Should I just go home? Have I made a mistake? I was having sex with random men before, but it was to get Steve back. Do I still want to do that? Of course, I still want Steve back, but is the Sex Project the right way to do it? I have a lot of experience now. I could try to seduce Steve without collecting any more data. I look at myself in the oval mirror above the sink. Nope, my mindset is not right for doing that yet.

I wash my hands and admire the antique pedestal sink. The taps are porcelain with hand-painted flowers. It's beautiful. Who is this hippie who lives in his grannies house? I haven't hooked up with a guy like this, but he does feel so good in my arms. I've been feeling so lost and this just feels right. It's just one night.

Outside the bathroom, I hear Mark call to me. I follow his voice and find him lying in a bed.

"Are you good?" He watches me carefully.

I take off my sports bra and slide into bed next to him. That should answer his question.

He turns toward me and I can feel the heat of his skin against my cool body. We start kissing and his hand slides up my body to my naked breasts. I can feel his hardness against my stomach. I kiss his neck and shoulder, moving on top of him. I start kissing down his body, under the blankets, licking his stomach and hip bones. He tastes salty from his sweat. It's different, but it's not horrible.

It's dark under the covers and I can't see much, but his erection looks like a good size. Average, I assume. I laugh to myself at my audacity. Now I'm ranking his penis size, like I'm some kind of connoisseur. He's a dart expert and I'm a penis pro.

Avoiding his shaft on purpose, I lick and kiss the area around him. I'm teasing him. Well, I hope I am. I can hear him moaning quietly. I think that's a good sign. I slowly lick the length of him, root to tip and he lets out a louder moan. He liked that. I start tonguing the tip and putting it gently into my mouth, sucking on it softly and then vigorously. I alternate between the two, getting into it and Mark is a very vocal about how much I am pleasing him. It's almost too much. He's loud. I smile to myself and keep going.

I put the entire length of him in my mouth and slowly withdraw. I do this at a slow pace for a minute and then begin to quicken. I can feel him at the back of my throat. I've got a good rhythm going and he is moaning so loudly that he's either going to burst or shatter the windows.

"Stop. Stop. I don't want to come that way," he says. I feel his hands on my head over the blankets.

I crawl up from under the covers and he pushes me gently on my back. We kiss some more and this time he straddles me, squeezing my legs together. I can feel his penis on my hips. He squeezes my breasts and dips his head down to bite my nipples. He goes from one to the other. He has my breasts so close together that my nipples are almost touching. He laps them like a cat. It feels incredible. I let out a moan and he stops. My eyes blink open.

"You like that?" He questions, unmoving.

I look at him with surprise. "Yes, it's great."

He smiles and does it some more. This time he bites and my moan is louder.

"You like that?" He stops again.

What is it that he is not getting? "Of course I like it." I'm irritated, but give him the encouragement. A moan means I like it. It's not difficult.

He lingers on my breasts for a while. Almost too long. I need more. Plus, I'm still annoyed by his questions. He needs validation? Just do it already.

"Mark," I say quietly and hopefully seductively. "I need you inside me."

His hands fly off my breasts. "You want to have sex?"

I am stunned. "Yes. Isn't that what you want?"

He nods vigorously and in one swift motion, jumps off of me. He goes to the left of the bed and rummages through a side table. He pulls out each of the three drawers, digging inside each one. I don't think he can find a condom. At least he's smart enough to get a condom. Finally, he pulls one out and holds it up to me.

"Better safe, than sorry." He winks.

I nod. Let's just get this over with now. This guy doesn't have any moves. I watch him start to put the condom on and he is having trouble. I close my eyes. I could fall asleep right now, but I feel the bed move and open my eyes in time to see him moving towards me on his knees. It's not a pretty sight. He is absolutely flaccid. I'm not starting over again.

Mark starts kissing me and I begin to melt, but he stops quickly. He takes my hands and pulls me up to sitting position. Surprisingly, it didn't take any time at all for him to become aroused again.

"Get on your hands and knees."

Oh. Ok. I do, but I'm not into it, at this point. Everything's so choppy and random.

He gets behind me and starts to tease my sex, but I'm pretty sure I'm totally dry. And the position... I don't like it. Mr. Baker did this position in my dream. Or was it Jack? It should've been Steve. I'm not aroused anymore. My dream comes back to me quickly. Jack had his hands on my hips, like Mark's are now. Jack was making love to me. No! I want it to be Steve!

"Stop! Stop. Wait." I pull away from him and crawl to the edge of the bed.

"What's wrong?"

"I can't do this. I'm not fine. I have to go home." I get up and find my panties on the floor. Where's my bra top?

"Really?" He grabs a pair of pants that are on the floor.

"Yes, really. I'm sorry. I just can't." I dig out my bra top from the bed sheets and put it on. Mentally, I map out where the rest of my clothes are in the house. I know my pants are in the hall and my yoga top is in the living room. I'm moving faster now.

Mark tries to catch up. He comes out of his bedroom with his head in a shirt. "Slow down. Did I do something? Is something wrong?"

"Yes. I mean, no." I slide into my pants. "You didn't do anything. It's not you." I look at him quickly and then go down a few steps to get my yoga top. "I'm going through something right now…" How do I explain this?

"I'm too small. That's it, right?"

I turn around to look at him, with my shirt half on. "What?"

He avoids my puzzled gaze. "My dick is too small." He turns around. "You fucking women are all the same. I don't have a big enough cock for you, so you run away."

"Oh my God, Mark." I walk up to him and touch his shoulder. "That's not it at all." What did I get myself into? "Mark, look at me."

He turns around, but he looks angry.

"I have decided to leave because I'm a mess. I'm not going to get into it with you, but I can't do this. Your… manly part is perfectly fine. It's great. It's average for a man."

"Average?" He turns away again.

Are you kidding me? "Mark, I couldn't handle more than average." The guy needs his ego lifted, so I can fib a little. "You're perfect."

"Really?" He turns to me again.

Holy hell. "Yes. Now, I have to go home. I need to sleep." Get me out of here.

"I'll walk you. Is your car at the studio?"

"I'm fine, Mark. You don't have to walk me."

"I can't let you walk to the studio, in the dark."

"I've lived in Toronto my whole life, Mark. I can walk by myself, no problem."

"Can I call you a cab, instead? It'd make me feel better."

"Fine."

After the call is made, we bundle up and stand outside silently. I don't know what to say to him. It got awkward very quickly. How do you recover from that?

When I see the cab approaching, I give him a quick hug and a peck on the cheek. "Thanks for tonight. I had a lot of fun."

"Could I have your number? Maybe we could meet another night?"

"I don't have a pen or anything." Thankfully. "I'll see you at the yoga studio again, I'm sure." I'll just have to go to different classes to avoid him. I've got that three month membership now, and I don't want to waste it, especially since I know I like yoga.

"Right. Will you be at the basic class again next week?"

"Quite possibly." I smile, but I doubt I'll be there.

"Great. Goodbye, Colleen."

I get into the cab. "Goodbye, Mark."

8.

It's Sunday and I try to sleep in, but my internal clock prevents it. I lie, looking at the ceiling and try to look forward to a quiet, uneventful day. Last night was too much, too soon. I should've gone home directly after yoga. I flip over to my right side and see that the time reads seven o'clock. I wish I could sleep!

Another yoga class could be on the agenda today, even if I run into Mark. I can handle that awkwardness. We didn't have sex, so there's nothing to be ashamed about. Yoga was too much of a pleasure, and a release, to give it up now. I kick my legs out from under the covers, trying to get comfortable.

It's funny how I don't want to run. Normally, I'd be up and out the door, running to the waterfront, enjoying the weather and fresh air, but I have no interest in doing that. I don't feel guilty about it and I don't care if my pace slows. I don't have the energy! I get back under my blankets and roll onto my stomach, pressing my face into the pillow.

I'm anxious about going back to work tomorrow. I'm sure that the busy schedule will keep my mind occupied, but I'm worried about little things setting me off. Obviously, I still obsess over what happened with Mr. Baker. Look what happened with Mark last night. Thoughts of Mr. Baker and Jack prevented me from having sex with Mark. Poor Mark! I cover my head with the pillow. I was so inconsiderate and he took it so hard. I guess it's true about men and the size of their penises. They worry too much. I thought I had issues.

If I can't stop these random thoughts, how am I supposed to deal with my patients? Will I be pleasant and interested in my patients' problems or will I have to fake it all day? I love my job, but how am I supposed to help other people when I'm such a basket case? I roll onto my left side now.

I'll have to face Margie, too. I haven't even called her to see how she's dealing with everything. The police told me the details of her escape, but I can only imagine how afraid she and Mrs. Baker were. Could she be dealing with the stress of it, like me? It was probably just as traumatic for her. I look up at the ceiling again and lay my arms over my head. I hope she's ok. God! We're more than co-workers, we're friends, and I'm being such a horrible person! Dammit! I just don't want to talk about it. I have that right. I don't want to think about it!

That's enough! I can't sleep. I kick the covers off of me and slide out of bed. A pillow follows me and lands on the floor. I kick it across the room and it lands underneath my dresser.

The jogging pants I wore a couple of days ago, are clean enough to wear again, so I put them on, as well as a long sleeve shirt that I find on my lounger. I pause to scratch at a stain that's on the cuff, but it doesn't come off. Oh well. I kick my through my yoga clothes from last night to get to the bathroom.

Mark was a nice guy, but he was only a distraction for me. I tie my hair back and splash cold water on my face. I should really figure out if I want to get back on track with my Sex Project. Am I going to go through with it? What's my motivation now? I've learned a lot and feel I'm ready, but I promised Christine that I wouldn't call Steve for two weeks. It's a smart idea, but it's only been a few days, and it feels like I made that promise months ago. Time is going so slow. I still have a week to experiment, I guess.

In the kitchen, I make a cup of tea and toast a bagel. Where did I put my research notebook? I scan the kitchen. The last time I saw it, I was hiding it from Jack. Right. I rifle through the mail and magazines on the kitchen table and find it between two pizza flyers. I butter my bagel and peruse the notebook as I eat.

All of my sexual experiences have helped me in some way. During the last couple of encounters, I was assertive, sexy and strong. Wow. I want to be that woman again. I shake my head and smile. I'm not referring to the sleeping around part. I just like how much confidence and strength I had. I can't believe how much this so-called trauma is affecting me.

I open the notebook to the next blank page.

Data Collection

Sample #7

<u>Seek persons who understand study & are willing to express inner feelings & experiences</u>
- Man, aged? (in his mid-30's), interested in yoga. Don't know what he does for a living.
- Inherited grandmother's house.
- Brunette, goatee, muscular body.
- First impression: hippie-vegan-yogi.
- Final impression: insecure-pro dart-playing-hippie.

<u>Describe experiences of phenomenon</u>
- We met at yoga and I didn't see him as a sample right away. We went to the pub across the street and drank beer and played darts. I hadn't eaten anything, so the beer went straight to my head. A bet was made that if he won the dart game, he would kiss me. I don't remember what I would get if I won. I don't think that it was decided. He kissed me before the game was over; it was a surprise attack outside the bathroom. It was a good kiss and I decided to go home with him.
- I performed fellatio on him and left before anything else happened.

<u>Direct observation</u>
- What is needed to be more sexual: Willingness to have sex, desire to be fulfilled and satisfied.
- I just didn't want to be alone. I wanted to forget everything and not be around people who reminded me of Mr. Baker and the abduction.
- Fellatio is pretty easy to do. Men seem to like it. There's no wrong way to do it, I suppose. I didn't swallow this time, he stopped me.
- Future goals: ??

Audio or videotape? n/a
- *Maybe this could be a future goal.*

Data analysis

Classify & rank data
- *2 out of 5*

Sense of wholeness
- *I did it because I lacked affection and security. This wasn't for the research. This was for me. I thought I could forget my problems. I stopped everything after I performed fellatio. I couldn't go through with it. It was for the wrong reasons.*

Examine experiences beyond human awareness/ or cannot be communicated
- *Guilt. He blamed his small penis on why I was leaving. It wasn't small. It was average, although it upset him when I said it was average.*
- *He seemed inexperienced and required validation for his 'moves'. I felt that I was more experienced than him. It bothered me.*
- *The experience was fine.*

The word *fine* isn't ideal for this type of research. I need specific, reliable and informative data. I'm disappointed with myself. .

Also, I notice in my past notations, that I felt like I was missing something during my experiences or after the experiences. It was a *something* that I couldn't figure out. I kind of felt it this time too. I lacked fulfillment. Mark didn't fulfill me, but was it because we didn't have sex? Because I didn't orgasm? Is that why? Is that the only sign of fulfillment? No, I had orgasms all the other times and I still felt empty or lacking in…*something*. Interesting.

This could be my motivation to begin again. If I want to get Steve back, I have to overcome all obstacles. What if I felt unfulfilled with Steve?

I can't have that. Should I start this research again, even though I haven't healed yet?

9.

Being lazy hasn't ever been my thing, but surprisingly, I lounge comfortably watching a home decorating show marathon. It's funny how during the last few days, watching TV has stressed me out, to the point of aggression, but now, I'm fine with it? Maybe I'm finally calming down and putting the past behind me. After the seventh episode, I stretch and figure that I should actually do something. Being a couch potato has its benefits, but I still feel guilty about it.

I lumber into my office and pick up the yoga schedule on my desk, but remember that it's not up-to-date, so I open my laptop and search for it online. I find it easily, print it out and see that there's a slow flow class beginning in twenty minutes. I can make it, if I hurry. I grab my mat and open the front door, but stop fast. Margie is standing on my porch.

"Hi, Colleen."

I'm immediately uncomfortable. "Hi, Margie." A warning would've been nice. I'm not ready to see her yet.

"Are you on your way out?" She looks at my yoga mat. "You're going to yoga?"

"Uh. Yes, I have a class. I joined a yoga studio." I can't even look her in the eyes.

"Well, I won't keep you." She looks disappointed. "I just wanted to see if you were all right." She turns to leave.

Come on, Colleen! This is Margie. *Talk to her!* "No, come on in. I can go to yoga anytime." I grab her by the coat and pull her back. I usher her inside and place my mat beside the door.

"I can come back another time."

"No, it's fine. Really. Would you like some tea?" I clear a space on the kitchen table and pull out a chair for her to sit down. Tea will help the situation.

She sits, but she looks strangely at me. "How are you holding up?"

"Me? I'm doing well. I had more than a few days off to relax. I'm sorry that I didn't call." I look away and busy myself with filling the kettle. I'm such an awful person. I picture Margie locked in the bathroom with duct tape on her mouth and hands. I feel sick. She's been through so much and I haven't even asked her how she is. I turn around and look at her. "How about you? Are you ok?"

"Don't worry about me. I'm good. I didn't endure all that you went through." Margie starts crying. "I was so scared for you, Colleen."

I take the coat out of her hands and place it on the chair next to her. I rub her back. "I'm fine. I'm perfectly safe."

She throws her hands up. "Look around, Colleen. You're not fine!"

I shake my head. "What? Sure I am."

Margie stands up and opens her arms. "Look at this mess. You don't live like this." She takes the dishes from the table and loads the dishwasher. "Your sink is filled with dishes, cups and…" She picks up a couple of soggy tea bags from the bottom of the sink. "You're not fine."

"Please. I'm just relaxing. I'll clean it all up later." I can feel my anger rising again. My body goes rigid and I grit my teeth, to try to stay quiet. This is *my* home. How can she walk in here and say that?

She stops cleaning and looks at me. "This isn't you. You're neat and precise and everything has a place." She shakes a plate at me.

Not this bullshit again. "Margie, people can change! I don't have to be Miss. Neat Freak! I like this mess." I take the plate out of her hands and throw it into the sink. It smashes into pieces. I'm horrified. The plate was a part of my Aunt Anna's good set of dishes. I'm so angry, that I want to throw another plate, but I start crying and pick out the ceramic shards from the sink. Why can't everybody just leave me alone?

"Colleen," Margie says quietly, and she helps pick up the pieces. We throw them into the trash. "What can I do to help you?" She hands me a tissue.

I wipe my tears. "Nothing, Margie. I'm sorry for losing it, but I don't need the constant reminder of what happened with Mr. Baker. I want to forget every detail about it. I just need time to forget." Please, just let me forget.

"Is that what you would tell a patient who went through a similar trauma?"

I stare blankly at her for a minute, before I speak calmly, "Margie, for me, it's fine. This is how I want to cope." She didn't go through years of school to get her name on the door. "Now, would you like that tea?" I hope that came out calmly. I want to change the subject. I'm the god-damned psychologist.

"Yes, please. As long as you use fresh tea bags," she teases.

Oh, that was hysterical. I turn toward the counter and take a deep breath. I'm just being sensitive. She's another friend just trying to help. I make the tea and she fills me in about the schedule for next week.

"I've arranged it so that you don't have to come in on Monday. I really think you should take a few more days off."

"I'm coming in on Monday, Margie." I'm not fighting with her about this.

She nods. "I thought you might say that, so I actually have booked you for a six hour day."

"Why only six hours?" It seems like a waste of a day and my time.

"You don't need to return to a full load of patients. Anyway, they all understand and are happy to wait for the next available appointment."

I panic. "What do they understand? What have you told them?" My career is finished. I'll be known as the shrink who lost it.

"Hey! Don't worry! When I rescheduled all of your appointments last week, I told them that you had an emergency situation you had to handle. That's all. No one knows a thing."

I exhale slowly. That's not too bad. "I still can work longer than six hours, Margie. I'm fine." I'm not helpless. I don't need to be told what to do, especially by my secretary. This is *my* practice.

"I can start booking more people in on Monday, after we see how you are. We can start slow. On Monday, you don't even have to come in until ten."

"Why come in at all?" I'm angry by her constant mothering.

"What?" She stares at me.

"Nothing. I just wish you could see that I'm--"

"Fine?" She interrupts me. "You keep saying that you're fine, but I know better." She gets up and starts putting on her coat. "Maybe I'm a trigger for you and I can totally understand that, but just know that you can talk to me about anything and I'll listen. If you don't want to talk to me, Jack and Christine are very eager to know how you are."

"You talk to Jack and Christine?" My voice cracks.

"Yes, they both call me to get updates, but I haven't had anything to tell them. I wish you'd call them both yourself."

"You guys are unbelievable. Listen, I just saw Christine yesterday. We talked. Everything is great. As for Jack, you can tell him that I am..." I stop myself. Margie tilts her head, waiting for me to finish. I will not say fine. "I'm perfectly capable of handling the stress of the situation."

"Honestly, Colleen, we've just been worried sick about you. Christine said that you avoid talking about what happened. If you'd just open up to one of us, we'd leave you alone."

This mothering has to stop. I force myself to hug Margie. "Thank you for handling the appointments and stopping by to visit. I'm sorry that I didn't call you. Please tell everyone that I'm dealing with everything the best way that I can." I'm seething inside. Are they all best friends now? Do they talk about how sad and pathetic I am?

"I look forward to seeing you on Monday, Colleen. Have a great day."

"You too, Margie." There's that phony façade that I wanted to avoid. I'm sure it'll reappear tomorrow.

As soon as I close the door, I clench my fists and want to scream. I want to hit something or throw something. I walk to the kitchen table and with one arm I heave all of the stacked up mail, magazines and even my Sex Project notebook onto the floor. That felt good. I kick a chair and it crashes against the table and falls onto its side next to the mess. Fuck!

I need to go out. I look at the yoga schedule again. There's a hot yoga class that begins in forty-five minutes. The class might be too hard, but maybe that's what I need. And there's no chance that Mark will be there either. Let's see if yoga can calm the beast inside me.

10.

Hot yoga is tough. The instructor's name is Caita and she's an older lady with long gray hair down to her bum, but she's not as frail as one might think. She teaches it like the basic class, in that every movement is linked to a breath and some of the same postures are used, but it's way more difficult. It's vigorous, fast-paced and it's hot!

There's isn't any time for adjustments or to think about what you're doing. I inhale and exhale loudly, like everyone else and pray for no more planks, but there are always planks. She's a monster.

Caita doesn't really participate, so I'm constantly looking at everyone else to see what I'm supposed to be doing. I'm sure that once I get the hang of it, I'll figure out what each pose is supposed to looks like. The sweat in my eyes makes it hard to focus, but I think I'm putting everything in the right spot.

Halfway through the class, I'm embarrassed by the amount of sweat dripping off of me, so I strategically place my towel on my mat during downward dog, so that the sweat falls on it. When I glance around the room, I see that everyone has sweat pouring off them too. I relax a little. I don't feel so gross now. I'm surprised that the room doesn't smell worse than it does.

We finish in corpse pose again and Caita starts walking around to the participants, rubbing their feet. That's new. Thankfully, it's the least sweaty part of my body.

"Hot yoga has many benefits. Your sleeping habits will become better, your energy will increase, and your moods will become more elevated and stable." I feel her rub the arches of my feet and then flex my feet toward my shins. It feels wonderful. "Hot yoga facilitates stress and anxiety reduction, and has even been shown to improve symptoms of depression."

Ding ding ding. Her comments hit home. At least I don't start crying this time.

When the class is over, I feel extremely limber and surprisingly calm. Yoga calmed the beast. I'm surprised and satisfied. It's like that 'something' that I was missing with sex. I'm completely content and fulfilled, and I didn't need a man to make me feel this way. I'll have to delve into that later.

My spandex is completely soaked and it's difficult to take off to change into the extra clothes that I brought. I struggle with my pants for a minute and then stick the wet clothes in a plastic bag, stuffing it into the end of my yoga bag. I wash my face and refill my water bottle in the sink. I've already downed three bottles, but I'm still thirsty. I gather my things and head to the front door to find my boots.

"Well, hello there!"

My stomach drops when I hear his voice. "Hi, Mark."

"Did you do hot yoga?"

"Yes, it was a great class."

"I'm going to the basic class next. I guess I won't be seeing you in the easier ones anymore." He looks like a sad, little boy. A sad, little boy with a hot goatee.

"You never know." I pull on my boots and smile up at him.

"I could skip the next class and we could go have a beer or something. I don't have any real plans tonight. I could even make you dinner. I was going to make lasagna and watch a flick on the movie channel. Or we could order pizza, but I'm a really good cook. You'd like my lasagna, unless you're a vegetarian."

He's really babbling on. He was so confident the other night, but I guess the whole small penis dilemma put him off his game. It's cute that's he's fumbling, but I just want to go home and shower. "No, go to yoga. That class really tired me out. It was pretty difficult. I'll see you another time."

"Oh. Ok."

"Have a good class. It was nice seeing you." I quickly leave the studio and don't look back.

Mark is sweet, but I know that a second date is bad. What did Christine say? *If you want to have casual sex, you need to play by its rules. No second dates!* That was her advice right after my first date with Dave the orthodontist. She was right then, and she's right now. I peg Mark as the insecure-slash-stalker type, so I don't need the aggravation of annoying phone calls or worrying about hurting his feelings. I dodged a bullet.

I take another swig of water and head outside. It's cold again. I quickly put my water bottle into my yoga bag and dig my hands into my pockets. My hair is wet with sweat and it's making me shiver. I should've brought a tuke. When I start to pull on my hood, I catch a glimpse of a man on the other side of the street. I think he's staring at me. I keep walking, but cautiously watch to see what he does.

Yes, he's definitely staring at me. What else could he be looking at? Don't get scared. Be strong. *I am a strong woman!* I stop dead and stare back. The man promptly puts his head down, but walks slowly in the same direction that I am. He's rather tall and reminds me of Mr. Baker, but I'm not sure if it's him. I begin walking again, keeping my eye on him.

This time, he stops to look at me. My heart begins to race and I start walking as fast as I can, looking for a place I can stop. This block only has townhouses and my house is still five blocks away. I can't breathe. I look at him again, and it seems like he's picked up his pace too. I'm just glad he's on the other side of the street.

There's a small convenience store about two blocks away, but I know closes early on Sunday. How early? I might make it, but I start jogging, just in case. What if it's not Mr. Baker? I could be acting crazy again. I slow my pace and give the man a quick glance. He's still there, but I can't tell if he's staring. I'm not going to take any chances. I sprint the last block and head into the store.

Inside the store, I peek out of the window and see the man turn down the next street, away from me. I keep watching to see if he looks back at me, while I try to catch my breath. My breathing is loud and erratic. I can't calm it down. After a few minutes, he still doesn't look back and I feel stupid and confused. I don't know if it was Mr. Baker or not.

"Are you ok, Miss?" The cashier looks at me strangely.

"I'm fine. Thanks." Embarrassed, I leave the store and sprint the last three blocks home.

As soon as I get inside, I deadbolt and lock the door, bending forward with my hands on my thighs, panting. I don't feel very good. I think it's a combination of hot yoga, running, paranoia and a lack of food. I may even be dehydrated.

I stand up and stumble to the side. I feel pretty weak. I definitely need something to eat.

Just as I open the fridge, there's a loud knock on my front door. My heart leaps out of my chest. Mr. Baker?

I back away from the door. "Go away! I'm calling the police!" I blindly find the phone on the kitchen counter. "The police are coming!" I start crying.

"Colleen? Colleen! It's Jack! Open the door!"

11.

Dammit! Jack can't see me like this! I wipe away my tears and take a deep breath.

"Colleen! I'm going to break down the door!"

"No! Don't do that!" I take a few recovery breaths. "I'm coming! Hold on!" This is all I need.

I slowly open the door, but Jack pushes through and storms into the kitchen, looking around.

"Are you ok?" He walks back to me and grabs me by my elbows. "What's wrong?"

"Nothing's wrong. I'm fine."

"Why were you yelling? Is someone here? Why is your house a mess?" He releases one of my elbows and points to the piles of letters and the chair that I had dumped on the floor earlier, in my rage.

"They fell this morning."

"I don't understand. Why you were screaming about calling the police?" He loosens his grip and gently rubs my arms.

"I wasn't screaming," I whisper softly. I pull away from his grasp and start filling the kettle. This kettle is getting a lot of use lately. "I'm sorry. My imagination went into overdrive and I was just seeing things. Don't worry."

"What did you think you saw?" Jack comes to stand beside me. His blue eyes filled with worry. I want to push his long hair off his forehead. He's so handsome. I take a step backward, after that thought.

"Oh, I'm so stupid. I was walking back from yoga and I thought I saw Mr. Baker." I giggle uncomfortably. Jack is not my type. "I obviously didn't see him. It was dark. I just panicked. It's nothing." I open up the cupboard door to grab a mug.

"Listen, I don't want you walking anywhere alone. I don't like it, especially in the dark."

"Don't start, Jack." I slam my mug onto the counter. "I can go anywhere I please. Besides, I don't have a car at the moment and I'm not going to be stuck at home."

"Ok. Ok. I'm sorry. You're right." He pats my hand. "When are you going to get a new car?"

"I was thinking I'd go tomorrow after work." I pour the boiling water into my mug.

"Do you want me to come with you?"

"No, thank you." The last car I bought was with Steve and I really didn't like his choice. I'm somewhat thankful I get to pick a new one and I don't want anyone's input on the matter.

"Hey, you don't look too good."

"Thanks for the compliment." I take off my coat and place it over a chair and cradle the mug in my hands. "Do you want some tea?"

"Colleen, when's the last time you ate something?"

"I had a bagel this morning. Why?"

"You've lost weight."

I look down at myself. I hadn't noticed if I had or hadn't. At the studio, I had changed into long tights and a skinny jersey shirt. Not really company-appropriate. I pull the shirt over my hips and try to stand behind a chair. "You've never seen me in spandex."

Jack comes over and cups my face in his hand. "I know your body. I can really see it in your face, especially in your cheekbones."

His touch is gentle. Flip flop. Wait! He knows my body? I wriggle out of his grasp and step back. Why did I get a *flip flop*?

"You're really pale, too. I'm making you dinner right now." He opens the fridge and freezer and starts rooting through my food.

I put down my mug and try to close the fridge on him. He pushes back. I put my hands up and roll my eyes. "I'm quite capable of making dinner, Jack." He's so frustrating.

"I'm hungry too. I'll make it for both of us." He takes out some chicken breasts from the freezer and vegetables from the crisper. "You're not going anywhere, are you?"

"No, I'm not." I take my mug to the table. "Fine. Whatever. Make me dinner." I *am* hungry, but I would probably just make myself another bagel. Let him make me dinner.

I poke at the tea bag in my mug with my finger. I should help him with the food, but I don't want to go near him. I'm puzzled by my reaction to him touching me. It'd be polite to engage in conversation with him, but I don't know what to say. I don't even know how to act.

I start jabbering nervously, "I'm pale because I just did hot yoga. It was pretty difficult and wiped me out. It's a really good class."

"Why did you think it was Mr. Baker?" He completely ignored me and changed the subject.

I shake my head at his rudeness. "It wasn't him. I was acting crazy. Just like when I thought I saw him outside the coffee..." My voice trails off. I shouldn't have said that. I quickly take a sip of tea, hoping he didn't hear me.

He stops chopping the vegetables. "You think you saw him before? When was that?"

"Oh, Jack. It's all me. I'm just being idiotic."

"When?" He demands.

"Last night."

"Where?" Another demand.

"I was at the coffee shop four blocks away. Really, Jack. It's my mind playing tricks on me."

He opens his mouth and then closes it. He goes back to his cutting board. "Please let me know if you think you see him again or if something out of the ordinary happens?"

"Why? He's not coming after me. He wants his daughter. I was just in the way before."

Jack stops again and stares at me. "Please," he stresses, "Just let me know."

"Ok, I will." He's so over-protective, like the big brother I never had. I felt safe as soon as I heard his voice outside yelling at me to open the door, but what was with the stomach flutters I had when he touched my face. I don't think of Jack in that way. I remember the dream I had about him and blush profusely. *Stop it!*

I hastily scoop up the mess of papers from the floor and pile them on the table beside me. I start rummaging through them to find a magazine to read. Jack is not an option.

"So, hot yoga?"

I look up and see him grinning at me. "What?" I ask.

"Is this a new passion of yours?"

"It's different. I like it." I smile back. "Why the wicked grin?" I like him when he's playful and not demanding.

"Does this mean that I might be able to defeat you in a run?"

"I wouldn't go that far." I smirk and thumb through a cooking magazine.

He bends down and when he stands up, I see that he has my Sex Project notebook in his hands.

I rip it out of his hands. "I got it." I wedge it under my magazine and place them both on the rest of the pile.

"What's in that thing?"

I feel my cheeks getting hot. "Why?"

"That's the second time you've hidden that book from me."

"I'm not hiding it."

"Sure, Colleen. Let me see it then."

"It's just work-related. You know patient info." I'm babbling again. "I can't breech the patient confidentiality agreement. You know how that is."

"Ok. I believe you." He turns back to the stove top. "Dinner will be ready in ten minutes."

"Let me go clean up and please help yourself to a beer."

I grab the pile of mail, along with the notebook, and take it to my office. I drop it all on my desk and close the door behind me. Jack doesn't need to see the contents of my notebook. How embarrassing would that be? And what if he talks to Steve? Oh no… If Steve knew that I was being promiscuous, he'd never talk to me again. I quickly walk back into my office and stuff the notebook into one of my filing cabinets.

12.

"Dinner was fantastic, Jack. Thank you so much." He made a chicken stir fry, using broccoli, canned water chestnuts and toasted almond slices. I'm impressed. I put my foot up on my chair and hug my knee. I poke at a hole in my black spandex pants.

"You're very welcome." He stands up and takes my plate from me.

"I can do the dishes, Jack. Just leave them in the sink."

"No offense, Colleen, but your housekeeping skills have really gone to shit." He chuckles.

"What does that mean?"

He stops laughing when he sees my face. "I'm kidding. You've been home for a couple of days and I know that you're still healing. It's ok to let the dishes pile up."

Healing? Is that what he thinks I need?

"You don't have to be perfect all of the time."

"Right. I can take off my robot costume once in a while."

"Colleen. Please. I didn't mean any harm."

"First of all, I'm fine. F-I-N-E. Fine. I'm sure Margie told you that already." I get up and grab the plates from him. "Secondly, I can be messy. I can be a slob. I don't have to be perfect. Please stop thinking that I'm this organized and logical person. I'm not." I drop the dishes in the sink and stare at him

"Why are you getting so angry? You do the dishes then. I'm sorry." Jack has his hands up in defeat, with a baffled look on his face.

He doesn't deserve my hostility. I put my hands on the counter and look down at my toes. "I'm sorry. I find myself on edge at times and I get angry really easily. Everything's still in the back of my mind, but I'm sure it'll be forgotten soon."

"Come on. Let's talk. You need to get all these feelings out. You'll go crazy."

I pause, thinking about where to begin. How do I tell him that I feel useless and weak?

"Have you had any more bad dreams?"

Does my dream about him belong in the good or bad category? There goes my motivation to start talking. I start wiping the counter. "You know what? I'm good. I don't want to talk about it. I talked enough at the police station."

He stops my hand. "You only told the police facts and opinions. You haven't told anyone about how you felt. I saw you in the elevator. You were torn apart. You were terrified and broken. Please open up to me."

I kissed him in the elevator. I wrench my hand away. "I can handle it." I try to smile. "Please believe me." I'm embarrassed that he saw me in such a vulnerable state.

"I wish I could." He takes a step closer to me. "I tore up the stairs that night you had a bad dream. I heard you screaming and I would've broken down your door to get to you. I had to help you." He pushes a curl away from my face. My hair is still damp from the shower. "I wanted to take all of your pain away, but I couldn't. I felt so powerless."

I turn my head to the side and avoid his eyes. I can't look at him. Why does he want to talk about this?

"All I could do was hold you in my arms and try to comfort you. I felt you relax, almost melt next to me." He takes a step closer and I breathe in his scent. "I could've left when you were calm, but I didn't want you to be alone." He lightly touches my cheek with his fingertips.

I close my eyes. "Why are you telling me this?"

He places his thumb under my bottom lip and turns my head toward him. "Colleen, I want to be with you."

I feel his lips on mine. Flip flop. I am surprised by the kiss, but I welcome it. His lips are soft and warm. My hands go to his chest and his arms wrap around me. I feel his tongue flicker out to meet mine. I respond and I hear his sharp intake of breath. He pulls me tighter and our kiss deepens.

He suddenly breaks away from me and looks me in the eyes. "I know you have feelings for me. Please tell me that I'm right."

I look at his face and I remember the dinner parties at my house. All of those women he dated... There were so many. He used and abused them and Steve high-fived Jack for his taste in women. He's definitely not my type and he was my husband's best friend. I can't be with Jack. I start shaking my head and pull away. "I can't."

"Colleen. Why?" He tries to pull me towards him.

"I love Steve. I should be with him."

He releases me. "What? You can't still want him?"

"I'm still married to him and I want to reconcile. That's all I want. I have to meet him one more time to see if I can make him happy"

"Meet with him? What do you think you can do in this meeting?"

I avoid his eyes and fiddle with my fingers.

"Sex? You think sex will change his mind?" He paces around the kitchen. "I'm sorry, but if sex with you didn't do it for him before, why do you think it will now?" His voice is getting louder.

"That's nice. A person can change, you know." That was hurtful.

"Colleen, Steve is an imbecile. All that man wants is sex, but from different women. He won't be happy with just one woman, even if you tried something new every night, he would eventually get bored." Now he's yelling.

"You don't know that. He loves me. We got married."

"And then he got bored. Wake up, Colleen!" He runs his fingers through his hair. "You're so frustrating!"

"I think you should leave."

"No." He takes two large strides to me and kisses me hard on the mouth.

I push him away, but he's holding me close. His tongue pushes into my mouth and I feel intense pressure swell between my legs. Flip flop. How is he making me feel this way? I'm not supposed to feel anything for Jack. Why can't I stop? It feels incredible.

His hands go under my cotton tee shirt and roam up my body. My skin burns where he touches it. I push my hips toward his and our kiss deepens. I'm grasping his shirt in my hands so tightly, I feel like I'm going to rip it off of him.

Jack pulls away again. I'm breathless. Why did he stop?

"How can you say that you don't want to be with me? Can't you feel the electricity between us?"

"It's just sex, Jack. I could feel that with anyone."

His hands drop to his sides and he stares at me blankly. "Do you really believe that?"

I've been drawn to other men and turned on by other men. This is no different. I know it's new and we obviously have a connection. I know he saved my life and maybe I feel indebted to him, so it's just a rush of out of control emotions. It does seem different when I kiss Jack. It feels natural, like we've done it all our lives, but it's not just that. There's something more. It's like when I kissed Steve for the first time. I shake my head violently. I don't love Jack.

"What? What are you thinking?"

"Jack, I can't do this. I have to follow through with my plan."

"You mean your plan to seduce Steve and miraculously get him to reconcile with you?"

57

He doesn't know how right he is. "Forget it. Listen, I love Steve. I'm sorry."

"You know what? *I* can't do this anymore. Every time I'm with you I fall deeper—God! There's no way that you don't feel it!" He throws his hands up in the air and pulls his hair. He comes back to me and takes my hand. His hair falls into his eyes. "If you can't figure it out and you can't get past Steve, I can't keep trying. I have to give up on you. Do you want me to do that?"

"I never asked you to try."

He looks like I just stabbed him in the heart. He drops my hand and steps away from me. When he speaks again, he is walking toward the door, "Listen, if you ever need anything, you can call me, but I won't bother you again."

"Jack, don't go."

He closes the door without turning back.

13.

Why do I always feel so empty after Jack leaves? I must feel indebted to him or some other kind of emotional or…psychotic attachment. I don't like it. What's that syndrome when abductees fall in love with their rescuer? Stockholm Syndrome? No, that would be me falling in love with Mr. Baker. I shudder. I'll have to research this later. And hold on, I'm not in love with Jack. He's just come to be a big part of my life. We went through an overwhelming ordeal together. It was traumatic and we experienced raw emotions that were involuntary and impulsive. Love? That's crazy.

I tap my fingers on the counter. I'm angry and frustrated again. Jack does this to me every time. I start rinsing the dishes to put them in the dishwasher, but I'm moving too hastily. A dinner plate slips out of my fingers and falls back into the sink with a loud crash. I inspect the dish and thankfully, it's not broken this time. I slowly place the dish in the dishwasher and dry my hands. The rest can wait. I need to go for a walk.

I grab my puffy, white jacket and mittens, and head out the door. The cold slaps my face, but I stuff my hands into my pockets and trudge on. I have no plan. I just walk aimlessly down the street. I smile smugly, remembering that Jack tried to forbid me from walking alone in the dark.

The moon is almost full, but I don't see any stars. Toronto's light pollution has changed the black sky of night to one with a dull orange glow, devoid of stars in the sky. That's one of the downfalls of living here, but the air quality in the city has been steadily improving over the past decade, with fewer smog days and less pollution. I'll still never leave the city. It's my home.

There are a lot of people on the street tonight and it makes me feel safe. The corner kitchen accessory store is holding some kind of sidewalk sale. There are bright lights and balloons, surrounding a table covered with pumpkins, apples and scarecrows. Isn't Halloween next weekend? I guess they're celebrating early. I watch some kids biting into candy apples and see that their faces are covered in red, sticky sugar. I smile at their cute, messy faces. I smell hot apple cider, too. When I spy the large urn, I stop to buy some, but keep walking. It's delicious.

I want to feel better and be my normal self again. I was so strong and level-headed before the incident. Despite the separation, I was in such a good place with goals and I had so much hope. The Sex Project helped and I still believe that the outcome will be positive. I don't think it would hurt to complete my research. Should I?

My mind/body connection seems to be strong tonight. In two more steps, I'll be at Mark's house. I suppose I consciously approved the continuation of my project, beginning with Mark. I'm content with my decision. I need to finish what I started and make our experience more inspiring. Leaving it partially completed, doesn't qualify my research. I didn't even find out his last name. Sure, it's unnecessary, since I refer to him as a 'sample' in my notes, but that lack of information leaves the research open.

I'm not really dressed nicely for seduction, but I take a deep breath and knock on his door anyway. I don't think he'll mind what I'm wearing. Look how much I've learned about men already. I mentally pat myself on the back.

The door opens slightly and I see Mark peek out. When he sees me, he opens the door wide. "Colleen! What a great surprise!"

"Hi, Mark. I hope you don't mind. I was bored and I remember that you were just going to watch a movie tonight."

"I'm glad you came. Come on in."

"Thanks." I undo my coat and he takes it from me.

"Are you hungry? I have lasagna leftovers."

"Thanks, but I've already eaten." It's a little awkward. I know what I came here to do, but I don't know how to begin.

Mark stands in front of me with his hands on his hips. "Come on in. I just sat down and was ready to pick a movie. You can help me decide."

"Ok."

He leads me to the living room and he offers me the oversized floral couch to sit down on. I sit down and rub the arm of the couch. It's really ugly.

He reads my mind. "Remember, this furniture is my grandmother's. I'm in the process of deciding what to do with it all, but it's tough. Work prevents me from getting it done quickly." He sits down beside me.

"What do you do?"

"I'm a doctor at the Children's Hospital."

"Oh." Scratch all my stereotypes about him. I never would've thought that. Dr. Mark. Should I ask him last name now? I don't really care.

"I'm only living here while the contractor and designer figure out the best way to fix it. I want to sell it or rent it immediately. I haven't decided. I can't wait to get back to my condo on the water."

I smile to myself. Here, I thought he was just a yoga enthusiast and dart pro. He's definitely not a hippie. He must get a lot of women just because he's a doctor. Then why did he have such a need for validation the other night? You would think that a doctor would know the average size of a penis.

"So, what choices do we have for movies?"

We peruse the listings together and I squeeze in closer to him. We tell each other what we've each seen in the theatres and what we liked or didn't like. We playfully tease each other's choices. I try to touch his arm and thigh as much as I can. I'm not here to watch a movie. I hope he figures it out soon.

Suddenly, I notice that he stopped talking and I look up at him. Before I say anything, we're kissing. It feels nice, but I need to pick up the pace. I propel my tongue into his mouth and grasp his shirt tightly in my hands, pulling it away from his body. I need more than a positive outcome for my research, I need a release.

Jack does this thing with his tongue when he kissed me. I've never experienced anything quite like it. Hold on! Don't think about Jack. This is Mark. I climb on top of Mark, straddling him and I push my sex into his hips. I can feel his hardness through both of our pants. I grind my pelvis against his and he starts tugging on my shirt, so I sit straight up and pull the shirt off myself.

He's staring at me with such a silly grin on his face. I smile back and he swoops down to kiss me again. When I kiss his neck, I taste salt. Did he not shower after yoga? He didn't taste like this last time. I go back to his lips, but I can't get the taste out of my mouth.

I have an idea. "Hey, you want to shower with me?" Steve and I snuck into the university showers quite frequently after practices together. It was usually later at night, when everyone was gone and they always ended very well. Sex in the shower stopped after marriage for whatever reason. I shake the thought away.

"Sure." Mark didn't even have to think about it. He stands up and takes my hand.

We walk upstairs to the bathroom and he turns on the taps, and then the shower head. He faces me and takes off his shirt. He's so lean and fit. I touch his stomach and lean over to kiss it gently, just like before.

When I stand up, he lifts up the bottom of my undershirt. I didn't put a bra on after my shower earlier. He seems to appreciate the ease at which my breasts become free, and fondles them quickly.

I tug at his elastic waist and he smiles and pulls his pants down. His erection springs free and I rub the length of it with both hands. He sticks his thumbs in my waist band and I release his manhood, while he slides my spandex down. I didn't put panties on either. I step out of my pants, open the sliding door to the shower and step inside.

Steam diffuses into the bathroom and I can feel the heat on my bare skin. I step into the water and Mark follows me. Facing him, I stand under the stream of hot water and lift my hands up to my head to get my hair wet again. He reaches for my breasts and takes them into his mouth. I watch the water run over his face and into his mouth.

I see a green pouf sponge hanging behind his head, so I reach for it and look for soap. There's a blue bottle labelled, *Shower Gel* on the bottom ledge, so I grab it and pour it on the pouf.

"Turn around," I tell him. He does and I start scrubbing his back, making him soapy. A fruity scent fills the shower. I go up to his neck and down to his bottom. I don't go too in depth there. That's awkward.

"I still have to do your front." I smirk at him. We switch places and the soap washes off of him.

Mark smiles and puts a hand on either side of the shower to brace himself. I start soaping his neck and chest, and then go lower to his abdominals. I purposely go around his erection, but then I squeeze the poof over top of it and soap covers it completely. I put the pouf's string around my wrist and begin rubbing the length of him in my hands. He's so slippery.

I look up at him and his hair is in his eyes. It reminds me of Jack and how he got me so hot with a single kiss. How did he do that?

"It's my turn," Mark says.

I'm not going to argue. My mind is elsewhere. I hand him the pouf.

He adds more fruity gel to it and soaps my breasts and stomach completely. He's not shy about soaping my sex, but drops the pouf and continues to gently finger my sex. Then, I feel a finger, or maybe two fingers, penetrate me. I have to hold onto the sides of the shower now.

His other hand comes around me and rests very low on my bottom. He turns me to face the back wall of the shower, so I am standing sideways to him. He enters my sex from both directions at the same time and leans his body against the side of mine. I moan loudly and put my forehead against the shower. My legs buckle as his fingers thrust into me steadily.

Mark gets on his knees and turns me again. His mouth is at my sex and he is tonguing it lightly. Does the soap taste like fruit? I look down and most of the soap has washed away. He spreads my legs wider and fingers me, as he licks. I pull his hair and relish the sensations that overcome my body.

He nudges me, wanting me to move, and I shuffle my feet in the direction he wants me to turn. My bottom ends up at his face and he kisses it, but continues to travel up my body. His hardness is now against my bottom and I want him inside me.

"We have to get out of the shower."

I look at him, confused. He doesn't want me?

"I don't have condoms in the shower."

Right. Very true, Dr. Mark.

He turns off the water, slides open the door and reaches for a towel. He wraps it around my body and grabs another towel for himself. We step out of the shower and he leads me to his bedroom.

Mark heads right for the bedside table and I hope he finds a condom quicker this time. He does and rips it open, rolling it on. His erection is steadfast. I'm impressed.

I follow him onto the bed and get on top of him, guiding him inside me immediately. I place my hands on the headboard and start rocking my hips back and forth quickly. I know it's too fast and I should probably slow down, but I just want to orgasm. I need this.

My breath quickens and becomes louder with every thrust. Then I'm reeling in sensation. It washes over me like the shower water. My core tightens up and I moan with delight. I hear Mark grunt a little, but I'm too involved in my pleasure to worry about his.

Finally, it's over for me and I collapse on top of Mark.

"That was amazing," he says.

Does that mean he climaxed? I roll off and peek over at him. He's not erect anymore and he's taking off the condom. Good. He was done.

I close my eyes and turn on my side. I feel Mark scooch up behind me. Spoons? Really? The spoons position is usually reserved for couples, not one-night stands. Uh oh. What did I say he was? An insecure-slash-stalker type. I lay there quietly and cross my fingers that he falls asleep.

Steve used to fall asleep immediately after sex. I'd come back from cleaning up, hoping to snuggle, but he'd be sprawled out on the bed, out cold. I'd squeeze in on the last quarter of our queen-sized bed and try to snag some blankets. His heavy breathing would eventually lull me to sleep. We used to cuddle after making love, when we were still in university. I sigh. Why did that stop?

After a few minutes, Mark's breathing changes and I assume he's sleeping, as his breaths are deeper and he's snoring quietly. I reposition my leg to test out some movement and he doesn't stir. I think I can sneak out of here. The bed creaks loudly, when I start to slide out of it, so I stop to make sure that he hasn't heard me. I can still hear his slow, even breathing. Mark's arm slowly slides off of me, as I get further away from him and I try not to let it drop onto the bed. It falls gently to the mattress, without any disturbance. Phew.

    I continue to slide away and ungracefully land on the floor, bottom first. I peek over the bed and he still didn't hear me. I get up and tiptoe to the bathroom, pulling on my clothes as quiet as I can. I also towel off my wet hair a bit more carefully. It's going to be cold outside.

    When I go downstairs, I walk on the outer edge of the staircase. I know that in Aunt Anna's old house, the stairs were creakiest in the middle. I only snuck up and down them in the middle of the night, to get cookies and hot chocolate. If she were to see me now….

    I find the rest of my clothes in the living room and put on my coat and boots. Finally, I steal a winter toque with a logo from the Children's Hospital on it, and quietly exit the old age home.

14.

Sleep is not a continuous state for me. I don't think I make it to the REM stage. I'm up every forty-five minutes and toss and turn all night. I have a quick dream about Mr. Baker and it ends when he pushes me down to the ground, in my office. This time, I'm not afraid when I wake up and I have enough sense to think of an alternate ending. Imagery rehearsal therapy focuses on changing a nightmare's ending to a more positive outcome, so I choose to stab Mr. Baker with the letter opener. It works for now, but I don't like the violence and can't actually picture penetrating his chest with the knife. There isn't really a realistic alternative. I could run for the door or hide in the bathroom, but both of those options are pathetic. Mr. Baker could change into a basketful of puppies.... I need to work on that one.

I get a glass of water from the bathroom at 3:23 a.m. I sigh. This lack of sleep isn't conducive to a productive first day back at work. I'm already anxious about my return, now I'm going to be cranky as well.

It's so quiet in the house. I hear the heat kick on and my heart jumps. I rush back to my bedroom anyway, looking behind me just in case, even though I know it's just the furnace. Silly girl. I jump into bed and snuggle under blankets. My bed seems more comfortable than before. I relax and fall asleep in no time at all.

Jack infiltrates my next dream. It starts out with me and Steve walking by Toronto's harbour, holding hands and laughing. I feel nervous and elated at the same time. It seems like we just got back together and we're celebrating. All of a sudden, Jack charges into us and knocks Steve down. I rush to help Steve, but Jack pulls me away. He tells me that I don't need Steve. I'm so confused. I look from Jack to Steve and Steve to Jack. I want to go to Steve, but Jack pulls me further away. I can't even see Steve anymore.

I wake up upset and my heart is racing. It's 5:17 a.m. What's the alternate ending to that dream? I could pull away from Jack's grasp and help Steve get to his feet. Then, Jack could leave and Steve and I would live happily ever after. That was pretty easy. Easier than it really is.

The bed is not comfortable at all now. I try the same routine and get up for more water, but now I have to go pee. After using the washroom, I pace around a little before I get back into my bed. Nope, I'm too awake. I'll have to try something else.

I put on my robe and slippers and wander downstairs into my office. I know that I shouldn't use my laptop because studies have shown that the screen's blue-spectrum light is known to impede sleep, but what else can I do at this hour?

The laptop blinds me, when I open it. I understand the correlation now, but my eyes adjust quickly. I check my email and determinedly delete the first one. It's a reminder for the Culinarium Cooking School. Apparently, Lebanese night is the theme this week and next week will be Spanish tapas. I feel a pang of regret. I enjoyed cooking class, but there's no way that I can go back. Sleeping with Chris was a great experience and I surprised myself when I seduced him, but I don't want to lead him on. His broken marriage was so fresh, that if I went to class and shared a kitchen with him again, he'd think that I was into him. I don't want him to believe he has a chance.

Oh my God. Listen to me. As if I'm some vixen! Oh, he's probably pining away for me! I laugh sarcastically. *Get over yourself, Colleen!* That's silly. He's probably been with other women since me or maybe he got back with his wife? I hope either of those cases is true.

Mary-Ann, from the book club, also sent me an email:

```
Hi Colleen!

I hope everything is ok. You missed the last
two meetings and I was wondering if you're
coming back. I hope you are! It was so nice
to be able to see you again.

My life is crazy with the kids and my husband
and I'm beginning to think that I took too much
on. Would you still be willing to take over
the Book Club on Thursdays? I still want to
participate, but I might not be able to come
weekly.

"Lady Chatterly" will be finished this week and
I was thinking that we could start John
Updike's "Couples". I don't know if you
```

read it, but here's the synopsis: The
novel focuses on a promiscuous circle of
ten couples in a small town. They are
basically swingers, and they struggle to
balance the pressures of their own sexual
ethics against an evolving outlook toward sex
in the 1960s. For that era, it's racy and
explicit. I thought it might be fun.

Please let me know as soon as you can. If you
can't do it, I might ask Miranda to take it
over.

Thanks,
Mary-Ann

Promiscuity? Pressures of sexual ethics? That book just hits too close to home. Not only that, Dave is another reason not to return to the book club. Another sample to avoid. God, I'm running out of places to revisit. I do save her email, promising myself to respond later.

An email from the *Island Air Aviation Academy* reminds me about my registration for the flying lessons. They start in two weeks. My stomach sinks. I don't know if I can handle that right now. I was so excited to start, but extracurricular activities aren't my priority anymore. I frown and sit back in my chair.

Is it wrong to focus all my energy on the reconciliation? Or the Sex Project? I still work, with the pitiful hours that Margie is setting me up with, but at least I'm not obsessing about Steve. Or am I? This is just too much to think about at six in the morning.

I slide the mouse in a clockwise circle over and over again and stare at my filing cabinet where I put the Sex Project notebook. I could write about Mark now…

I slam my laptop shut and walk over to the cabinet. I hesitantly take the notebook and sit back down.

Data Collection

Sample #7: PART TWO

Seek persons who understand study & are willing to express inner feelings & experiences

- Man, aged? (in his mid-30's), interested in yoga.
- He's a pediatrician with a condo. Surprise! Surprise!
- Inherited grandmother's house.
- Brunette, goatee, muscular body.

<u>Describe experiences of phenomenon</u>
- I went back to his house the next night. I knew he was going to be home, watching a movie.
- I wasn't interested in watching a movie.
- He tasted like sweat, so I suggested we take a shower.
- We soaped up each other and fondled each other
- We finished quickly in the bedroom, me on top.

<u>Direct observation</u>
- I seduced him. I went there with a plan. I executed the plan.
- Future goals: ??

<u>Audio or videotape?</u> n/a

<u>Data analysis</u>

<u>Classify & rank data</u>
- 3 out of 5

<u>Sense of wholeness</u>
- I did it because .... why did I do it? It went against my rules for casual sex. Only one date is acceptable. Jack instigated feelings of loneliness and I went to Sample #7 because he was a sure thing. It was for the wrong reasons.

<u>Examine experiences beyond human awareness/ or cannot be communicated</u>
- I remember thinking that I just needed that orgasm. Was it the release of it? I was stressed.

- *The experience was fine.*

I brush the tears away. Why do I feel so empty? This is supposed to be constructive and helpful research. These samples are supposed to help me to get Steve back. I shouldn't think about the why, it's more about the what!

I erase the last part and write more:

<u>Sense of wholeness</u>
- *My self-confidence has increased greatly. I suggested we shower and I got naked in front of him easily.*
- *I am spontaneous and creative!*

<u>Examine experiences beyond human awareness/ or cannot be communicated</u>
- *I'm more aware of my mind/body connection. Perhaps it's the yoga helping.*
- *I'm stronger, confident, and thus, sexier than I was at the start of this project.*
- *I should be proud!*

Crying about how lonely I am won't change a thing. Enough of the negativity! What would I tell my patients? I think for a minute and strategize my own positive self-talk: Acknowledge my negative thoughts and feelings. Release them. Replace them with positive emotions and thinking. Don't focus on problems. What's the solution? I am not alone. I am in transition. I will be happy.

Words spoken aloud can also be influential to the mind. "I can get Steve back. I will get Steve back."

I make my way upstairs and get into bed. Work starts in about three hours. Another hour of sleep couldn't hurt. I repeat my mantra a few more times and fall asleep.

15.

The relentless ringing of my cell phone wakes me in a panic. Where am I? What time is it? I scramble to the bedside table and fumble with it, trying to press the button to answer it.

"Hello?" There's silence at the other end. Whoever it was, already hung up.

I fall back onto my pillows, still trying to figure out what day it is. Then, my home phone rings. Of course, that phone is on the other bedside table. Stupid queen-size bed. I throw my body to the other side.

"Hello?" I'm breathless.

"Colleen, are you ok?" It's Margie.

My eyes open wide and I sit up straight in bed. "Oh my God! What time is it?" It's Monday! I look at the clock. 10:01 a.m. I have to stop closing the black-out blinds.

"It's ten o'clock."

"I'll be there in twenty minutes." I'm about to hang up, but I hear Margie say something. Annoyed, I put the phone back up to my ear. "Pardon? What did you say?"

"I said that it's ok. Take your time. I've rebooked your first appointment, so you don't have to come in until eleven."

"What? Oh, ok. Fine. Fine," I mutter. She didn't have to do that. We could've just pushed everyone back a half hour. I've done it before, especially when a patient needs extra time with me. I thought *I* was the doctor in charge. She's doing it again. Margie needs to ask me before she does things like that.

"I'm just trying to help."

"I know. I know. Thank you."

"See you soon."

I hang up and take a deep breath in, slowly releasing it. I can't be mad at Margie. It's not her fault.

There's no time for the leisurely shower that I had planned for this morning, so I do my usual five minute routine and get dressed quickly. I get frustrated when can't find the brown suede boots that go with my beige sweater dress. I kick around the clothes that are on the floor, check the racks in my walk-in closet and finally find them under the oversized sweater that I wore a couple of days ago.

I put on my wool coat and collect my things, but as I reach for the doorknob, I lift my head up in exasperation. "Fuck!" I don't have a car to drive to work. I drop everything onto the floor and call a cab.

I'm extremely perturbed now. What did I say wouldn't help with trying to have a good first day back to work? Anxiety, lack of sleep and now, pure perturbation, will not likely help with my day.

What would help? I ponder the idea of asking the cab driver to stop for a latte. The hot liquid would feel so comforting. Technically, we could go through the drive through. I shake my head. It's not good etiquette.

The bagel and orange I stuff in my bag aren't as appealing. I need caffeine! I pace in front of my living room window, hoping the cab arrives soon.

16.

"Good morning, Dr. Cousineau," a soft voice says.

I thought I was early enough to avoid my patient in the waiting room. I turn around, irritated. It's Janie, the one who has a slight learning disability and self-esteem issues. She must be early. I need to compose myself, she doesn't deserve my crabbiness

"Good morning, Janie. I'll be right with you." I nod to her parents, who are seated beside her. Let me get into my office, please.

I nod to Margie too, and she annoyingly follows me into my office. Such a little puppy dog.

"Here's a vanilla latte for you. I figured that you wouldn't have time."

I feel guilty for thinking badly. "You're a life saver. Thank you so much." I take a sip and the warm liquid soothes my body and my mind. The day might turn out better now. "I have no excuse. I just overslept."

She has the worry lines on her forehead. "We can reschedule your patients if you want to go home. I don't want you stressed out."

Yip! Yip! Yip! I should spray her with water. "No, Margie. Just send Janie in, please."

Like every Monday, play therapy is the theme of the day with all of my patients. It's a perfect and easy way to get back into my routine and I'm looking forward to it. However, I can't find Janie's file.

I leave Janie on the couch and stick my head out the door. "Margie, where is Janie's file?"

"It's on your desk."

"Oh." I look and see that I placed my purse and briefcase on top of it. When I try to slide the file out, my latte pours all over the desk and just misses the file. "Oh sh…" I stop myself from swearing.

"Janie, please take anything out from the shelf and start to play with it. I made a mess." I scurry toward the bathroom to get paper towels,

72

cursing under my breath, hoping Janie doesn't hear me. Why the hell did Margie put it there?

"Do you need help, Colleen?" Margie stands up.

"I'm fine," I say a little too sharply. "Please leave the patient's file on the door next time."

"Ok."

I know, wholly and completely, that I've always asked her to put the files on my desk, but I don't care. I almost ruined the fucking file. I scramble to clean up the latte and hurry to join Janie, who took out the same puzzle that we played with during her last visit.

"We've played with this before. Don't you want to try something new, Janie?"

She stands abruptly and starts putting the puzzle pieces away. "I'm so stupid," she whispers and looks like she's going to cry.

"I'm sorry, Janie. If you like the puzzle, we can play with it. It's my favourite too." *Good job building her self-esteem, Colleen.* I take a deep breath and adjust my attitude and approach.

Janie looks at me and slowly sits down again.

"I really like the chocolate lab. He's cute."

"I love dogs," she says, smiling. "My parents don't think I'm responsible enough to have one, but I'd take care of it and feed it and walk it. I wish I could get one." She starts putting all the puzzle pieces face up.

We chat more about dogs and different names for dog, while putting the puzzle together. When there are only a few pieces and a couple of minutes left of our session, I step outside to talk to her parents.

"Janie is doing well. She seems to like her visits with me."

"Yes," her mother says. "She adores you and talks about you for a couple of days after the visit. Unfortunately, by the weekend, she tends to get upset again."

"That's what I thought and I don't want her to depend on me. She still seems to perform negative self-talk." I think for a second. "Is anyone allergic to animals in your family?"

"No. Why?"

"Well, this is a big investment, but a pet might help. Animals can provide unconditional love with no regard to limitations and could help strengthen Janie's sense of self."

"I've read about that type of bonding with horses," her father says.

"We can't have a horse," her mother exclaims.

"Not a horse, but maybe a dog?" I suggest.

Her mother smiles and nods.

"Janie's unable to express physical and emotional comfort and closeness with others, but she might be able to fully and freely form that type of bond with a dog. The bond can serve to help Janie develop a number of positive characteristics, including acceptance, confidence and assertiveness."

Janie's parents look at each other in consideration.

"It's something to think about," I say. "I'll finish up with Janie and be right out."

After I say goodbye to Janie and her family, Margie tells me that my next patient called to say that she was running late.

"Good." I have a few minutes to collect myself and finish my latte. I start to walk back into my office.

"I need to run out and buy some stamps. Is that ok?"

She should've done that when she got my latte. "Sure. Whatever." I grab my latte and sit at her desk, as she walks out the door.

I look around the office and notice that the woodwork around the bathroom door, and even the door itself, is different. It's new and shinier. I walk over to inspect it. Margie must've had it fixed while I was off work. I wonder how much damage was done to it when Margie and Mrs. Baker broke it down. To have the whole thing replaced means that it wasn't an easy fix.

Where's the invoice for the repair? I hope Margie's not hiding it from me. Does she think I might get stressed out? She's driving me crazy!

Inside the bathroom, I don't see any damage or new fixtures. I picture the women taped up and frantic. It must have been awful for them. I lean against the bathroom wall and close my eyes. How could I let that happen to them? I should've stabbed Mr. Baker with the mail opener when I had the chance. Those women didn't deserve to be treated that way.

I hear the door to the practice open and I freeze, holding my breath. All I can think is that it's Mr. Baker. He won't find me in here.

"Hello?" A male voice calls out.

It doesn't sound like him, but I still can't move. My heart is beating wildly and I feel dizzy. It's really hot in here.

"Excuse me? Is anyone here?"

I slowly inch towards the door. It's not him. He wouldn't be pleasant. Breathe. *Don't be so stupid.*

I step out into the office and see a man holding a large, somewhat flat package. I take a deep breath and exhale through my mouth. It's a postal worker, not Mr. Baker. Why do I have to think the worst? I suppose triggers like these are normal, but that was almost delusional. I quickly regain my composure.

"Good afternoon. I have a package for Colleen Cousineau." He's young and I see a tattoo on his collarbone, coming out of his shirt, up the sides of his neck. I can't make out what it is.

"I'm Colleen."

"Well, here's your package." He's being flirtatious. His eyes travel down and up my body. He smiles and winks.

He's cute, but I don't need the hassle. I ignore him. "Do I have to sign for it?"

"Nope. It's yours. Just take it."

Was that an innuendo? "Thank you." I walk up closer, to take the package and see that his tattoo is of a dove. The wings travel up his neck. "I like your tattoo."

"Thanks. A dove mates with one partner for the duration of its life. It represents steadfast love and devotion."

"That's beautiful. Have you found your partner?"

"Not yet." He winks and eyes me like a piece of meat.

"I'm sure you will." I walk to the door and open it for him. He should leave now.

"Have a wonderful day, miss."

I smile slightly and watch him walk to his truck. I don't think the tattoo suits him. He doesn't seem to represent a lifelong, faithful partner. He's too flirty and assertive. I wonder if women fall for that sort of thing. I couldn't just ask a mailman to come in to have sex. I guess I've done worse. What's so different from that and having sex in a nightclub's back office? Or going home with the multitude of men that I have been going home with after knowing them for only a short period of time? There's no difference.

The return address on the package is from the *Art Barn School*. Flip flop. I carefully rip off the tape and open the box. It's my own painting of the countryside. I'm surprised. Did Shawn send it? Oh, there's an envelope too. I open it and pull out a hand-written letter.

Dear Colleen,

You weren't in class this past week and the way you left me the other night, after my Gallery opening, makes me think that you won't be back and that saddens me. I sent you your artwork, not that I never want to see you again, but because I'm hoping that it will lead you to return. No strings attached. You have natural talent and a creative mind. I don't want to see that go to waste.

I did have a wonderful time last Friday and would love to see you again, even if it's just on a completely professional level.

Take care,
Shawn Lauzon

Wow. He is sweet. I look at my half-finished canvas. It was such a great experience painting again and I learned a lot from Shawn. Should I go back? Never mind. I could never go back and face him again, after I snuck out of his apartment. I bring the painting into my office and slide it onto a low filing cabinet. I might be able finish it at home.

Shawn was an amazing experience for my research. I remember how chaotic my emotions were when I was waiting for him at *Gallery 123*. I wanted to see if I could seduce him, but then I became scared and almost left. I giggle to myself. I was ridiculous. It all turned out perfectly and I went home feeling accomplished.

I could use a few more experiences like Shawn. I have one week left before I can call Steve. I can meet one or two more men, couldn't I?

17.

It's only four o'clock when my last patient of the day leaves. The five hour day flew by, just like I knew it would. No break-downs. No stress. What did Margie think I would do? I could've handled more, but I'm also glad I'm done.

Now, I have energy to burn. It's my volleyball night… Could I handle seeing Ryan? I grit my teeth and shake my head harshly. Nope, I don't think so. I could go to a hot yoga class? I'm totally up for that and it's early enough that Dr. Mark may still be at the hospital. I'll keep my fingers crossed. I'll have to go home and change and check the schedule.

I root in my purse for my keys, but stop suddenly, maddened by the fact that I don't have a car. "Fuck!" That's the second time today.

"Margie?" I hope she's still here. I run out to the front. "Margie?"

She comes out of the bathroom, drying her hands. "What? What? What's wrong?"

"Nothing's wrong. I didn't know if you were still here and I needed—"

"You scared me!" She touches her heart and shakes her head. "Don't do that to me."

Enough with the drama already! I tap my foot impatiently and wait for her to catch her breath. "Could you please drop me off at that car dealership in Scarborough? It's a little past your house, but not too far."

"Of course, and I can stay with you, until you find something."

"It's just a car. I'll be fine. I know I'll find something appropriate." I don't plan on drawing this out and I'd rather be alone.

"Are you ready?"

"Yes, let's go."

Margie's minivan is luxurious, with all the bells and whistles, but I quickly find out that she can't handle the vehicle. She's a nervous driver.

She's heavy footed on the brake and grasps the steering wheel tightly, all the while squealing under her breath when she thinks someone's going to hit her. I keep my eyes closed, until we get on the 401.

"New van?"

"Yes, I got in an accident with the last one."

"What? When did that happen?" It's not surprising to me at all.

"Oh, it was about a year ago. It was completely my fault and my car was totaled." She looks at me, like she wants to say something, but changes her mind. She squeals when she passes a semi-truck.

Ok, so she's not good on the highway, either. "That's awful and you weren't hurt?"

"Not at all," she says, smiling, "Unfortunately, it was my third accident in four years."

I grasp onto the door handle tightly.

"I'm not the best driver, but Jerry never blames me. He went out immediately and bought me this beauty. He's such a good man." She glances at me quickly. "We all have things we're good at and things we can handle, but when we're overwhelmed, it's good to have someone on your side. We talk all the time and we get through the problems."

"That's good." I don't know why Jerry wasted his money on a new car. He should've bought a beat up, used piece of crap. I don't think she'll become a better driver, anytime soon.

"If I need to vent, he doesn't give advice or try to fix the problem, he just listens. I feel so much better afterward. If he was angry after any of my accidents, what good would come from it? I'd be more stressed. Instead, he listens, calms me down, and we go out for Chinese food. We're there for each other."

All right, I see where she's going with this, but I'm not going to bite. "You're great for each other."

"You know that you can always—

I point up ahead, "Here's our exit! Turn right onto Kingston Road."

Margie follows my directions and we see the dealership, as soon as we turn. I quickly gather my belongings and grab at the door handle, prepared to leave. I don't need another lecture about talking about my feelings.

"Thank you so much. I'll see you tomorrow with my new ride." I quickly step out of the car and close my door.

She opens the passenger side window. "Call me if you can't find a nice one. I can take you to a different dealership."

I curtly wave goodbye and start walking down the car lot, happy to get away from her. Enough negativity! Time to buy a new car!

The dealership has a lot of options. There are new and used cars, including SUV's and trucks. I've always driven a small, compact car, so maybe I need a change. Everything else in my life has changed. Why not?

A dark blue Expedition Max catches my eye and I look inside the driver's side window.

"She's a beaut, isn't she?"

The voice surprises me and I step away from the vehicle. I turn and see a man in a well-tailored suit, with a name tag that reads, *John*.

"Hi. Yes, I'm looking for a car to buy today."

"Today, huh?" He has a dimple on his chin when he smiles. "What are you driving now?"

"Long story. I don't have a vehicle."

"Perfect. My name is John Blake and I'd be happy to help you find your new car." He shakes my hand. It's a firm grip, but his hands are soft. His light blue tie matches his eyes. He's a very good looking car salesman.

"Thank you." When Steve and I looked at cars, we were lead around by a female or an older, bald gentleman. I didn't expect this windfall.

"Do you want an SUV?" He walks closer to me and I can smell his cologne. It smells spicy, almost like cinnamon.

I step away from him and focus on his question. I put my hand on the SUV. I'd love this, but it'd be a poor decision on my part. "No," I say sadly and walk away from the Expedition. It wouldn't always fit in the underground parking in Toronto, it's bad on gas, it's horrible for the environment, and the list goes on.

"What type of car are you looking for?"

"I don't know." I hope he doesn't think I'm a brainless twit. "I've always driven compact cars."

"Good to know. Do you normally commute or are you a city driver?"

"A city driver."

"Great! Let's start with what you know. We have some great deals on compact cars." We walk across the lot and he points to a blue Corolla. "It may not be the most exciting choice on the market, but the Corolla is reliable and has good fuel mileage. The 2014 is stylish, but it has one hundred and fifty-five horsepower and one point eight litre cylinder.

Ugh. It's boring. "What else do you have?" I look around. "Oh, and omit the horsepower, blah blah, mumbo jumbo, car talk. I don't care about that stuff."

He laughs. "Sounds good. He points to a silver Passat. "Here's a lavish executive car. It has front and rear parking sensors, cruise control, and a six-inch colour screen with DAB radio, USB input, Bluetooth and audio streaming. It has low emissions, however, the diesel engine is still punchy enough that you don't feel like you're living with a gutless car for the sake of keeping emissions low

    I caress the rear end. It's very nice.

    "You'd look great in that one."

    I look at him and he's eyeing me. Is he flirting or is this how he sells? "It's ok, but what about that?" I point to a very modern and sleek, black car.

    "That is the Infiniti Q50. It looks like a sports car and drives like one. It's built with power to spare, easy to handle and has style both outside and inside. It's great in the city and on the highway."

    "You sound like a commercial." I smirk. "I like it very much. Can we go on a test drive?"

    He squeezes my shoulder. "Solid choice for such a beautiful woman. I'll go get the keys." He flashes me a million dollar smile.

    I swoon and watch him walk away. Screw the car, this guy could definitely be a sample. Screw in the car? I do a full turn, giddy all of a sudden.

    John quickly comes back and unlocks the door, holding it open for me. "This is going to be fun." He stares at my legs, as I get into the car.

    I let my sweater dress ride up a little. Yes, it is going to be fun. I smile up at him.

    When he gets in, I start driving and pull out of the lot. He directs me around a few neighbourhoods and he talks about the car.

    "Infiniti introduced a first-of-its-kind steer-by-wire system as an option. It's called Direct Adaptive Steering. It lets drivers choose from three steering settings."

    I roll my eyes at him and smile.

    "Really, it's a great option. You can choose heavy, standard or light modes to reflect your needs or your mood."

    "I just want to drive."

    He puts his head back and looks up at the roof of the car. "Women!"

    I don't take offense. "I do like the way it drives. It handles well and the acceleration is…" I step on the gas. "Wow!"

    He puts his hand on my thigh. "Slow down." He starts laughing. "What's your name, crazy lady?"

    "Colleen." I take my foot partially off the gas and look at his hand. This is going in the right direction.

    "Nice to meet you." He slowly takes his hand off my leg and his fingertips tickle my skin.

    "Anything else I should know about this fine vehicle?" I know I'm going to buy it, but I figure he should at least, try to sell me.

    "Park here." He points to the side of the road.

I don't question him. I pull over and put it in park.

"Put it in reverse, but keep your foot on the brake."

Again, I obey him.

"Look at the backup camera system. It has a 360 degree view. It seems a bit excessive, but once you use it, you'll miss it when it's gone." He laughs. "I used to have this car, but upgraded a while ago. My new car doesn't have this."

"Aw, you miss it," I tease.

"Yes, I do. Now, put it back in park." He points to the dashboard. "This is a new InTouch infotainment system, with dual touch screens and gestural support. It offers the Infiniti Connection, which is a security- and concierge-related telematics service that provides remote monitoring, SOS call and collision notification, as well as a personal assistant service."

"How do you remember all of this stuff?"

"It's my job." He stares at me for a minute. "Are you ready to go back?"

I nod. "Sure." It's hard to tell if he's interested. Maybe he's just selling a car. He does work on commission.

We drive back to the dealership in silence and I pull back into the same parking space. "I like it and it's a great price. Can I drive it home today?"

"That was super easy. I thought I could spend a little more time with you, before you decided." He smiles bashfully. "Sorry, I shouldn't have said that."

He does like me. "No, it's ok." He's pretty cute.

"Maybe we could finalize everything over dinner?"

Without a thought, I say, "Sure." Let's see where this takes me tonight. I'm ready for another sample.

"Perfect. I know a restaurant just down the street. Let me get the paperwork and we'll walk there. Is that ok?"

I nod excitedly and wait for him to come back. It doesn't take him very long and he comes out with a briefcase. We chat on the way to the diner, which is just a short distance away and he holds the door open for me when I walk in. He grabs two menus and we seat ourselves.

"Hey, Amy! Can we have two cups of coffee?"

A waitress behind the counter nods.

"I come here all the time. You like coffee, right?"

I'd rather have tea, but it doesn't matter. "Sure. Sounds good"

When Amy comes with our coffees, we order our meals and I ask for a glass of water.

"Water? I hate that stuff."

I shrug. Who hates water? "Let's do this paperwork."

The contract is straightforward and we finish going over it, just as our food arrives. John stuffs a napkin down the neck of his shirt and smooths it over his tie. He looks ridiculous.

"Can't get myself dirty."

I put a napkin on my lap and begin eating my salad, but I pause in shock, as he devours his spaghetti. It's a good thing that he is wearing that napkin. The tomato sauce has splattered all over it, narrowly missing his shirt.

"Is your salad good?" He asks with his mouth full.

I nod and avert my eyes. He has meat sauce all over his chin and mouth. Gross. I don't know if I can take another bite of my lettuce, but can't help watching him. I've never seen anything like it. He twists the spaghetti on his fork, but instead of using a spoon to manage the hanging pieces, he lifts his fork up high and slurps the spaghetti strands into his mouth, slowly lowering the fork to devour the load. He slurps it loudly and finishes the plate in minutes. I've barely had a couple of bites.

"What's with women and salads?"

"I don't know what you mean?"

Amy comes by and takes his plate. "I'm not impressed by watching you eat leaves and vegetables. I know you'd probably rather eat a big, thick steak." He pretends to hold something big in his hands and takes a bite out of it.

"I wanted a salad. I like salads."

He starts to tap his fingers annoyingly, so I start to eat slower. Is it that you're supposed to chew twenty or thirty times before you swallow? He can strum his fingers as much as he wants. I'm beginning to rethink the whole idea of adding him as a sample. Would he be this impatient and sloppy in bed?

"I read somewhere that, on a date, women use the content of their plate to transmit a subliminal message to potential suitors."

I almost drop my fork. "What?"

"Yeah," he starts, but covers his mouth a burps loudly. "Excuse me. A woman thinks her salad leaves say that she's attractive and that she takes care of herself."

I look at my plate, contemplating his statement. "I can appreciate that and understand the concept behind the analysis, but I actually like to eat salad." He seems pretty intelligent. "Where did you go to school?"

"Oh," he laughs, "I dropped out of high school. I just read a lot."

I nod and scrutinize my ability to read men. I suppose the expression, 'you can't judge a book by its cover,' encompasses this situation.

"Are you almost done?"

I look at my plate. There are a couple pieces of lettuce, slices of tomato and cucumber and a piece of chicken. I'm obviously not done. I eat the chicken and push my plate away. What was I thinking? I can't stand being with him for another minute.

"Amy, you can take her plate," he yells over his shoulder. Amy is with another customer and she ignores him.

"Can I sign the papers now?"

"Yes, you can, sweetheart." He pulls them out of the briefcase, takes the napkin from his shirt and wipes up a spot of spaghetti sauce from the table, before putting them down. "Sign here." He hands me a pen.

I sign at the bottom and he gives me a copy. "Congratulations," he says.

"Thank you. Ready to go back?" Please say yes.

John throws a twenty dollar bill on the table and stands up, rubbing his stomach. "Ready, willing and able." He winks at me.

Ten dollars doesn't even cover tip. Poor Amy. I can't even look at her. I just get up and follow him quickly out the door.

Just past the diner, John stops me. "Listen, I know this was quick, but I just wanted to say that it was great meeting you. You are a fun lady."

Fun lady? Who is this guy? "Yes, it was great meeting you too." I turn to start walking again.

He pulls my arm and I end up in his arms. He's hugging me. It's not what I expected from him, but it's a nice hug. I actually don't mind it.

I start to pull away, but he doesn't let go. I feel his lips at my neck and they travel up to my ear. I feel his breath in my ear as he gently bites my earlobe. Hold on a second. This feels nice. So what if he lacks table manners and proper tipping etiquette. Maybe he's good in bed. It sure seems like it.

"I knew you wanted me," he breathes into my ear. "From the moment I walked up to you in the lot and saw your sexy legs."

That's a little presumptive and over exaggerated, but he can keep complimenting me.

"Let's go back to my office. No one will be there."

We walk quickly back to the dealership and he unlocks the front door. After he locks it behind us, he leads me to a tiny office at the back of the building and closes and locks that door too. At least, I feel secure about no one walking in on us.

"Take your coat off."

I do it slowly, still not sure about the whole thing. I suppose it doesn't have to happen. I can still make a quick getaway, if needed.

He stares at me. "Are you wearing panties?"

"Of course." What kind of question is that? I need to stop him from talking. I don't have a gag, so I take a step forward and start kissing him.

John doesn't offer me his tongue and the open mouth kissing is gentle, but I need more. I want to feel his tongue, so I lightly nudge mine out. I lick his upper lip and then his lower one.

"Oh, you like tongue, do you?"

I wish I hadn't bothered. Our kiss turns slobbery and he sticks his entire tongue in my mouth. It's like a dead fish. He's now licking my teeth and the roof of my mouth...is that my uvula? I gag and pull my head away to wipe my mouth. I try again, holding my head back, so that he can't shove it in again, but he grabs my head and pulls me closer. I breathe through my nose and try to relax, but the feeling is gone. I can't have sex with this guy.

I jerk my head away and take a step back, but he takes my hand and makes me rub the length of him through his dress pants. He seems quite large.

"Do you want that?"

I keep looking down. Does his size make up for the bad kissing? He feels my breasts over my dress and that arouses me. Then he starts to kiss my neck and ear again. If he sticks to this, I can handle him.

He backs me up against his desk and pulls my dress up. I sit down and he pushes me all the way back, so that I'm lying on his desk with my dress at my waist. He pulls down my panties and I feel his fingers at my entrance.

"Do you have a condom?" I ask.

"Right. Shit. I almost forgot." He rushes to the other side of the desk and rummages around his desk drawers. He pulls one out and rips the foil with his teeth. I close my eyes. What am I learning from this?

I feel him between my legs and he drives into me immediately. He does have great girth and I get excited immediately.

He doesn't move. "Wow. You took that no problem. Some women can't handle it."

If that wasn't bad enough, he goes at me like a rabbit. Now I understand that cliché. He bangs into me so fast that my butt sticks and painfully, unsticks all over the cold, laminate desk. I look at him and he's in some sort of zone. Is that his tongue sticking out of his mouth? This is not good. It's not good at all. I think I'm getting rug burn on my lower back, but without the rug. Desk burn. Do I say something? This is awful.

His breathing becomes short and he starts to grunt repeatedly. I think he's going to orgasm. I can't let that happen yet.

"Hey. Hold on. Slow down."

John opens his eyes. "What's wrong?"

"I'd like you to go slower. We're not in a rush, are we? No one is going to walk in on us?"

"No. You don't like it?"

"I like it," I lie, "But let's try something different." I sit up and point to his desk chair.

He withdraws and moves to the chair. "You like things kinky, don't you?"

"Sit down."

I straddle him, putting him deep inside me. My toes still touch the floor, so I slowly lift up and when I come back down I rock my hips forward. It feels amazing. I repeat the slow, delicious process. Now, this is how you do it. I wish he would play with my breasts or kiss my neck though. Do something. His hands just stay unmoving at my hips.

John's grip on my hips suddenly tightens and he starts lifting me up and bringing me down hard onto him. Just like before. Too fast and uncontrollable. It does nothing for me. I try to tighten up my body and not move. My legs are flexed, but I can't hold it for long. He's bouncing me up and down in no time.

I give up and let him use me. The cinnamon-smelling cologne is nauseating me now. I will never have a cinnamon latte again.

Within seconds, he explodes and I stare blankly at him, watching. His is face scrunches up and a vein pops out of his neck. After one loud grunt, he relaxes and his face falls into my chest.

Well... That was interesting.

I stand up and pull my dress down over my hips. I take a few extra seconds to smooth out the imaginary wrinkles. I don't know what to do. That was not worth my time.

John remains seated and I turn away, as he pulls the condom off. I don't need to see that.

"That was great, babe."

Babe? Get me out of here. "Yes. It was... nice."

On his way to the garbage can, he smacks my bottom. "I sold a car and a got a shag to boot. It's my lucky day."

My skin crawls. I thought that about him, when I first saw him. "I should be going. It's getting late and I have to work in the morning."

"You're my kind of woman. Slam, bam, thank you, man." He laughs and grabs a small glass bottle off his desk. He lifts it to his neck and I see a spray come out of it. "I'm usually gnawing my arm off to get away from a chick."

An extreme cinnamon odour fills the air. It's disgusting. He's disgusting. How could I have thought he was good enough to get experience from? Let's end this fiasco. "Do you have my paperwork?"

"Right here, babe. Just give me a kiss goodbye to get it."

Oh no. I try to peck his cheek, but he turns his face and I kiss him on the lips. I'm sickened at how wrong I was about him.

"Gotcha! Here are the papers." He unlocks the office door. "I'll even be a gentleman and walk you to your car."

Great.

As we get to the car, he swings the keys from his fingers. "You're going to need these, babe."

I try to smile, grab the keys from him and rush to get into my new car. I start the engine and he gestures for me to put my window down. What now? I just want to take off. I'd even consider running him over, so I don't have to hear another word out of his mouth.

When the window is down, I quickly say, "Thank you for helping me find a car. I love it."

"I aim to please."

Whatever. He should stick to selling cars.

"I'd be lying if I told you that I was going to call you. You're a big girl. You know what this was."

I breathe a sigh of relief. His honestly is the best thing about him. "Yeah, no problem. See you around."

I think he wants to say something, but I quickly put up my window and speed out of the lot.

18.

When I get home, I sit in my car for a few minutes to admire it. I hope I don't think about John every time that I'm in it. What an awful experience. I really should have gone to volleyball instead. Seeing Ryan again wouldn't have been as painful or horrible as that debacle.

Inside my house, I throw my bags onto the floor, put my coat over a chair and head straight to my office. I rummage through the file cabinet and find my Sex Project notebook.

Data Collection

Sample #8:

Seek persons who understand study & are willing to express inner feelings & experiences
- *Man, aged? (in his mid-30's). Car salesman.*
- *Light brown hair, brown eyes, dimple on his chin.*

Describe experiences of phenomenon
- *He sold me my new car, had dinner together and had sex in his sales office.*
- *During the sales experience, he was professional and suave. He was even shy and sweet.*
- *During dinner he lacked table manners, tucking a napkin into his shirt and slurping his spaghetti. He even talked*

differently. He called me sweetheart and was impatient. (Why did I sleep with him??) His tip was awful too.
- Outside the diner, he turned me on when he kissed my neck and ear. I decided I'd sleep with him. BAD MOVE!! He was horrible. He could only go one speed: Fast and Furious! I guess I could have stopped him, but I let him orgasm and I went home.
- I did not climax, not even close!

<u>Direct observation</u>
- Sex with a random guy isn't always good.
- Partner must have similar personalities, ethics, behaviours, and a good character to have good sex.
- If I don't like the inside package, I'm not going to like the outside package (even if the 'package' looks ideal!)
- Future goals: Make sure that I like the sample, before I have sex with him. Be choosy.

<u>Audio or videotape?</u> n/a

<u>Data analysis</u>

<u>Classify & rank data</u>
- 0 out of 5

<u>Sense of wholeness</u>
- I am continuing with this research project because the more I can learn, the better equipped I'll be to seduce Steve. However, I feel used by this sample. He had sex to have sex, not to please me or make me happy. He was selfish. I didn't know that men do that.

<u>Examine experiences beyond human awareness/ or cannot be communicated</u>

- *I need a commitment, crush or attraction to a sample to continue with sexual experience.*
- *I didn't get a 'flip flop'.*
- *I left unfulfilled, but didn't feel empty, just used and annoyed. I'm mad at myself.*

A long shower would feel amazing right now. I run upstairs, desperate to wash away the memory of John Blake, the car salesman.

I undress, step into the shower and scrub my body with a loofah. The coconut scent of my body scrub smells nice. Cinnamon is now banned. *Don't dwell on it, Colleen.* It was my first bad experience. I guess that can happen.

In university, Christine told me a few stories about her sexual experiences, where she was left feeling unfulfilled. One guy lasted two minutes in bed with her. She thought it was hilarious and told everyone in our dorm. The poor guy was called Two Minute Tom for four years.

Then there was Niles, who couldn't get it up. She said the foreplay was amazing, but when it came down to the deed, he froze. He blamed it on the beer, but they only shared a single six-pack. Christine told people that it wasn't enough alcohol to affect performance with her. Limp Dick Niles transferred to another university mid-year.

Even with the disappointments, Christine never gave up and she definitely didn't become abstinent. She obviously had more conquests than failures and enjoyed sex too much to stop. That's the difference, though. Christine is doing it for pleasure and I'm doing it to learn a few things. Should I stop? Is it harming me? I don't think so. It's experience. Plain and simple.

I don't have any clean towels left on the rack, so I pick one up off the floor. I dry off and dress in the sweats that are on my unmade bed. I survey the mess, but surprisingly, it doesn't bother me. I drop my used towel on the bedroom floor and grab fresh ones from the hallway closet, piling them on the counter.

It's still early, so I go back to my office and prepare my work files to be recorded. I stare at them in my hands and groan. I really should record my patient's sessions. I flop down in my bright yellow chair and stuff them back in my briefcase. I can do them tomorrow morning before work. With that thought, I start to skim through my Sex Project notebook. I've gone so far. I can't stop my research because of one dud. I'd like to experience a few more things before trying to seduce Steve. I make a list on an empty page.

Sex talk/dirty talk

Role-playing

Bondage, like handcuffs or silk ties

Videotape

Sex toys

Blindfolds

Sex in water (may be difficult due to the condom issue)

Sex in a car

Sixty-nine

I blush and erase the last point. It was always taboo to talk about it growing up. Boys loved to joke about that position and girls would get embarrassed.

What comes after 69?
Mouthwash.

Yeah, that joke still isn't funny. I should ask Christine how awkward it would be to get into that position. I'm sure she's done it. What about anal sex? God, I don't think I'm ready for that either. I think my short list is reasonable for me. I'm motivated to learn more.

Before I head to bed, I take my cell phone out to charge and spot a business card at the bottom of my purse. I take it out. It's Zack Brown's, the new pilot I met at the airport.

I look at the clock. It's 9:23 p.m. It's not too late. I dial Zack's number.

"Zach Brown."

"Hi Zach. This is Colleen Cousineau." There's a pause. "I met you at the flight school two weeks ago."

"Colleen... Yes, I remember. To what do I owe this pleasure?"

"I was wondering if your invitation to take me up in the Cessna is still open."

"Of course. I'd love to take you up. How about this Thursday at five o'clock? I can't go out much later than that. It's getting dark earlier now."

"Five o'clock is great. Thank you so much."

"Just meet me at the same hangar."

"Of course, I'm looking forward to it."

"Me too. Good night, Colleen."

"Good night."

That was quite easy. I didn't even feel nervous. I'm surprised and happy that my confidence is finally increasing. This date with Zack will just fill the time, before I'm able to see Steve. I'm anxious, but looking forward to that day of reckoning. I just hope that I have the patience and strength to get through this last week.

19.

Through one eye, I see that the clock reads 8:15 a.m. I close my eyes again. Why hasn't my alarm gone off?

My eyes flash open. I forgot to set it! Now I have to rush to get to work on time. Again. I growl and throw on whatever I can find, putting my hair in a low ponytail. It'll have to do.

My new car drives effortlessly, but I'm not used to where the lights and windshield wiper levers are located. I try to get the wipers to spray fluid and almost rear-end the car in front of me. That was too close for comfort.

I'm not late, but when I step into the office, I suddenly realize that I forgot some important files at home. "Fuck!" I stomp my foot. If I didn't have to rush, I wouldn't have forgotten them. Margie needs them to document the appointments and submit the paperwork to the patients' insurance companies. She'll be all over me about that.

Margie looks at me strangely from her desk. "What's wrong?"

"Nothing. I just forgot to bring some files back," I snap.

"Oh."

"It's not a big deal, Margie. You can do your thing with them tomorrow." I walk past her without looking at her. Yes, I'm fully aware that I don't normally forget things. Get over it, Margie!

I almost stomp my foot again, when I remember that I didn't do my recordings this morning. Dammit! Those will pile up quickly, if I don't get to them soon. My God! Can anything else go wrong today?

Margie knocks softly on my door. "Janice Clarke is here."

Great. I cannot handle a patient like Janice Clarke right now. "Give me a few minutes, please."

Janice is fourteen and lost both her parents and her three sisters in a house fire on Christmas Eve. She very understandably suffered a mental health crisis and ended up in psychiatric hospital where staff seemed to be overwhelmed by her. They didn't give her the treatment or the attention that she needed. I was told that Janice was left alone for much of her stay at the hospital. I understand that sitting with clients with unsolvable pain is much harder than coming up with solutions to crises, but more experienced caregivers should've helped. I should've been called in sooner. I take a few deep breaths to calm myself and prepare for the session.

When she comes into my office, I can see that she's already having a rough day. She's not crying, but her eyes are red and puffy. She grabs the box of tissues from the table and cradles it in her arms, as she sits down. I'm not sure that I have the patience for this today. I feel like I'm having my own mental health crisis.

Before I even say anything, she begins to speak, "No, I'm not myself. Yes, I'm sad today. I'm sad every day." She keeps her eyes on the tissue she pulled out of the box and is now, crumpling it in her hands. "I promised myself that I wouldn't cry while I'm here, but don't count on it."

"Hey! I'm not judging you. It's only been a few months since the accident. I'd be worried if you weren't sad."

She looks at me blankly. "How long will I be like this?" The tears start to well up in her eyes and she blots the tissue at them.

I regurgitate from memory, "Grieving is a personal and highly individual experience. How you grieve depends on many factors, including your personality and coping style, your life experience, your faith, and the nature of the loss. The grieving process takes time." I pause to reiterate, "Lots of time. Whatever your grief experience, it's important to be patient with yourself and allow the process to naturally unfold."

"Some days I'm really good. I go out with friends or my cousins and I laugh and have fun, but some days, I can't even get out of bed."

"The grieving process is a roller coaster, full of ups and downs, highs and lows. Like many roller coasters, the ride tends to be rougher in the beginning and the lows may be deeper and longer, but the difficult periods should become less intense and shorter as time goes by. It takes time to work through a loss." My life is certainly a roller coaster lately. I have to start listening to my own therapy sessions.

"Everyone says that. Time. Time. Time," she repeats, annoyed.

I take a moment to figure out what I want to say next. I'm rattled as to how close to home this hits. "Think about time this way instead. Balance the time you spend working on your grief, with the time you spend coping with your day-to-day life. Balance the amount of time you spend with others with, the time you spend alone. Balance seeking help from others, with caring for yourself." I'm such a hypocrite.

"I guess."

She doesn't get it. Time to focus on Janice and gear my help towards her age. "Do you use Facebook?"

"Who doesn't?" She rolls her eyes.

That's a typical angry teenager response. "Have you thought about doing a memorial page on Facebook?"

"A what?"

"A memorial. Some people, who have lost loved ones, create a Facebook page to inform a wide audience of a loved one's passing and to reach out for support. You can post pictures, quotes and memories and your friends and loved ones can post their own tributes or condolences. Reading such messages might provide some comfort for you."

"That's a good idea." She smiles and sits up straighter.

Success.

We brainstorm ideas for her Facebook memorial page and we end the session early, as Janice wants to get started immediately. She hugs me briefly before she leaves.

"Thanks, Dr. C."

I smile and feel better about the day. My day starts *now*. "Margie, could you please get me a coffee?" We could sit down together and enjoy the caffeine buzz.

"Sure. Why did you end early? She still had ten minutes."

"Because I did." Uh oh. That pushed my buttons. How many chances do I get to start my day over?

"Oh."

Margie walks into my office. "So, you got a new car, eh?"

I'm annoyed at her intrusiveness, but walk past her, to the front window and admire it. "It is nice." I'm proud of my purchase.

Margie comes to stand beside me. "It's a little flashy, isn't it?"

Anger flickers inside me. "Flashy?" Why is she picking on me?

"I don't mean anything by that. It's just more… More luxurious than your last one. I think you should have slept on it. You might regret your decision. Hey! What's that?" She's pointing at me.

Oh my God! What now? I look down, but I don't know what she sees. "What?"

She touches the collar of my shirt. "You have a stain."

"Dammit." I inspect the collar. It looks like coffee… or chocolate? I guess that's what I get for wearing a shirt from the dirty laundry basket. Thanks for pointing it out, Margie. It's not like I have a change of clothes in my office. Is there anything else she wants to criticize?

"Are you ok, Colleen?"

Such a simple phrase and I feel my anxiety rising again. "Of course." I whip my hands down to my sides and roll my eyes. "Can you please stop asking me that?"

"Sorry."

"Just go get me my coffee," I bark.

Margie stares blankly at me.

I want to apologize. I never speak to her that way, but I'm angry that she keeps calling me out on my behaviour. I ignore her look and walk back into my office. She thinks I'm a mess. First, it's her reaction to my forgetfulness. Then, she questions my therapy techniques and my choice of a car. Now, it's the stain on my shirt. Give me a break. I ignore her look and walk back into my office.

Sitting at my desk, I put my head in my hands and close my eyes. What happened to taking my own advice? *Balance seeking help from others, with caring for yourself.* How the hell am I supposed to reach out for help, when I'm criticized for my behaviour? Behaviour that's absolutely normal for a normal human being! So what if I forget files at home? So what if I end my session early? So what if I have a stain on my shirt? It's still me. I'm fine!

I look at the stain again. I know I've been a little lax with laundry and cleaning. I mean, I did pull out a shirt from my dirty pile to wear today. And, of course, I noticed the dishes piled up in the sink before I left for work. I'll get to it all soon. There's no problem though. People get busy. People do it every day.

Even my desk has pencils and pens scattered across it. I've never let this happen before either. Everything has a place, right? That's the way I used to be. I take a swipe at the pencils and a couple roll and drop to the floor. Fuck that! I'm not that person anymore. That person wasn't happy. That person couldn't keep her husband happy. I like this new me.

Margie knocks and then walks into my office. "Here's your coffee." She places it on my desk, looks at me briefly, looks at the pencils on the floor, and then walks out of the room.

"Thank you," I call out, as she closes the door.

A moment later, she buzzes me, "Your next patient, Nolan Watson is here."

"Send him in, please." I don't need to seek help from Margie. Margie and I need to maintain a doctor-receptionist relationship. It's best.

"His parents want to talk to you first because it's his first time."

Shit. I forgot. "I'll be right there." I take a quick sip of coffee and it burns my tongue.

As I come out of the office, I hear Mr. Watson telling Nolan to 'go away' and I see him shove Nolan a bit. Nolan looks to be about five or six years old. He's a cute kid with freckles splashed across his nose. He's probably bored and trying to get his parents' attention, but the interaction bothers me. I brush it off and make a mental note to update the toys and books in my waiting room.

"Hi, Mr. and Mrs. Watson. I'm Dr. Cousineau."

"Hi, Dr. Cousineau," Mrs. Watson says.

"Listen, Nolan has been wetting his bed and we've had it. We're so embarrassed. He slept over at his grandma's the other night, and he peed on her pull-out couch," Mr. Watson is loud and that his lack of tact must be humiliating Nolan. Even preschoolers get embarrassed.

I put my hand up, to let Mr. White know to stop talking and I turn to the little guy. "Hi, Nolan. I'm Dr. Cousineau." He doesn't even look up at me. He stares at his feet, as they kick the coffee table softly. Poor kid. "Margie, can you please take Nolan in my office to colour?"

"Sure." She scowls at Mr. Watson and quickly ushers Nolan out of the room.

"I understand how frustrated you must be, but you need to reassure, encourage, and express confidence in Nolan. Let me talk to him and I'll come back and let you know what I found out." My aggression levels are rising again. You don't talk negatively about your child right in front of him. What kind of parents are these people?

When I walk in to my office, Nolan is just sitting on my couch, looking at his hands. "He didn't want to colour?"

Margie shrugs. "No, and he won't talk to me, either." She pats Nolan on the shoulder and walks out of my office.

"Nolan, I have a pile of games, puzzles, play dough and other fun stuff, right behind you. Go ahead and get something that we can play with together."

Nolan slowly looks behind him. "I can pick anything?"

"Anything you want."

"Can I play with play dough?"

"Absolutely!" I smile. "Bring it over."

He runs to the cabinet, grabs two cans and skips back to me. "My mom never lets me play with play dough. She says it's too messy."

"I love playing it with this stuff." I open the cans and dump it out onto the table.

Nolan smiles at me and I see that he's missing his two front teeth. He takes the blue dough, squishes it in his hands and then rolls it out with his palms. He takes a piece of the red dough and sticks it in the middle of the blue, blending it together. That would've bothered me as a child, but now, I can just throw it out and purchase more.

"What's new in your life, Nolan?" I know that a stressful home, as in a home where the parents are in conflict, may sometimes cause a child to wet the bed. Also, major changes, such as starting school, a new baby, or moving to a new home, are other stresses that cause bedwetting. I pray that he hasn't been physically or sexually abused. Children sometimes begin bedwetting due to that atrocity.

"Nothing."

"Nothing? Come on, there's nothing new happening at home?"

He bangs his fist into the dough a couple of times. "I have a new baby brother."

Bingo. "What's his name?"

"Adam." He picks up the dough and looks at me for a second, before he bashes it back down on the table. He looks at me again and I give him no reaction. Bang away.

"Do you like Adam?"

Nolan wraps one of his hands in the dough and then puts it all down, wiping his hands on his legs. Bits of red dough stick to his pants.

"Do you like your baby brother?"

He makes a face, like he wants to say something, but looks down at the dough.

"What you say in here is between you and me. I won't tell anyone, I promise."

"Really? You won't tell my mom."

I cross my heart with my finger. "I promise. I'm here to talk to you and to be your friend. This is our time together."

"Adam cries all the time." He lifts up the dough and starts banging it on the table again.

"Oh, that's not good."

"My mom yells at me to be quiet, even when I'm not even doing anything. Adam's the one being noisy, not me."

"I'm sorry that she yells at you, but it's not your fault. Your mom probably doesn't like the crying either. When Adam cries, your mom gets stressed out. Do you know what stressed out means?"

"No." He looks at me shyly.

"It means that crying and loud noises bother her. When Adam cries, your mom probably gets upset and can't handle normal day-to-day things. She may even yell, cry or get angry."

"My mom cries a lot."

"It's not your fault."

Nolan and I keep talking and I find some cutting tools and cookie cutters for the play dough. He makes a pizza and I pretend to eat it. I don't mention the bed-wetting at all. We talk about how to play quietly with his toys and how often he plays outside with his friends. He's a sweet kid and his parents need to be taught how to handle his bed-wetting.

I ask Margie to sit with Nolan, while I talk to his parents. "Margie loves pizza," I say.

When I step out of my office, they ambush me. "Did you find out why he's wetting the bed?"

"I think so, but let's talk about how you handle his bed-wetting. What do you do when he wets the bed?" I try to whisper, hoping that they keep their voices down.

97

"We punish him. We know he's just being lazy, so we took away his television privileges, but it didn't work. He's wet the bed every night this week," Mr. Watson states brashly, appalled at his son's behaviour.

Margie lets out a gasp and when I look at her, she puts her head down. I want to strangle Mr. Watson too, but we need to remain professional.

I close my office door, so that Nolan, and Margie, can't hear our conversation anymore. "Punishment often results in more bed-wetting and if you punish him further, by say, taking away his toys, it'll never stop."

"I told you." Nolan's mother pokes her husband and he sneers at her.

"Please don't punish Nolan anymore. Bed-wetting isn't caused by laziness. I talked to Nolan and it seems that the new baby stresses him out and he doesn't know how to tell you." I turn to Mrs. Watson. "Does Adam cry a lot?"

She nods her head. "Yes, he's a little colicky."

"I'm sorry to hear that. I hope you're getting help at home and resting when you can." I look at Mr. Watson and he's playing with his phone. "Mr. Watson," I pause.

"Uh, yeah?" He puts his phone in his pocket.

I'm not getting paid for marriage counselling. "Shaming Nolan for wetting the bed will lead to poor self-esteem. You need to be supportive and reassure him that you love him."

I sit them down in the waiting room give them more tips and strategies about how they can help Nolan. They listen intently, which gives me hope. They do want to help him.

"Reward him consistently for dry nights and if he has an accident, have Nolan take an active part in cleaning up. Ask him to help strip the bed and put the sheets in the laundry." I stand up. "Margie will give you some pamphlets and I'll finish up with Nolan. I'll be right back."

As I open my office door, I hear Nolan's mother say, "I told you not to blame him or criticize him."

"Shut up," Mr. Watson hisses.

He's such a jerk.

Before Nolan leaves, I make sure that I build up his confidence, so I tell him that he's smart and very creative with the play dough. His smile is incredible. I brush his pants off and let him take the play dough home. I ask him to play with it at a table, or on newspaper, so that it's not so messy and his mom won't get angry.

When they're gone, Margie grabs my arm, "Why didn't you suggest that the parents take some counselling?"

I'm stunned by the question and I release her grip on my arm, finger by finger. "This was Nolan's first visit. I don't think it seemed necessary."

"Really? He told his wife to shut up and he treats his child horribly. I can't believe that a father was mortified about his six-year old son peeing the bed. It's absurd! You heard him degrade Nolan. The kid was so embarrassed. What an appalling man!"

"Margie, I can handle my patients and their parents." I walk back into my office and start to close the door, but Margie puts her hand out to stop it.

"Can you handle it, Colleen?"

I stop and click my heels together. "What does that mean?" She must see the fury in my eyes.

"Oh, nothing." She looks down and walks out of my office. She saw it.

That's right, you did step over the line. I want to scream at her, but I pace around my office instead, with my arms tightly across my chest. When I get close to the door, thinking I want to reprimand Margie, I stop and throw my arms down. I'm too angry. I might say something I'll regret.

Margie talks through the intercom. "Your next appointment just cancelled."

"Good. Cancel the next one too. I'm going home."

Margie suddenly opens my door and rushes to my desk. "What's wrong?"

"Nothing." I turn my back to her and start packing up my belongings. Are you kidding me? Enough with the coddling already.

"Did you reschedule your doctor's appointment?"

I look at her and snap, "What? Isn't it next week?"

"No, it was yesterday." She clicks her tongue disappointedly.

I missed it? Dammit! I completely forgot. It takes months to get in for a yearly physical.

She walks to my desk and rummages through the pile of papers. "I gave you the message, just before we left last night. It's right here." She picks it up.

"It's under control." I snatch it out of her hands and toss it back on the desk, turning my back to her again. "Just cancel my appointments."

There's a pause. "Sure."

When she's gone, I slump down in my chair. What's wrong with me? I unclench my fists and stretch my fingers out. I shouldn't be this upset. It's not Margie's fault, but she's not helping. I should apologize to her, but I don't know if I can be sincere.

As I think about the right words to use, my cell phone rings and I see that it's Christine.

I pause, unsure if I want to answer it, but catch it on the last ring. "Hey, Christine."

"Hey, Ci-Ci. Can you sneak out of the office for an early dinner? And when I say dinner, I mean margaritas at *Jose's*."

This is why I paused. I pull my ear away from the phone and throw my head back in frustration. Not now! I'm not in the mood. "I'm done work, but I don't really want to go drinking tonight."

"Come on. We need to go to a bar. It's been awhile."

Yeah, it's not really what I want to do. "I was going to have a nap and do laundry—

"Ci-Ci, you promised me, not too long ago, that we would hang out more. Come on, bestie. I miss you."

Her words appease me. How does she do it? "Ok. Ok. Ok. I'll go."

I hear her smile on the other end of the line. "Be there for five and you'd better show up! I know where you live!" She threatens.

I hang up, collect my belongings and walk out of my office. Margie is on the phone and I pause to wait, but the new bathroom door catches my attention again and I feel sick. Apologizing to Margie can wait. Or I might not even apologize at all. She's so… unnerving. I'm so torn. I can't stand this confusion of thoughts and emotions. I need to get out of here.

20.

    This time, it's my cell phone alarm that jolts me awake in a panic. Why did I set it for four-thirty? What day is it? It slowly comes back to me. Oh, right. I groan. I don't want to go to the bar with Christine! I hug one of my pillows and close my eyes again.
    When did I become so dominated by alarms and getting to places on time? It never used to be such a hassle. I guess I've never had to take naps because of sleepless nights before either.
    My bed feels so comfortable and warm. I don't want to move. I don't want to go anywhere or deal with anyone. Can't I just hide here?
    Half the comforter falls of the bed, when I fling my arms and my legs open wide in defeat. Fuck! Christine will be waiting for me and her threats are never empty. She *will* come to my house if I'm not at the restaurant by five o'clock.
    I roll out of bed and pull off my wrinkled work clothes, finding jeans and a sweater. I re-tie my hair back and don't give myself a second glance. I don't care.
    Jose's is a Mexican-American restaurant, specializing in enchiladas and pasta. It's a weird mix, but we don't go there for the food. Their lounge is comfortable and they have great two-for-one drink deals. Today's special is margaritas. What I didn't know is that on Tuesdays, *Jose's* has a live band. It's loud and crowded already and the band isn't even playing yet. Don't people work? I just want to eat the free basket of nachos and salsa and leave as fast as I can, but Christine orders a second strawberry margarita for me, even when I say no and I feel obligated to drink it. She's good at making me feel bad, but I honestly don't mind. I feel more relaxed now, than when I first sat down. It feels like old times.
    We're sitting in a booth, in the lounge area, furthest away from the band. "Are you still going forward with your Sex Project?" She slides her finger along the rim of the glass and then licks the sugar off of it. Without

a thought, she puts the entire strawberry garnish in her mouth, holding onto the stem, and bites off the fruit. She places the leftovers in front of her.

I place my strawberry on the napkin in front of me. I don't know how many people have touched it. I certainly don't want to eat it. "It's funny that you ask that. What's the worst experience you've ever had?"

"Uh oh." She licks the strawberry juice off of her fingers.

"What?"

"You must've had bad sex."

"Kind of." I smile and look down. I fiddle with the strawberry and pick it up. Before I change my mind, I quickly take a small bite. Old Colleen would never do that.

She laughs. "You have to tell me the details."

"You first."

"I've really nailed—excuse the pun—nailed down tactics to prevent bad sex. I have certain questions to ask before I go home with a guy."

"You're going to have to teach me those, but first, tell me your bad sex story."

Christine thinks for a few seconds. "A couple of years ago, I met the most gorgeous guy. He could've been a movie star or a model, or something. He was smooth and sweet and he had the hottest body. Sex was unbelievable. God, was he hung." Her hands come off the table, about shoulder-width apart, to indicate how big he was.

I laugh, but I'm confused. "I don't hear a problem there at all."

"At around six in the morning, we were still going at it, when the police showed up at his apartment. They broke the door down. It was scary. Before they took him away in handcuffs, he wrote down his lawyer's number and told me to call it, to tell the lawyer that he was arrested. I was in shock. I stayed and talked to the police, and every question they asked, I answered with, 'I literally just met him last night.' It turns out that he committed fraud."

"Christine! He could've been a serial killer."

"Any guy could be! That's why I have sound strategies now."

"Jeez. You were lucky." I shake my head, worriedly. "But that wasn't even bad sex. That was just a convenient escape from a one-night stand."

"Wow! Ci-Ci, you really understand casual sex now! You never would've said that before. Sounds like you might've experienced an escape yourself."

I blush. "Come on, what's your bad sex story."

"Right. Ok." Her eyes close for a second and open animatedly. "I've got one. I went home with a nurse."

I look at her dumbfounded. She's been with a woman?

"A male nurse." She laughs. "I don't do women. Anyway, his version of dirty talk was, 'Aw yeah, hump that shit.' He must've said it thirty times. Hump that shit. Hump that shit. It was really hard to keep a straight face."

"I guess." I giggle. "What did you do?"

"I finally had to stop him. Told him that I had a headache and bolted. He was buck naked, at his front door, watching me run down the street!" We laugh loudly.

"Oh my God! That's awful!" I laugh loudly. "Good for you for getting out of there. I don't know if I could've left."

"So, what was your bad sex?"

Slowly, I tell her about John the Salesman. I've never really given her such explicit details and I find myself blushing, but I get though the story.

Christine shakes her head. "I can't believe that self-centered guys still exist at our age. Do they not know that women like to be pleasured too? We're not just here to get them off them."

"Seriously, I felt I was just a prop or a toy. I don't think he cared that I was in the room." I take a sip of the margarita. "He used me, but I think he believed I enjoyed it."

"He's an immature idiot. Don't take it personally."

"Oh, I don't. He's probably used to doing it by himself at home. His hand would've been just as fast."

"You're so bad! Jackhammer John, eh?"

We start giggling uncontrollably.

"Hey, Colleen."

I turn around, still laughing, but stop awkwardly when I see Jack standing there. He's wearing a thick, black sweater and jeans. His blonde hair is unruly and it looks like he hasn't shaved in a few days. Flip flop. I don't want to admit that he looks hot, sexy almost. Whatever. He's not my type. I do sit up straighter and pat down my hair. I wish it wasn't in a ponytail.

"Hi, Jack. What are you doing here?" What was with the flip flop?

"I'm here with some guys from my pick-up hockey league."

He plays hockey? "Oh." I feel Christine pinch my arm. "Jack, this is my best friend Christine."

"Hi, Jack. I've heard a lot about you. It's very nice to finally meet you." Christine's on full flirt mode. She swishes her hair back, and when they shake hands, she places her other hand on his forearm.

"Nice to meet you too." He stands at the table, between us, and I watch their eyes lock.

I look at Christine and her breasts are heaving forward. Obviously, Jack's responding to her sexuality. His eyes are devouring her cleavage. I hear her ask him about his hockey league and she throws out some NHL statistics. She knows how to talk to men. They'll probably hit it off. I look down at the floor and toe a beer cap with my boot. They both love casual sex. They'd be good for each other, even if it's just one night.

I kick the cap across the floor. Well, Jack used to date a lot of women, but maybe his crush on me ended that. I know I hurt him the other night, he's probably not ready to date yet, especially Christine. He's definitely still getting over me.

"Do you two want another drink? I'm buying." Jack asks.

"Yes, please." Christine bats her eyelashes.

"Sure. That'd be great." I wish I could throw my hair over my shoulder. Stupid ponytail.

"I'll be right back with two more…What are they? Strawberry margaritas?"

We both nod and he walks away.

"This is *the* Jack. The Jack that saved your life." Christine fluffs up her hair and pinches her cheeks.

"Yes."

"He's hot! Wow! He's one fine specimen." She watches him at the bar for a minute and then suddenly focuses her attention on me. "I'm sorry. Do you—Are you interested in him?"

"No!" I shake my head furiously. "Of course not. I'm not interested." I don't know why my stomach is turning.

"Would you mind if I had a go?"

A go? What kind of talk is that? Would I mind? I don't think he'd go out with her. "Are you going to ask him out?"

"I'd like to see if he's interested first. He has to meet my criteria." She taps her lip with her finger. "But you didn't answer my question. Would you care if I did?"

Should I tell her that he wants to date me? No, I turned him down. It shouldn't make a difference at all. "He's free game. Give him a go."

"Perfect." Christine pulls out a lipstick from her purse and applies it expertly. She smacks her lips, just as Jack returns.

I smile. Jack doesn't like lipstick.

"Here you are, ladies."

"Thanks, Jack." Christine smiles and touches his hand.

"No problem." He turns to me, hands me my drink and I barely look at him. "Everything all right, Colleen?" He asks so only I can hear.

Before I get a chance to answer, I feel a tap on my shoulder.

"Excuse me."

I look to my side and then up, until my eyes rest on a very tall, good looking man, smiling down at me. He's olive-skinned and wearing a pale blue button down shirt and jeans. His eyes look like amber. He's beautiful. Can I say that about a man?

"Hi," he says.

"Hi."

"I'm sorry to interrupt, but do you work on Charles Street?"

"Yes, I do." I cock my head to the side. Do I know him?

"I think we're neighbours. I'm a marriage counselor at 375 Charles Street."

"That's just a couple of buildings over. We *are* neighbours."

"I'm Kevin MacLean." He extends his hand.

I take it. It's a strong grip and he has soft hands. "I'm Colleen Cousineau."

Jack steps towards me, making Kevin take a step back. "Hey, I'm Jack."

I scowl at Jack. "Jack, this is Kevin."

They shake hands, but they seem to be sizing each other up. Kevin is about three inches taller than Jack, but I don't think that what's bothering Jack.

"This is my friend, Christine." I tug Kevin's arm toward the table. This time Jack takes a step back and throws daggers into Kevin's back, with his eyes. What's his problem? He's got Christine.

"Hi, Kevin." Christine's smile is inviting. Looks like she's keeping her options open.

However, Kevin is immune. He moves back to me, cutting off Jack's access to me. "How long have you had your practice?"

"Almost two years. You?"

"The same."

"I'm surprised that I've never seen you before."

"I think you arrive earlier than me, but I stay later. Adults can stay out later than children," he jokes.

He knows that I work with children. What else does he know about me? He must be interested. I smile and attempt some of Christine's flirting techniques, while we engage in light conversation.

Out of the corner of my eye, I see Jack and Christine doing the same. Christine is touching his elbow and he's looking into her eyes. I'm bothered, but I don't know why. I try to ignore the feelings.

After a few minutes, Jack excuses himself, "I'll leave you two ladies alone." He looks at Kevin. "They're having a girl's night out."

"Oh, right. Sorry to bother you. I'm sitting over there with some friends. I'll come back later," Kevin says, but doesn't leave. I think he's waiting for Jack to go first.

"Sounds great, Kevin. Have fun." I glare at Jack and he glares right back at me. He doesn't budge.

"Have fun, boys. Make sure you say goodbye before you leave, Jack." Christine has her hand on his elbow now.

"I will," Jack says, but he doesn't take his eyes off of me, even as he steps away from our table.

Then, the men stare at each other, backing further away. At the same time, they walk away in opposite directions. It's like a western showdown, but without the big gunfight.

"Are you sure there's nothing going on between you and Jack?"

"Absolutely not."

"Ok. I just felt some vibes. If you say there's nothing between you, then I believe you. He's passed my criteria and now I just have to get the confirmation." She laughs to herself. "Anyway, Kevin sure is a tall drink of water."

Good luck getting that confirmation.

"Did you know there was such a hot therapist on your block?"

"Not at all. Kevin is so…"

"Hot!" She finishes. "If it wasn't for Jack, I'd be using my feminine wiles on him instead."

I want to inform her that she shouldn't be so confident. Jack is likely to turn her down because of his feelings for me. I'm sure she's used to a little rejection and she'll get over it. I really don't like the way that she's acting. I can win over guys too, just as much as her. More even. She has no clue about how much Jack wants me. I should burst her bubble.

We finish our third drink and I'm ready to leave. It's not worth telling Christine about Jack. I don't care if she dates him. It doesn't bother me at all. Really. I just want to go home.

We ask the server for our bill and while we're waiting, Kevin comes back over to our table.

"I see you're settling up. I wanted to catch you before you left." He looks at Christine briefly and then asks me, "I was wondering if you wanted to go out tomorrow night."

Before I have time to answer, Jack comes back. "Are you ladies on your way home?"

Christine answers, "Yes, we are. Can I talk to you for a second, Jack?"

"Sure." I watch them walk toward the bar.

"Colleen? Do you want to go out for dinner with me?"

Christine has her hand on Jack's chest and she throws her head back as she laughs. God, she's a natural. How can Jack not fall for it?

"Hello? Colleen?"

I whip my head around to look at Kevin. "I'm sorry. Yes, I'd love to have dinner with you tomorrow."

"Great. Here's my card. Can you call me tomorrow, during the day, so we can finalize things?"

"Sure, it sounds good, Kevin." I put his card in my purse and look up to see Jack and Colleen return to the table.

"It was great to finally meet you, Colleen. I look forward to seeing you tomorrow." Kevin smiles at me and starts backing away. "Nice to meet you two, as well."

Jack gives him a dirty look, and when he's gone, he glares at me again.

"I have to visit the ladies room. Jack, if you aren't here when I get back, I'll talk to you later?" Christine asks, eyeing us both suspiciously.

"Yes, I'll call you." He smiles at her, but quickly returns his gaze to me. "You're going out with Kyle?"

"His name is Kevin, and what does it matter?" I stand up and put my hands on my hips.

"There's something about him. He's not right."

"What do you care? You're going out with Christine."

"Are you going out with him to hurt me?"

"No, that's asinine. Why would I do that?"

"Colleen, you are infuriating." He slams down his beer bottle on the table. "Have fun on your date." He turns and walks away.

I want to run after him, to stop him, but why? I can't worry about his feelings. I've told him that I don't want to date him? I feel guilty though, and my stomach is churning. I don't want him to be hurt. He's a great guy. I'm about to go after him, when Christine grabs my arm.

"Going somewhere?"

"No... I thought I saw someone I knew, but I was mistaken." Jack will be fine.

"Are you positive that nothing's going on between you and Jack? I sense some hostility or some kind of really intense sexual tension."

"What? Oh no. Definitely not. That's crazy."

"The lady doth protest too much, methinks."

"Look at you quoting Shakespeare." I grab her arm and squeeze it. "Christine, I promise you. There's nothing going on with Jack."

She grabs my hands and squeals. "He hits all of my standards. I can't wait to see what he has contained in his jeans!"

My stomach continues to churn.

Christine and I hug our goodbyes and I head home wondering about all of these feelings that are coming to the surface. Rage, depression, impatience, jealousy... I think I need to make an appointment with a psychologist.

21.

The next morning, when I get out of the shower, I read a text on my cell phone from Margie: *Call me*.

I pull the towel tightly around me and dial her number immediately.

"Hi, Colleen."

"Is everything ok, Margie?"

"No, I'm too sick to come into work today. I'm sorry for the late notice, but I started feeling bad around three this morning."

"Oh, that's awful." Margie hasn't ever taken a sick day and I'm concerned, but nervous. I still haven't apologized for my behavior and I don't know the right words. Do I bring it up now?

"Do you want me to call a temporary receptionist?"

"No, I'll be fine. Just get better quickly." Now is not a good time to apologize. I'll send her flowers today to let her know I care.

"Thanks. Have a good day."

I hang up quickly and pause, staring at the phone. For the first time this week, I'm punctual and I'm not rushing to get to work, so the interruption is a surprise. It throws me off a bit, but I should be fine without a receptionist. I can handle it.

As soon as I walk up the pathway to my office, two patients are standing outside, waiting for me to open the door. They both have the same exact time for an appointment. I don't know how it happened, but I talk them into shorter appointments. One patient and his family go to the coffee shop down the street, while I see the other patient. I quickly call my next appointment, asking her to come in thirty minutes later. All of my other appointments have to be pushed back too, so somehow, during my breaks, I manage to call and organize everyone.

Most patients' parents aren't bothered by the time change, but one mother is outraged. I haven't even had an introductory appointment with her daughter and she has been rescheduled a number of times because of my incident with Mr. Baker. I'm shocked to hear this, as Margie hadn't informed me of any problems. Usually, she handles my schedule very professionally, but the parent obviously doesn't know about my whole ordeal. All she knows is that her daughter needs therapy and she is getting 'screwed' around by me. I'm completely empathetic and squeeze her daughter in on Friday. She seems to be calmer when we hang up.

All of this does not make for a perfect day. Plus, I forgot the files at home again, I didn't do my recordings and after seeing patients without a break, I'm starving by mid-afternoon. I feel my irritation levels increasing and my patience levels decreasing. I have a few minutes in the afternoon to scarf down a granola bar and my cell phone rings.

"What?" I bark into the phone with my mouth full.

"Colleen?"

"Yes."

"Hi, it's Kevin."

I forgot that I was supposed to call him. I quickly chew and swallow a hunk of granola bar. "Hi."

"Are you busy?"

"Kind of. My receptionist is sick. It's been a hell of a day. I missed lunch and I'm eating a snack that I keep just for my patients. I really don't have time to chat."

"No worries. I can call you back later."

"I don't know if I can go out later, Kevin. I look down at the wrinkled wraparound dress I'm wearing. I didn't even dress for a date.

"Oh," he sounds disappointed.

"I'm sorry."

"That's ok. I understand. I'll call you another time."

"Thanks. Take care."

As soon as I hang up, my next patient, Trudy arrives. No rest for the weary. Or is it wicked?

22.

    Trudy skips ahead of me, out of my office, and I'm surprised to see Kevin in the waiting room, sitting with Trudy's mother, Mrs. Courtier. They are casually talking and don't see us come out. Kevin looks at-ease and particularly handsome in a pale green sweater.

    "Hi, Mommy." Trudy crawls onto her mom's lap and Kevin stands up, walking towards me with a plastic take-out box in his hands.

    I pat my hair, hoping it's not too flyaway. "Hi, Kevin. This is a surprise. Could you wait a minute please?"

    "Sure." He steps aside.

    "This nice, young man has brought you lunch," says Mrs. Courtier. "Aren't you a lucky girl?" She winks at me.

    Kevin waves the plastic box at me. "Am I?" I smile at Kevin and run my hands over my dress, hoping to flatten out the wrinkles.

    I turn to Mrs. Courtier, "Please call me tomorrow to set up an appointment for Trudy. My receptionist should be back and things will be under control by then."

    "Ok, thank you, Dr. Cousineau. Enjoy your lunch." She takes Trudy by the hand and leaves the office.

    "She's right, you know. I am a very nice, young man." His smile makes me weak in the knees.

    "That's for me?"

    He nods and hands me the takeout container. "I bought it from the deli down the street. It's nothing, just some fresh cut veggies, hummus and some cheese and crackers. Oh, and I got you this." He reaches behind him and pulls out a bottle of water from his jeans pocket.

    "Kevin! You didn't have to do this." Wow. He's so thoughtful. "I wish you could stay and share it with me, but I really don't have a lot of time. My next appointment will be here any minute."

    "That's ok. I understand."

"Thank you so much."

"I'll get out of your way now." He walks toward the door, waves and then, he's gone.

I sit down at Margie's desk and dig into the hummus with a carrot stick. Maybe I'll go out with him tonight. He seems like a good candidate for sex. I'm sure he wouldn't mind sleeping with me. It's pretty clear he's interested. I'm not sure that I'm in the mood, though. I'll have to primp and be seductive. That takes a lot of work.

Listen to me! How did I get to be so flippant about having sex? Who am I to pick and choose sex partners, like I'm shopping? And what makes me so confident that he'll actually even agree to it? Or want it with me?

Wow. I'm not sure that I like this new me. I'm almost egotistical! I shake my head and bite into some cheddar cheese. Men like Kevin, are the reason why I'm so self-assured…or cocky. These men I've been with have given me the boost of confidence that I've been pursuing. That's what I wanted, right?

Can I be this direct and confident with Steve? That question makes me instantly nervous. I have more confidence, yet it scares me to the core to think about seducing Steve. Other men give me strength and make me feel good about myself, but Steve turns me into an insecure, quivering ball of nerves. I don't want to be shot down. How do I change that?

I guess I do need this extra week to prep. I'll call Kevin on my next break.

23.

As I lock the door to my practice, I glance down the street toward Kevin's office and see him locking his door too. Nervously, I giggle to myself and slowly make my way to the sidewalk.

When I turn the corner towards him, I feel shy all of a sudden and put my head down. Maybe having a date with someone on the same block isn't a good idea. What if he turns out to be another dud?

He's on the sidewalk now, heading towards me. Too late to turn back now.

"Hi, Colleen."

"Hi, Kevin."

He stops in front of me and buries his chin underneath his scarf and I see him sink his hands deeper in his pockets. "Listen, are you sure you don't want me to drive to the restaurant? It wasn't this cold this afternoon."

"No, it's not that far. Let's go." I tuck my arm into his elbow and pull him down the street. My head reaches the top of his shoulder. He's a giant.

"How was your day?"

"You know how my day was," I say laughing. "But you totally made it better. I appreciate the special delivery." We pass his office and I see stark white walls through a window. "Thanks again. It was really tasty."

"I could only imagine how you must have been without a receptionist. I felt your pain." He looks down at me and smiles. I notice how completely straight his teeth are. And super white, too. They're almost blinding.

"How was your day?" I ask.

"Very slow after you called me. My afternoon dragged on and on."

"I hate those days. Patients are late, they want to go over their time slot or their problems just get to you."

"No, I didn't mean that. I meant that I've been anticipating our date ever since you called. I couldn't wait."

"Oh." I blush and look down at my feet. On the phone, he did seem very excited to go out with me tonight. He said 'see you soon' about five times and 'great' around six times. I thought he sounded cute. I look at him now and notice his great profile. His dark hair has some curl to it and hangs low over his eyes. He looks almost Arabic, like Aladdin. Kevin suddenly looks at me and I smile, but quickly look away.

"Have you been to this restaurant before?" We're going to *Chicory's Steakhouse*. It's right beside *Il Fornara*, the Italian restaurant I went to with Dave the orthodontist. I've come so far since that date.

"No, I haven't. I'm glad that you suggested it. I see it on the way to work and I've always wanted to go. Is it good?"

We talk about the menu and our favourite foods and we arrive at the restaurant, just before six o'clock. Kevin opens the door for me and I feel his hand on the small of my back, when we walk through the door. Even though I'm wearing a coat, I still get goose bumps.

The hostess finds the reservation that Kevin made and she seats us at a plush leather booth, next to an impressive fireplace. Tall candlesticks stand in the center of the smartly made table, complete with a freshly ironed tablecloth. It's a great spot, partially secluded and away from heavy traffic. The dim lighting makes it very romantic.

"Perfect," he says, and I see him hand the hostess some cash when he shakes her hand. He paid for this spot. I wonder if when he called to book it, he promised her a tip. In any case, he knows what he's doing.

Kevin's actions remind me of Steve. Steve always wanted the best of the best and over-tipped everywhere we went, even if the service was horrible. Actually, he gave an even better tip if the service didn't live up to his high standards, but it wasn't for a compassionate or sensible reason. Steve saw waiting tables as a most pitiful profession and called it a 'white trash' job. He assumed all wait staff were uneducated and often humiliated them. He gave the worst ones a higher percentage because they were 'never going to go anywhere in life'. I was always embarrassed by this behaviour and I tried to calm him down during his rants, but he wouldn't listen. At least, he wasn't like Jackhammer John, a very poor tipper. I shake my head at the thought.

As I'm about to pull out my chair to sit down, Kevin quickly pulls it out for me. "Thank you." Then he helps me with my coat and hangs it up on a hook near the fireplace. So sweet.

The waiter arrives, tells us the specials and Kevin orders a bottle of red wine immediately.

"I hope you like red," he says, after the waiter walks away.

"Yes, I do." It's strange that he didn't even ask me my opinion, but I quickly brush the thought aside. I like red wine, so there's no problem.

"Do you enjoy what you do?"

It's a specific question, but I appreciate his directness. "Of course."

"I only ask because you chose to specialize in children, not adults. You must really like children and I suppose, they would be easier to work with."

Odd and untrue statement. "I do like children and it can be fun to work with some of them, but to say that they're easier than adults is an impudent statement. Some children have problems, just like the rest of us, that don't have an easy solution. I use the some of same treatments and strategies that you would use for adults." Any psychologist would learn this in school.

He touches my hand lightly. "I meant no harm by that. I'm just trying to get to know you better."

"Oh." I need to let my guard down a little.

"Why did you choose child psychology?"

I take a deep breath. "I lost my parents when I was very young and my aunt raised me. She took me to a psychologist and that's who I talked to about my grief, not my Aunt Anna." I play with the napkin on the table. "I saw the psychologist for years. We played games and read books at first, but as I got older, I felt I could tell him anything. I looked forward to seeing him every week." My aunt didn't want to hear about my problems, she wanted to solve them, but I just needed to vent.

"I'm so sorry about your parents."

"Thank you. Anyway, I just want to be that kind of person for a child. I want to be someone a child can confide in."

"It makes sense. Thanks for sharing." He touches my hand again and stares into my eyes, but moves away when the waiter comes back with our wine.

The waiter pours the wine and Kevin says, "We are ready to order."

"Ok, sir. What will you have?" The waiter looks at me.

"Oh, I'm not ready. Please just give me a—

"We'll both have the surf and turf special." Kevin takes the menu from me and hands it to the waiter, along with his. "Have the chef cook the steaks medium."

I guess I'll have the surf and turf special. Why is he ordering for me? That's awfully controlling. I *was* going to order the surf and turf, but he didn't know that. Should I say something? It's a good thing that I like my steak cooked medium too or I would've let him have it.

He hands me my glass of wine and holds his own up. "Cheers to you, Colleen, and to an enjoyable evening."

I hold my glass up hesitantly and try to smile. He only ordered for me, right? I wasn't upset when he opened the door for me and pulled my chair out. He's being chivalrous. It's a nice change and thankfully, it's only for one night. It's not a big deal.

I make my smile larger and say, "Cheers." We clink glasses and I sit back in my chair, trying to relax. "What about you, Kevin? Why couples therapy?"

"I'm actually a sex psychologist."

"Really?" A sexologist. This interests me greatly. I can pick his brain about my situation and my Sex Project, in a roundabout way.

"Yes. I usually don't go into detail about what I do because people don't understand it. They actually think that I have sex with my patients."

"You don't?"

He looks at me like I'm insane. "No, of course not."

"I know. I'm just kidding." I smile.

"Phew!" He wipes his brow and starts laughing. "I was going to ask to see your credentials. I didn't think you'd be that that stupid."

"Ok, that's a little harsh." I won't put up with name-calling.

"No, you're not stupid. I know that." He squeezes my hand briefly. "I figured you'd understand my profession, even though you work with children. You probably just don't know too much about what I do."

He's getting on my nerves. "I know what couples counseling is, Kevin."

"Colleen, it's not just couples counseling." He clicks his tongue, like Margie did. "I treat erectile dysfunction, premature ejaculation, anorgasmia, compulsive sexual behavior—"

I have to interrupt, "What is anorgasmia?" At this point, I don't care if I look like an idiot? I'm interested in what he does, not in *doing* him anymore.

"Anorgasmia is people who have trouble reaching orgasm."

"Oh." I have no trouble there.

"Anyway, the list goes on. I treat individuals and couples."

Even though I don't like his personality too much and can't wait for the date to end or wish that it never happened, I'm eager to ask him questions. "Do you have patients who come to you with no experience at all, wanting experience to please their spouse or significant other?"

He thinks for a second. "I did have one, but I had to terminate our relationship immediately. The patient thought I would be the surrogate."

"Aw, poor thing. She wanted to have sex with you to give her experience? I bet your rejection and dismissal didn't help her self-confidence."

"The patient was male."

"Oh my. No way." I cover my mouth in disbelief.

"Scouts honour." He holds three fingers up.

Jack does that same gesture. I shake off that thought. "How did you not burst out laughing?"

"In my profession, it's all about the poker face. You should know that, Colleen." He tilts his head to the side, studying me. "I guess treating children wouldn't be as serious as treating adults."

"It's just as serious, Kevin. I'm just trying to make a joke." This guy is so condescending. Jack wouldn't talk to me this way. Or Steve! Steve would never talk to me like this.

"I'm sorry. I don't see the humour there."

I stifle my frustration and press on. "Have you had any female clients with the same problem?" I might as well get my money's worth.

"Yes, I guess I have. Sometimes the problems women come to me with initially, stem from a lack of experience."

"How do you treat a woman who is inexperienced?"

He stiffens up and actually seems taller. "You ask a lot of questions."

"I'm just curious. We don't have to talk about work." I don't want him to think I'm asking for my own personal gain.

"No, it's ok. I like to talk about psychology with people who aren't educated about it."

I open my mouth and then close it. It's not worth it. It's really not worth it.

"If a woman is inexperienced, I try to explain that she would need to get out and date, maybe even have casual sex. I had one woman who was married for fifteen years and her husband told her that she was horrible in bed. They ended up divorcing and she lost her self-confidence and had little self-esteem. I told her she needed to experience sex and find out what was right or good to her."

"So, you support casual sex?"

"Sure, but only for the right reasons. Obviously, I don't promote it in a self-hating or damaging sort of way, but for a release or a non-committal experience, why not? As long as no one is gets hurt." He smiles.

I think about the disappointment that some of my samples felt about me using them for a one night stand. Dave, Charlie, Ryan... "Don't you think casual sex hurts no matter what? I mean emotionally."

"Basically, if two adults hit it off on a first date and they have sex that night, in this day and age, I can say confidently that each adult knows that there's a chance that it's just a fling."

"Why?"

"No sane person talks about a future together on the first date."

"Right." Essentially, I know that he's correct. My whole project is based on this reasoning and I liked that he confirmed it. I take another sip of wine and Kevin fills it up again. It was barely empty.

"And if your date does talk about the future—run!" He laughs loudly at his joke.

I smirk. "Very true." Or run if he is a big-headed, egotistical jerk. How can I blow off the rest of the date?

The waiter comes at that moment with our meals. Before he places mine on the table, Kevin grabs my napkin and lays it on my lap. He also inspects my steak when it's in front of me. I mean, he really inspects it. He takes my steak knife and cuts into it.

"I don't know, Colleen. Does this look medium to you?"

I look at the juicy, pink hunk of meat. "It looks great to me." I nod to the waiter. "Thank you, it's fine." I'm not a child. I can cut my meat.

"If you're satisfied with it, then I won't cause a scene. Let's see mine." He summons the waiter. When it's on the table, he cuts into it and takes a bite. "It's fine." He waves the waiter away and focuses on his steak.

I smile at the waiter and roll my eyes. The waiter smiles back at me. Kevin is unreal, but I'm not about to leave now. The steak looks delicious, so I dig in. Didn't John the Car Salesman say something about women and salads on a first date? I wonder how it looks to Kevin when I bite into a honkin' piece of steak.

"Oh!" Kevin exclaims, making me jump. "I had this patient today. He's a sex addict. Talk about casual sex!" He laughs loudly and I see a chewed piece of steak in his mouth. "I'm sorry for laughing, but I haven't seen such a severe degree of addiction before."

I thought he refrained from humour in psychology. "What are his tendencies?" I ask smugly.

He finishes chewing and explains, "First off, he was married. When his wife became tired of his incessant, unfulfilled sexual appetite, he went outside the home. He had affair after affair, numerous one night stands and paid for a slew of prostitutes. He was forced to see me after his third arrest."

"Wow."

"The tough thing about treating sex addicts is that they are masters at deflecting any negative comments about themselves. This guy topped the charts. When I referred to his deviant behaviour, he implied that I was inferior. What a joke. Me. Inferior." He shakes his head and waves around a chunk of steak on his fork

This hits home. Kevin continues talking, but I fade off and remember a time that I had called Steve out on his inappropriate sense of humour. Steve had been in a bowling league and would go out with his three teammates on a regular basis. One night, I had invited them and their wives to our house for dinner and having never met any of them, I was nervous. I had found the wives to be quiet and, somewhat proper, but we got along well.

The men had started to drink heavily, doing shots and getting more boisterous, as the night went on. Steve had told a bowling joke that basically compared women to bowling balls. The punch line had been that no matter how many times you pick them up, stick your fingers in them, and throw them in the gutter, they always come back for more. The women had been horrified and I learned at that moment, to let Steve have his own friends.

Later, I had told him that I was embarrassed and he turned it around. He had told me that I was too uptight and I needed to relax. He had been extremely angry with me and slept on the couch that night.

"Am I boring you? Your eyes have glazed over."

"No, I'm enjoying this. You're very intelligent." I'll feed his ego, since he is feeding me this wonderfully delicious meal. He can pay for it, too.

"Well, thank you. Did you know that sex addicts can have numerous undesirable habits at the same time?"

It's like he fed off my compliment. "No." I like pretending that I'm 'uneducated'. I pick up a shrimp and bite into it. So good.

Kevin gets really animated. "This guy hoarded porn magazines, books and videos. Boxes full of them."

Steve had kept two file boxes of pornography that he moved into our new home. He had laughed at me, telling me that it was just 'guy stuff', brushing it off. I had then started finding it in his bedside table, under the couch and even under the kitchen sink. I had wondered when or why he looked at porn in the kitchen.

I force a smile at Kevin. "Doesn't every man own some type of pornography?"

"Perhaps, but if he can't throw it away or it invades his everyday life, then it's not healthy."

Holy hell. Steve wouldn't throw it out and it actually accumulated. He had started keeping it in his man cave, in the basement. Did he have a problem? I sit back in my chair and stare at my steak. *Come on, Colleen!* Steve's not a sex addict. It was just magazines and videos. I should've looked at that stuff with him and maybe he wouldn't have gotten bored with Saturday night sex night. Men have needs.

Sitting up straight, I ask seriously, "What's the difference between a sex addict and someone with a healthy sexual appetite?"

"First, I'd have to ask if the person is preoccupied with sex and if he's unable to resist sexual urges or can he stop despite negative consequences."

"What if you don't know those answers?"

"For sex addicts, cheating or having serial affairs is part of a larger pattern. They also use porn, as we have discussed, but also internet sex, phone sex and even flirting."

"So, sex is their most important need?"

"Exactly. They think about it night and day. They even make sexual jokes or awkward sexual references in social situations."

Wow, I was just thinking about that. I look at my half-eaten steak and pile of shrimp. I lost my appetite. I gulp down my wine.

"Serial cheaters, on the other hand, may or may not engage in other kinds of sexual behaviours. Cheaters who are not addicts probably cheat in other areas of their lives." Kevin fills my glass to the top again.

Steve had cheated when we played board games and he could never keep track of our scores when we played volleyball. He had always argued that he was winning. Am I grasping?

"Cheaters may be secretive, but only because it would be very inconvenient if people ever knew the truth."

This is crazy. Steve is not a serial cheater or a sex addict. He wasn't satisfied by me and he wandered. I understand it. Technically, he should've told me and we could have changed things, but I know it was my fault. I take a few more sips of wine.

"Are you sure I'm not boring you? I've been talking non-stop for the last ten minutes."

"No, not at all. This is fascinating." I take another sip of wine. I know I can satisfy Steve now, with what I've learned. If I can satisfy the men I've been with, I can certainly please Steve. And, even though Kevin seems like a hard sell, with his mightier than thou attitude, he's just like any other man. I can gratify him too.

"Perhaps we should change the subject? Enough about cheaters." I give him my best seductive smile and whisk my hair off my shoulders. "I need to know more about you. Why don't you have a girlfriend?"

Kevin starts to talk about his education and background. I listen, but I'm distracted with thoughts of Kevin's sexual prowess. Being a sexologist, he would have to know how to please a woman. He has all that sexual and anatomical knowledge. Sex therapists would have to acquire a greater awareness about the physiological processes of human sexuality. He would surely be great in bed, wouldn't he?

24.

We finish dinner and Kevin tells the waiter that we don't want dessert, without consulting me. Again, I don't actually want dessert, but he could have at least asked me. He has some major flaws that I would definitely mention to him, if I was serious about dating him. I can't stand his arrogance and controlling behaviour. But...I can't believe I'm thinking this...I want to have sex with him. I smile at the thought. I think he's going to be an expert and I need that in my research. I can't pass it up. Hopefully, he won't criticize me during sex.

The walk back toward our offices is colder than before, and I snuggle against his arm, trying to keep warm. I'm pretty sure that he won't mind having sex with me. Kevin approached me at the bar, already knowing who I was. He kept eye contact, constantly touched my hand and I felt his leg against mine during dinner. I roll my eyes. He's a man! Of course he wants to have sex with me.

"Would you like to see my office?"

"Sure." We could do *it* there, I suppose. I'm sure he has a couch or a desktop.

"My office is quite different from yours, as you'll soon see. Yours is more childish and immature, obviously suited to your clientele."

I release my grip on his arm. Does he not know that he just insulted me? Whatever. I start walking faster. I just want to see what the guy has to offer me, but if he keeps saying stuff like that, I'm better off going home.

He unlocks his office door and as I step inside, I can see why he said that his office is different. Those stark white walls that I saw when we passed by earlier are in his waiting room. It's extremely harsh, austere and unwelcoming. There isn't any artwork or depth. The straight, black chairs are the generic doctor's office fixtures, but there are no magazines or books. He doesn't treat his patients very well.

The receptionist's desk is cold, hard steel and the chair is the same as the others. I cringe, thinking about Margie having to sit there all day. How depressing.

"What do you think?"

"It's great. Very professional," I lie.

He nods with enthusiasm. "Now come see my office."

I follow him in and stop in the doorway. My jaw drops. The contrast between the rooms is astounding, but not in a good way. I feel like I've walked into a boudoir. The walls are painted a deep, blood red and crystal pendant lights hang from the ceiling. The couch in the center of the room is black velvet with a number of soft throw pillows. Is that velvet wallpaper behind his desk too? I honestly expect to see bondage restraints hanging from the ceiling. None of this seems like a professional psychologist's office.

"I can see that you are in awe of this place." Kevin's smile is overwhelming. He's proud of his lair and he's waiting for my reaction.

"I'm speechless." I really am. I would think that his patients would be uncomfortable talking about sex in this environment. It's too sexual. Too extreme. I can see why people think he has sex with his patients. His office is a sadomasochist's domain.

"Come sit on my couch." He takes me by the hand and we sit together. "This is my life. I had a vision and it came together easily. I hope I can re-create it at my new location."

"New location?"

"I didn't tell you?"

I shake my head. *I just met you, you crazy freak.*

"I'm moving out of here at the end of the month and going closer to the downtown core. I have a sweet, new office. Anything is an improvement coming from this area."

There he goes again. He has to know that he's offending me. I rub my hand on the soft velour. It's not worth it to say anything. I'm not here to like the guy.

"You'll have to come visit me."

"Oh, sure," I say, not meaning it. I want him to think I'm interested, even though it *is* difficult. Now that I know he's moving, I suppose I can get past his ego and downright rude attitude. I won't have to see him ever again. Having sex with him will be a lot easier now. I reach up and fondle the hair around his ears. "It's too bad that you're moving."

Kevin slowly registers what I'm doing and leans in closer. "I won't be that far away." He kisses me gently. I thread my fingers through the back of his hair and pull his mouth firmly onto mine. He bites my bottom lip gently and I tug his hair.

He pulls away and gazes at me. I smile, but see that he looks different, almost angry. I stop smiling and question him with my eyes. He doesn't say anything, but he suddenly, grabs my head and kisses me harshly. Our teeth bump and his tongue mashes into my mouth. He starts pulling my hair, wrenching my neck backward, and I try to fight it, but can't get away from the tongue battle in my mouth.

I finally pull away by shaking my head back and forth and closing my mouth.

"What's wrong?" He asks, breathing heavily.

"I couldn't breathe and you were pulling my hair too hard." I rub my scalp and wipe the saliva off my mouth.

"Poor little thing. You're not used to a dominant man."

Is that what he's calling himself? I'd say forceful and overbearing. "I like you, Kevin, but could we take it a bit slower?"

"Fine," he huffs, looking angry.

We begin kissing again and this time, it's nice and gentle. This is the pace I like. He slides my coat off my shoulders and fondles my breast over my dress. I feel his hand slide under the vee neck, onto my skin, and then under my bra. He pinches my nipple and I moan into his mouth.

"You like that?"

I mumble my appreciation and he pinches it again, rolling it between his fingers. I pull his shirt out of his pants and put my hands on his lower back, massaging upwards. His muscles are hard and defined. It turns me on.

Kevin pulls his hand away and stands up. "Come here."

Standing before him, I don't know what to expect, but his change of attitude makes me trust him. He undoes the sash of my dress, letting it fall open, revealing my lavender bra and panties. He doesn't even stop to appreciate. He rips the dress off of my shoulders and lets it fall to the floor.

"Turn around."

What? Ok. I slowly turn around and when my back is to him, I feel his body push against me. He places one hand on my breast and the other at my head, pushing it to the side. He kisses my neck and continues to fondle my breast. Then, both hands glide down my body and he cups my bottom in his hands, dipping his fingers gently into the middle, pulling my cheeks slightly apart. He gives a good squeeze and continues to bring his hands to the front of my hips. He keeps his thumbs at my hipbones and slides his fingers under my panties. His fingers find my wetness and I feel penetration. I don't know how many fingers he has inside me, but the feeling is intense. I feel weak in the knees and I buck against his hands.

I lift my arms and cradle his head in my hands. I try not to pull his hair again. I don't want him to get aggressive. His skilled fingers press and plunge into me and I feel myself start to tighten up and my legs become unsteady. I can feel an orgasm coming on quickly. It's unreal. Kevin's awareness of the human body is astonishing. I think he recognizes my impending state and stops, moving to kneel in front of me.

"Feet apart."

Quickly obeying him, he pulls down my panties to my knees and reaches up, continuing to finger me again with one hand, while his other hand is on my bottom, pulling me close. The feeling is rougher now. He is filling me up, but his hand is harder than what I'm used to. Is that his fist? It can't be. It's almost too much. Almost.

The fingers on his other hand gently stimulate my other, more unmentionable entrance. At first, I'm shocked, but it's just a faint tickle. The feeling is incredible. I can handle him touching the unfamiliar territory.

Standing is starting to become difficult. I want to lie down and enjoy this. The probing gets a little stronger and he starts to plunge into the taboo opening, at same pace that he's fingering me. I'm not sure how I feel about this. It's different and very carnal. I'm losing my breath. He then, starts licking my clitoris and I lose control. I pull his head into my rigid hips and feel everything tighten up. My breathing is hard and fast and the pressure is building up quickly. I moan loudly and climax hard.

I feel Kevin pull away and he pushes me backwards. The back of my legs hit something and I end up sitting on his desk. He gets on his knees again and licks my wetness. It's so sensitive. I want to push him away and close my legs.

"You taste good."

I don't know what to say. 'Thank you' doesn't seem appropriate. I just close my eyes, but open them quickly when I feel Kevin stand up between my legs. He starts taking off his sweater and pants. I was right about him working out. He has an amazing body. His rock hard abs lead to the clearly defined vee disappearing in his boxer briefs. His bulge is very noticeable.

He walks over to his desk and quickly pulls out a condom. What kind of psychologist keeps condoms in his desk drawer? I guess a sex psychologist. Still, very weird.

Kevin stares at me, as he pulls off his underwear, like he's looking for a reaction. He's a good size, above average. I can understand why he has an ego now, I guess, but I'm not going to congratulate him. I watch him roll on the condom.

"You ready for this?" He's holding it in his hand.

I want to laugh, but I just nod.

"Tell me you want it."

What? I look at him strangely.

"Tell me you want my cock."

Is he serious?

"Do it."

"I want your cock?" It came out as more of a question.

"Say it again."

"I want your cock."

"Oh, yeah you do." He proceeds to force it inside me and push me backward at the same time, so that I'm lying on his desk.

It feels good, but I don't think I'm in the mood anymore. I close my eyes and as soon as I do, an image of Jack comes to mind. What the hell? I brush it away and try to picture Steve. That's better. I imagine that Kevin is Steve and I become aroused again.

Kevin pushes hard and fast into me and it feels sloppy. I wrap my legs around his waist and squeeze tight. That slows him down and I begin to enjoy it. Steve and I have to try this position.

I don't think Kevin likes my control and disentangles my legs, straightening them up, placing a calf on each of his shoulders. He holds onto my hips and starts thrusting hard and fast again. The change of position is decent, but again, I'm losing interest.

Jack wouldn't be so rushed. I mean, Steve! Steve wouldn't be so rushed! I have to end this. It's not doing anything for me.

"Are you going to come soon?"

Kevin looks at me. "Am I boring you again?" He looks angry and pulls out of me.

"No, it's just that I have to get home. I have an early morning."

"You should've told me that you wanted a quickie. I wouldn't have wasted so much time pleasing you."

"I'm sorry. I did enjoy it."

"I know that. I licked your juices, remember."

Gross. "Ok. What can I do for you?" Just continue with the same position and get it over with, please.

"Now that you're offering..." He walks to a cabinet and opens the doors. He rummages through a box and pulls out this black thing with straps. As he brings it closer, I see that it's a strap-on.

"You want to do that to me? What? Why? You're more than ample."

"No, Colleen. I want you to wear it for me."

I'm stunned. More than stunned. He wants me to do him? "I don't think...I can't....No, I can't do that."

He drops it onto the ground. "Fine. No problem. Turn around and I'll fuck you from behind."

I quickly spot my panties on the ground. "I think I should just say goodbye." I rush to pick up my panties and put them on.

"Really? You're going to go?"

"Yeah. I think it would be best."

"I thought you'd be more open to new experiences. You're an intelligent woman, Colleen. We're two intelligent, sexual adults experimenting with sex. There's no harm. It's not taboo."

Hell yeah, it's taboo. I grab my dress and hastily tie up the sash. "Like I said before, I have to work early tomorrow. This was fun."

Kevin walks up to me, still naked. "I'll be moving to my new office during the next couple of weeks, maybe we can get together next month." He takes my hands.

"Maybe." His penis is touching my coat. I pull away, but kiss him on the cheek. "Goodbye, Kevin. Thanks for dinner. It was great."

"Goodbye, Colleen."

I look back at him and he looks so pathetic standing there, with his deflated penis and ego.

25.

Wearing heels doesn't prevent me from jogging to my car. What's the euphemism for having sex and running away? It's not dine and dash. I laugh to myself. The old in and out? It's funny, but I don't think it fits the situation, either.

I get in my car and turn it on, waiting for it to warm up. He had a strap-on! What a weird man. I think that's worse than sixty-nine or anal. But *he* wanted anal! I understand that everyone has their fetishes and passions, but I just met him. Why did he think it was ok? And why did he keep the strap-on in his office? I can't wait to tell Christine.

As usual, the drive home is so quick, that my car isn't even warm by the time I get there. When I pull into my driveway, I don't recognize the car parked in front of my house, but it's normal for neighbours to have their friends' park there. I don't give it another thought.

Inside, I turn on the gas fireplace when I get inside and stand in front of it. I'm still a bit chilled and it's odd that I feel a breeze in the house. Maybe I should get someone here to check my windows for drafts. I'm not sure when it was last done. I do feel the heat immediately and keep my bottom close to the glass. When I feel warmer, I'll make a cup of tea.

On the street, I hear a car door slam and through the living room window, I see headlights of the car in front of my house turn on. I watch the car make an abrupt U-turn, squealing its tires in the process. What a jerk.

I wander into the kitchen, turn on the kettle and then, head upstairs to change my clothes. I need some comfy pajamas. It's so chilly in here. I stop to turn up the thermostat. It's set at sixty-seven Fahrenheit, but it's only at sixty-one. That's odd. I bump it up to seventy-two.

When I walk into my room, I notice my keys on the bed, but continue to my walk-in closet. As I pull out my flannel pajama pants, a realization hits me and the panic flows through my body instantaneously.

Those keys. I look toward my bed. Those keys. I can't move. I'm frozen. Those were the keys that were lost in Windsor. Mr. Baker had them last. Why are they on my bed? How did they get there? Was he here?

I need to move. I need to get help. *Move, Colleen!*

The slam of my bedroom door, echoes through the house and heightens my distress. I lock it, and pull my lounge chair over to barricade the door. Next, I avoid the bed altogether, trying not to disturb the keys, and reach for the phone. I dial the police slowly. My hands are trembling.

Dispatch tells me that a cruiser will be by within ten minutes and that I should stay on the line until officers get there. "With a break-in, sometimes the perpetrators will hide in the house, if the homeowners come home."

Now, I am petrified. Mr. Baker might still be here? Maybe he was the idiot who pulled the loud U-turn outside my house, when I got home. I hope so. I hope he's gone.

I inspect the keys from a distance, as I talk to the female dispatcher, and I see that my wedding band is gone from the key ring.

26.

While two officers process the house, I tell them about Mr. Baker and the entire ordeal, but I think they're immune to my trauma. They nod their heads and make notes, without sympathy. They must deal with issues like mine, all the time. I watch them place my keys in a plastic bag, expertly dust for prints and comb for DNA, but they don't seem to find anything. The officers tell me that they can get a restoration company out tonight to fix my broken backdoor window, but then offer to board it up themselves. I must seem unstable or incapable.

"Here's the number for the restoration company. Call them in the morning and they'll fix it properly," Officer Nicholls says.

"Thank you." My hand shakes as I take the business card.

"Are you sure you want to stay here tonight, Dr. Cousineau?" Officer Nicholls is the more empathetic one.

No, but where can I go? "Yes, I'm fine. I'll turn on the alarm." I've never used the alarm before. It should keep me safe, right?

He nods, "The alarm will definitely help. Maybe you could think about getting a watchdog."

A dog? I don't want a dog.

"We'll file the B & E report and get the Windsor Police Department to send us the information that they have on Mr. Baker. It'll help your case," Officer Leeds says. He seems to be all about moral codes and professionalism.

"You should think about filing an 810 peace bond with the Justice of the Peace. Do you know what that is?"

"Sure, it's like a restraining order."

"Right. If you need anything, call dispatch and ask for us specifically." Officer Leeds hands me his card, nods his head and leaves abruptly.

"We'll look into Mr. Baker's previous addresses and, if he's in Toronto, we'll find him," Officer Nicholls explains, trying to pacify me, I'm sure.

"I hope so."

"Tonight, we'll drive by a few times and even, park out front. You'll be fine, I promise." He smiles, but it doesn't help. "Here's my card, too. This is our neighbourhood. We're always nearby."

When he leaves, I put my back against the door and close my eyes, trying to calm myself. Am I safe in my own home? I quickly turn on the alarm and back away from the front door. Where do I go?

I keep all the lights on in the kitchen and living room and head to my bedroom. My bedroom has to be the safest part of the house. It's far away from the front door and it's on the second floor. I'll be safer there.

I run upstairs to my bedroom and lock the door, placing the lounge chair in front of it again. I jump into bed, thinking that the blankets will keep me hidden and, in my mind, safe. I know it's absurd, but I snuggle beneath them with my eyes open wide, staring at the ceiling, listening for strange noises. It's going to be a long night.

27.

I watch my alarm clock change from 7:44 to 7:45. I didn't sleep at all. I'm not looking forward to work and I hope Margie is back. I can't handle another day without her. Dammit! I forgot to send her flowers! Now I really need to apologize to her and really, I just can't handle the office without her. That's one thing I thought about all night. I've been horrible to her and she doesn't deserve it.

My body aches from all the tossing and turning I did. The stress probably didn't help either. I rub and stretch the kink in my neck. I guess I should get up. I slowly sit up and bend forward at my waist, reaching for my toes. When my nose hits my knees, I feel a bit of relief in my back, but it does nothing for my achy neck.

Standing up, I immediately step down onto a belt and yelp in pain. I sit back down on my bed and rub my foot, looking at the clothes that are piling up on my floor. I kick them all towards the walk-in closet, as I make my way to the bathroom. The laundry basket is just inside my closet, but I don't have the energy to pick them all up. I'll do it later.

The hot water feels great on my skin and refreshes me. I let it pour down my body, as I mentally pump myself up. I can handle today. No problem. If I'm tired later, I can come home right away and sleep. I've had worse nights. A lack of sleep won't kill me. But will I be able to sleep?

Christine could possibly sleep over to keep me company. That means I'd have to tell her what happened last night and she'd be worried. I don't need that annoyance. I'd do anything to get some sleep, though. I stop rubbing my scalp to get the shampoo out. Hold on. She would've had her date with Jack and I don't want to hear about it. Ugh. I scrub my head roughly. I'll just go buy the homeopathic sleeping remedies that I used in university. They'll do the job.

I trudge back to my closet and pull off random clothes from hangers. They're clothes I haven't worn lately, but I don't have any favourite clean clothes to choose from. I look in the mirror at the outfit I'm wearing. The black dress pants are too loose and hang low on my waist, but the oversized gray sweater hides it. It's fine.

Back in the bathroom, I diffuse my hair, but my dryer cuts out. When I inspect it, I see and smell smoke coming out of the back, so I blow on it. It's done this before. It just overheated. After waving it around for a minute, I try to turn it back on, but it won't start. Half-dried hair. Great. I twist my hair up into a tight bun.

Perhaps I should just stay home today. I look like a homeless woman, with my baggy clothes and scraggly hair. I even have dark circles under my eyes. Ugh. No, I have to go. I can't reschedule my patients again.

I move the lounger away from the door and unlock it, slowly opening the door. I take a moment and listen for any sound. Mr. Baker is not in the house. He's not in the house! I take a deep breath and let it out, as I go downstairs.

Like a zombie, I make tea and toast, and sit at the table eating slowly. I pick up my cell phone and see that there are a few messages, so I listen to them.

The first one is Christine, wondering how my date turned out with the 'tall drink of water'. I do want to gossip with her about my experience with Kevin. She'd crack up and give Kevin a new name. What name would she give Kevin? Egotistical Kevin? No, not funny enough. Kinky Kevin! That's a good one! But again, if I talk to her, I'm sure she'll tell me all about Jack and I don't know if I want to hear about it. That's another reason why I shouldn't have her sleepover. I delete her message.

The second message is from the Art Barn School, reminding me about registration for the next watercolour session. It wasn't Shawn who left the message, it was some woman. I don't think I'll ever hear from Shawn again, which is fine and I won't go back to that school, either.

The last message is from Zack. He called to confirm our date for tonight at five. I look up at the ceiling in regret. I'm too tired! I'll wait and see how I feel this afternoon. Dammit! I'm not dressed for a date right after work. A feeling of anxiety starts to rumble at my chest. I'll have to decide now, if I want to go. Let me get moving and I'll figure it out. God! Dating is stressful.

I finish my breakfast and walk past my office to look at the broken backdoor window. I shiver at thought of Mr. Baker being in my house. For some reason, I sniff the air. I can't smell any booze, thankfully. I don't know why I would. Now I'm being crazy.

I pull my shoulders back and walk back to my office. I can see my Sex Project notebook on my desk and it compels me to record my newest experience.

Data Collection

Sample #9:

Seek persons who understand study & are willing to express inner feelings & experiences
- *Man, aged? (in his mid-30's), Sex psychologist.*
- *Longer, dark hair, Arabic-looking, Aladdin*

Describe experiences of phenomenon
- *I met him at a restaurant the night before.*
- *He knew me from our street; his practice is a couple doors down from mine.*
- *We had dinner and went to his office/boudoir/S & M whorehouse.*
- *Foreplay was amazing; he entered both "holes" and performed cunnilingus—Orgasm was immediate.*
- *He wasn't great at sex; he was rough and fast, he liked it hard.*
- *He offered me a strap-on to wear, I assume to penetrate him, but I declined and got out of there as fast as I could.*

Direct observation
- *He seemed like a normal guy, very intelligent, in the same field as me.*
- *His personality turned me off at times; he had quirks: egotistical, arrogant, talked down to me, controlling, etc.*
- *I didn't end the date because I thought he would provide me with exceptional experience.*
- *If I don't like the inside package, I'm not going to like the outside package (even if the "package" looks ideal!)—This remains true from Sample #8*

- *Future goals: Make sure that I like the sample, before I have sex with him. Be choosy!!! Why didn't I learn from Sample #8??*

<u>Audio or videotape?</u> n/a

<u>Data analysis</u>

<u>Classify & rank data</u>
- *1 out of 5*

<u>Sense of wholeness</u>
- *I think that if I was in a loving, secure and safe relationship with this man, something like a strap-on wouldn't intimidate me or scare me away. Being as this was our first date, it seemed too soon, or too normal for him.*
- *I think there was more to him in the sense that I shouldn't have trusted him so easily.*
- *I have the feeling that he is a shady character; there's something dishonest or disreputable about him.*

<u>Examine experiences beyond human awareness/ or cannot be communicated</u>
- *I need a commitment, crush or attraction to a sample to continue with sexual experience.*
- *I didn't get a 'flip flop' (again).*
- *I may be looking for experiences that I can't get with a one night stand.*

    I still have a few days until I can call Steve. I might as well go out with Zack. I can keep practicing how to flirt and seduce, but this time, I won't expect too much. I'll just go with the flow and if there are any red flags, I'll get out of there immediately.
    There. I've decided. Now, to change out of these hobo clothes and fix my hair.

28.

I'm half into my blouse, when the phone rings.
"Hello?" I move the phone slightly away from my ear and pull my blouse on.
"Did you sleep well last night, Dr. Cousineau?"
I don't recognize the deep, male voice and I'm not sure if I heard him correctly. "Pardon? Who is this?"
There's a click and then the dial tone. What? I stare at the phone in my shaking hand. My heart is beating so fast, it feels like it's coming out of my mouth. It had to be Mr. Baker. I struggle to hang the phone back up.
After I finish getting dressed, I run downstairs and gather my belongings. I quickly reset the house alarm and fly out the door, to my car. As soon as I get inside the car I lock my doors and bang my head into the headrest. I will not cry! Wait a minute! I frantically look out the windows and search the back seat of my car. He could be watching me. *Stop!* I can't live like this. I inhale sharply and exhale with force a few times. He can't scare me.
I'm in a daze when I drive to work, overthinking and imagining dangerous situations that Mr. Baker might put me in. I envision him attempting to abduct me and his daughter again, but this time I knee him in the groin and get away. I'm working myself up. I do some more deep breathing techniques, but it doesn't help. I need to take a self-defense class. I'll look that up today. *Shit!* I completely missed my turn and have to drive around the block.
Scurrying up the walk to my building, I almost drop everything, when I unlock the door, but manage to get inside. Margie hasn't arrived yet, but I lock the door behind me anyway. She can let herself in. I need to feel safe. Walking into my office, I lock that door behind me, too.

I immediately search the internet for self-defense classes in the area and copy down some phone numbers. There's one this weekend that's runs for only two hours. That I can do. I draw a star beside that number.

The front door to my practice squeaks open and I freeze to listen. I tiptoe to my office door and put my ear against it. Is it Margie? It has to be. I shake my head. No one else has a key. I unlock my door and peek through the crack. I immediately see a face looking at me. It scares me and I yelp in surprise.

"What are you doing?" Margie demands. "You scared me!"

"I scared you?" I hold onto my chest, feeling how fast my heart is beating.

"Why are you peeking out your door?"

"I don't know." I open my door completely and walk back to my desk. How embarrassing. I tense up, fully expecting Margie's concern and pity.

"Are you all right?"

There it is. "Yes. I'm just jumpy today. I didn't sleep." I pull some files out of my bag, keeping my back to Margie.

"I can rebook your appointments, if you want to go home and sleep?"

"No!" I snap and turn around. "I can't do that to my patients anymore. It's not fair to them."

She places her hands on my desk and leans in. "But if you're not getting sleep, how are you helping anyone?"

Does she mean her? "Margie, I can handle my work load." I'm getting angry. I wanted to apologize to her, but she won't let up!

All of a sudden, there's a giant crash in the reception area. We both jump and look at each other and then, towards the reception area. It sounded like glass shattering.

We rush into the room and see that part of the front bay window has been smashed. Sharp, jagged edges are still left in the frame and there are glass shards all over the floor.

"Oh my God," Margie whispers.

I quickly open the front door to see if I can see anyone. I don't know why I'm so brave.

"There's a brick on the floor."

I close the door and spot a red brick in the middle of the broken glass.

"Who would do such a thing?"

I pace back and forth staring at the mess and a chill runs down my back. "I think I know." I pick up the phone and call the police for the second time in twenty-four hours.

Margie listens in, as I talk to the police and when I hang up, I fill her in about my house break-in, the returned keys and the disturbing phone call this morning.

"Why is Mr. Baker doing this to you?"

"I don't know." I wrench my hands together, trying to get the shaking to stop. "Listen, we need to call my patients and reschedule them." I need to collect my thoughts.

"I'll take the morning patients, you take the afternoon ones," Margie says and picks up her reception phone.

I go into my office and pick up my phone, but put it down immediately. I sit in my chair, place my head down on my desk and breathe deeply. What does Mr. Baker want? I close my eyes and see him with a knife in his hand. I feel my heart start to race again. This can't be happening.

Margie walks in some time later and I'm still in the same position. "I called all of the patients. They're all rescheduled."

I slowly look up, not caring that she can see how upset I am.

"Do you want to stay at my house for a while? Jerry won't mind. We have a spare room."

I sit upright and attempt a smile. "No, Margie. I couldn't. I have an alarm that'll keep me safe. Thank you for offering."

"You haven't been yourself lately and I've been awfully worried."

"Margie, I have been a horrible boss and person to you lately. I've been meaning to apologize. I've been on edge and I shouldn't take it out on you." I reach my hands out in front of me, toward her. I let them fall on the desk in front of me. "This place doesn't function without you and I don't function without you. I appreciate everything you do and I'm sorry that I've treated you so poorly."

"It's ok, Colleen. I can't imagine what you went through. I understand how you could be put on edge." She smiles and cocks her head to the side. "I was going to give you my resignation letter though."

"What?" I look at her in horror.

"Just kidding." She pats my hand. "I'd never leave this place."

I smile. "Don't joke about leaving. It's not funny."

We walk to the front office and survey the mess.

"Why would he do this? It's not like you foiled the abduction. Jack did. Why isn't he tormenting him?"

"I don't know."

"He's an angry man. He just wants to scare you."

I don't know what to say. I've seen Mr. Baker angry. I don't want to see it again.

"Hey, the police are here."

A black and white squad car pulls up and parks behind my car. I hope it's not the same officers as last night. I'm going to look pathetic.

"Margie, could you call a window company and get them here immediately?"

"Sure. I'd ask Jerry to do the handy work again, but I think this is too big of a job for him."

"Did he fix the bathroom door?"

"Yes."

"Please thank him for me and tell him to send me an invoice. I need to pay him."

"He did it for you, for free. We won't take your money."

I hug Margie quickly. "Thank you."

"Sure thing, boss." She smiles, touches my arm and walks into my office.

I turn and open the door for the officers. "Good morning." They aren't the same officers, but they do look familiar. They enter and I explain what happened, including everything about my abduction again. Officer Lavoie writes everything down and Officer Ackerman processes the room. He places the brick in a plastic bag. It's disturbing how emotionless I am about the whole process. I'm numb.

"We've been here before." Officer Lavoie nudges his partner. "There were two other women here that were locked in the bathroom. So, you must be the woman who was abducted and taken to Windsor."

"Yes, that's me."

"And we were here before that, too. Do you remember, Corey?" He looks at Office Ackerman for help, but he shrugs. He's the quiet one. "Yeah! Yeah, I remember you. You called us about a disturbance... No, it was a domestic dispute."

I think for a minute and it comes to me. "That's right. It was about the same man too. Mr. Baker was threatening me and his wife." That's why I recognize the officers.

"You've been through a lot lately. You should really apply for a peace bond."

"Yes, I know." I tell them about the incident last night and named the officers that were involved.

"Here's my card," Officer Lavoie says, "This is our jurisdiction. It's different from where you live. Please call dispatch and ask for us, if you need anything else."

I'm not too impressed by my growing collection of business cards from police officers. I thank them and they leave, without erasing the ominous feeling in my stomach.

Margie and I sweep up the broken glass and I tell her to go home, while I wait for the window company to arrive.

"I don't want to leave you alone."

I need to be alone. I think she'll just annoy me and I don't want to say anything mean. I need to test out my courage, too. "If you stay, I'll make you reorganize the children's toys." She hates doing that.

She raises her eyebrows. "You're mean! Call me when you're done here." She grabs her purse, but stops. "Are you sure you don't want me to stay?"

"Yes, I'll get some work done. Just go home and spend some time with Jerry."

Her eyes light up. "He'll be so surprised to see me. I can finally bring some sushi for him to try."

"Enjoy!"

Margie leaves and I use the reception phone to dial the self-defense studio to book a spot for Saturday's class.

29.

The new window is finally installed by four o'clock. I wasted my whole day watching two guys make a mess on my carpet, with their dirty boots, and drink cup after cup of coffee. They were really nice though, so I didn't mind making it, but I ran out of creamer mid-afternoon. I didn't feel right, leaving them alone to run to the store, so I made up an excuse about being too busy to go to the corner store. How were they to know that I was just playing *Sticky Blocks* on Margie's computer? I *looked* busy. They were fine without creamer. I saw them drink their coffee black.

They hand me the invoice and linger, so I assume they want me to pay them. "I'll get my cheque book."

"No, you can mail us the payment," the tall one says.

"Oh, ok." Then why won't they leave? I don't have any more coffee.

"Here are our mugs."

I take them and place them on Margie's desk. They still don't budge. I need to get ready for my date with Zack. I'm glad I have a date. I really don't want to go home and worry about Mr. Baker breaking in again.

"Oh, hey! My backdoor window was broken into last night. Can you fix that?"

"Absolutely! When do you want me there?" The tall one looks at the short one and the short one turns to the door.

"Can I have your card? I have an appointment tonight, but I'll call you tomorrow."

He hands me his card. "That's my personal cell number, right there," he points, smiling at him. "You can call day or night."

"Oh, thank you." You wish. "I really have to go, so thanks for fixing my window. It looks great." I basically push them both out the door.

I'm going flying! The butterflies suddenly replace the sickening feeling that I had all day. I'm excited about going up in a Cessna with Zack. I thought I'd be exhausted by now, but I guess the adrenaline and tension of the day energized me. I smooth down my hair, apply some lip balm and look at my reflection in the mirror. I'm glad I changed into a sexier outfit. I pick some lint off my black tights and pull the longer, baby doll blouse over my hips.

After walking to the waterfront, I take the ferry to the airport, and as I get closer to the island, I can see that Zack is waiting for me. I exit the ferry and walk towards him. He's wearing the same leather jacket as before, but is now sporting a brown leather aviator hat. The hat looks silly.

"Long time no see." He gives me a big smile and his eyes crinkle at the corners. He's very handsome, but he still can't pull off that hat. He kisses me on the cheek and the rim of his hat, bumps my forehead. "You are still just as beautiful as when I first met you. What have you been up to?"

He's being flirty. "Hi, Zack. I've been busy with work, I guess. Nothing too exciting."

"Well, it's about time someone shows you a little excitement. I'm going to give you the ride of your life." He winks.

"I'm so excited! Let's do this!"

Zack takes my hand and pulls me towards the hangar. "She's all ready for us. We just have to hop in."

When we get to the plane, he opens the passenger door and picks up a quilted, black jacket with a logo on it, that I recognize from Zack's business card. "Wear this. It'll be colder up there."

He helps me into it, over top of my own coat. I feel big and bulky, but warmer already. He then, motions for me to get into the plane. He waits to see if I can fasten my seatbelt, but I don't know where to start. I can't figure it out.

Zack smiles and leans in close to clip the harness together. I smell a woodsy, outdoor scent on him. It's very masculine, but also mature. How old is he? I can see flecks of gray in his hair and wrinkles around his eyes and mouth. I take another deep breath. I decide that I like the scent. Who cares how many years he has on me? He tightens up the belt and then tests it by tugging on it. He's sexy.

His hand remains on the chest strap. "You're all secure. A man could do pretty much what he wants, when a woman is tied up like this."

I'm not sure how to respond. Is he saying he's some sort of a sadomasochist? Or is just trying to be flirtatious? Is he kinky, like Kevin? I hope not. I don't need another sample like that. I avert my eyes to my harnesses and start to rethink my plan.

"I'm kidding. I'm not into whips and chains. I'm a lover, not a dominatrix." He laughs and flicks my nose softly.

I smile and relax. I know he's just flirting now, but I do want to correct his vocabulary. A dominatrix is the female who takes the dominant role in a sadomasochist relationship. I think a male would be a master or just a dom. I should be relieved that he doesn't know the difference. Game on.

Zack closes my door and I watch him, as he disappears beneath the plane. I sit up straighter to see out the window, but I can't. How can I see the view when I can't look out the window? I finally see the top of his head, at the nose of the plane, and he tosses the chalks away. I remember that from the last time I was here.

He climbs into the Cessna, closes the door and starts turning on various knobs and instruments on the panel. His hands are nimble and watching him is overwhelming. There's so much to do. How does he remember it all? The propeller starts to turn slowly and then, it's a blur. It's so loud.

Zack inches towards me holding a head set. "Put these on, so you can hear me," he yells over the roar of the engine. He adjusts them carefully, when I get them on. "Can you hear me loud and clear?"

I nod. "Yes, I can hear you."

"Take these, too." He holds a pair of sunglasses out to me and I put them on immediately.

He gives me a thumbs up. I put my thumb up too, in response. He smiles.

After touching a few more gadgets overhead, and in front of him, I hear his voice in the headset, "City Centre, this is Piper Tomahawk Golf Tango Zulu Yankee."

"Golf Tango Zulu Yankee, this is City Centre."

"Golf Tango Zulu Yankee is by Hangar 4B. Request taxi for local scenic flight, departing east."

"Runway two four. Winds are at zero at five."

I hear more communication between the tower and us, but I don't understand it. The plane starts to taxi towards the runway and he grabs my knee. "You ready?"

"Absolutely!"

"City Centre, Golf Tango Zulu Yankee is ready for takeoff." Zack's voice booms over the headphones.

"Golf Tango Zulu Yankee, cleared takeoff on runway two four."

"Cleared takeoff on runway two four, Golf Tango Zulu Yankee."

Finally, we are off. We are speeding down the runway, travelling faster and faster. I see the end of the runway, with a building and trees beyond it. It doesn't seem like we'll ever get up in time. Suddenly, I feel us lift up.

Zack is pulling back on the yoke and our nose is headed towards the horizon. All I can see are blue sky and clouds. The lift off forces me back into my seat and my heart jumps into my throat. It's been years since I've been in a little two-seater. My dad was a great pilot and loved taking me out every weekend, but I don't remember it being this loud. It's really noisy. I feel like the engine is working too hard or something is going to bust open. I swallow to pop my ears. The climb is scary.

After a few minutes, we level out and Zack points for me to look out the front window. We are over the city and the water is on my right. The view is breathtaking. Buildings go for miles in front of me and the lake merges with the horizon. I can't believe how clear the view is. I thought there would be more clouds.

Closer to the water, I recognize the different beaches along Woodbine Park. I'm not surprised that there aren't any swimmers today, but I can still see a lot of people down there, sitting and walking along the sand. The long boardwalk that runs along most of its length, and a portion of the Martin Goodman Trail bike path, are both scattered with people, too. I like Woodbine Beach for volleyball and Kew Beach is good for relaxation and there are rock sculptors on summer weekends. Balmy Beach is the quietest of the three and ideal for seeking seclusion. I haven't been to any of them in a couple of years.

Steve and I had gone to Balmy Beach when we were dating and he talked me into having sex under a blanket on the sand. I had been so nervous that someone was going to catch us, but he assured me that because it was dusk, no one would know. He had made sure that we were secluded under the trees. There hadn't been anyone near us and no one would see us, he begged. After much discussion, he had spooned me, lifted up my sundress and entered me from behind. At first, I had tried not to move and kept scanning the beach for curious eyes, but it felt so taboo and so sensual, that I got into it. I had closed my eyes and enjoyed our closeness. He had been right. No one had seen us. It had been amazing. I think that was the only time we had sex in that position.

Oooh! I just got that falling feeling. I glance over at Zack and he smiles when he sees me. "You'll get used to it the more you fly," he says. I smile at him, thrilled that I might be able to fly on my own, one day.

Next, I see the magnificent fall colours on the ground below and recognize that they're a part the Scarborough Bluffs. My Grade Six oral presentation had been about the Bluffs and I remember it vividly.

The Bluffs were formed primarily by erosion of the packed clay soil. In some places, such as the western end of Bluffers Park, the erosion has shaped the clay into interesting shapes. I smile proudly. I had practiced my speech repeatedly and I still remember it.

In university, I used to go for walks on the trail around the Bluffs, that hugs the lake and I'd sit on each of the fifteen benches along the way, to relish the view. It had been a great way to unwind from the stress of my classes. My therapist had suggested it.

Just as I spy the Pickering Nuclear Generating Station, Zack turns us around toward the water. The flight seems smoother now, less turbulent. I wonder if it has to do with the smoothness of the water, compared to flying over buildings. I guess I'll learn that in flight school.

I should be talking to Zack. We *are* on our first date, but the view is just so breathtaking. What would I talk about? I'm sure he's seen the same sights before and I don't want to annoy him. We can talk later. I'm sure our date won't be over when the plane lands.

We're back, flying over the city, and the CN Tower is ahead in distance. It looks like we might fly straight over it. The buildings in the downtown core seem so small from up here, but when you're on the ground they're so overpowering. Even the Trump International Hotel & Tower is teeny tiny. And look at those enormous banks, like TD and Scotiabank. They aren't so monstrous now.

I feel like a child, like it's my first time in an airplane, even though I've been in one numerous times before. I'm so giddy and completely stimulated by the sights. I can't wait to become a pilot and see this whenever I want. I'll have to bring Steve up with me. Would he be just as thrilled? I know Jack would. He seems so impressed by whatever I do. *God!* Why do I keep thinking about him?

We're so close to the CN Tower now! I've been inside the tower many times before, for dinner and to look out from the observation deck, and seeing Toronto from that view is great, but viewing it from way above it, is even better! This is so exciting. We're right above it!

"City Centre, this is Piper Tomahawk Golf Tango Zulu Yankee," Zack surprises me in my headphones.

"Piper Tomahawk Golf Tango Zulu Yankee, this is City Centre, go ahead."

"Golf Tango Zulu Yankee is two miles south City Centre. Inbound for landing."

"Winds are one nine zero at five. Cleared straight in runway one nine, Golf Tango Zulu Yankee."

That's it? We're done already? Zack is all over the instrument panel again, flicking switches and pressing buttons. I'm in awe of his expertise. The flight was so quick, though. I want to keep flying, but I do see the sun setting in the horizon. I understand that we have to go back.

My ears pop as we descend and I want to grasp onto something, but there aren't any armrests. I clasp my hands together instead. My nails dig into my skin. It's just so loud and bumpy. We aren't going to crash. We aren't going to crash. We aren't going to crash…

As we get closer to Toronto Island, I can see the runway that starts at the inside the edge of the island. The lake is on all sides of us. We're flying so close to the water now that it makes me nervous, but I'm confident Zack can land this thing.

In a heartbeat, we're on the ground with a light bump. It was a graceful landing and we slow down immediately and taxi to the hangar.

30.

Zack tugs on the corner of Cessna's protective cover, to make sure it's snug.

"Good job, Colleen."

"Thanks!"

He takes my hand and we walk over to the hangar. I feel his hand on me, when we walk through the door. I'm still wearing his oversized coat, so I don't feel it, but I know it's on my bottom. He leads me to the empty lounge.

"I'm still on such a high!" I exclaim and jump up and down a few times. "I'm definitely hooked on flying." I throw the black, quilted coat onto a stool.

"It's almost as good as sex."

I think about it and nod my head. I'd agree with that statement. I flop down on the couch and undo my own coat, letting it fall open. I look at Zack and he's eyeing me seductively. Oh, I get why he said that now. He wants me.

He takes a drink from a silver flask and Mr. Baker's black eyes flash in my head and it repulses me. My stomach turns and I look away, trying to erase the thought.

"Would you like a sip?"

I pause and look at him again. Mr. Baker doesn't wear a goofy hat. "Sure." I pull off my coat and take the flask from him, as he sits down next to me.

"I don't drink anything else. It's Chivas Regal Royal Salute, aged fifty years. The stuff costs a fortune and it's the best."

I nod, but have no clue about the price of whiskey. I take a sip and it burns down my throat. I start coughing. I didn't know it would taste so bad either.

"Good stuff?" He laughs and takes the flask, downing the rest.

"So, what's flight school like?"

"Colleen, do you really want to talk?" He rubs my upper thigh.

I do, but I can tell that he doesn't. "I'm just so thrilled about our flight together, I want to know what to expect." His advances don't bother me. I think I'm actually turned on by the whole experience. I move a little closer to him and press my chest against his arm. I think my eagerness is a part of the adrenaline rush. I want his hands on me.

"I'll tell you what to expect." He leans in closer. "Expect the night of your life." With that, Zack flops on top of me, kissing me and pushing me back onto the couch.

Even though it's not the sexiest gesture, I'm caught up in the moment and I respond with equal enthusiasm. The first thing I do is rip the hat off his head and throw it to the ground, smiling to myself. A low growl escapes from Zack. He thought it was an act of passion.

His hips push roughly into mine and he grabs at my breast through the material. I think I hear it rip, but I'm too caught up in the moment to care. I push my sex into him, pulling his hips toward me and I bite his lower lip during our tongue battle.

He growls again and slides down to the floor, to sit up on his knees. He pulls off his shirt and I admire his strong chest and hint of abs. He looks great for a man his age. I'm assuming he's in his early to mid-forties. Not that he's old, I just haven't been with a man his age before.

"Are we safe here?" Do you think anyone will walk in?" I caress his chest with both hands.

Zack huffs, gets up and walks to the door of the lounge. He locks it, flips off the light and walks back to me. The glow from the single computer screen is the only light in the room.

"Is that better?"

"Yes, thank you. Now, get back over here."

He stands in front of me, picks up my feet and whips off my boots at the same time, then, pulls my leggings down forcefully. I lift my hips, to make it easier. I don't want him to rip them. I need to wear my clothes home. He kneels down on the floor again and pulls up my blouse, revealing my bra.

"Fuck, you have a hot body." He starts kissing my stomach and up further, to my breasts. He flips down the cups of my bra to release my nipples and bites each of them. I moan and reach for him, but he stays on the floor, pleasuring me. I arch my back and throw my head back in ecstasy.

All of a sudden, I feel him tear my shirt open. I open my eyes in horror and look down to see the raggedness of my pretty baby doll blouse. How could he do that? He's already prying up my bra and attacking my breasts.

"I'll buy you a new one." With his mouth on my nipple, one of his hands reaches between my legs, over my panties and he presses hard with his fingers. I feel his fingers inside me, through the silk. I push my hips up to meet the pressure, instantly forgetting about my blouse.

"You like that?"

I moan to respond. The urgency of our desire increases the pleasure that is building up inside me. My whole body tenses and my sex aches with desire. My response to his advances is so innate, it surprises me. I didn't know that I was this attracted to him. I'm sure it's still the adrenaline stimulating and heightening my senses. Whatever it is, I want him badly.

Zack suddenly stands up and takes his pants off. I watch his sizeable erection spring free when he pulls down his boxer shorts. Then, he's swiftly between my legs. I want him inside me. He pins both of my hands over my head, with one hand and his other hand rips off my panties. It's extremely erotic, but my guard goes up. He doesn't need to be so aggressive.

He clenches his eyes shut and forces himself inside of me. Hard. It rips me open and it hurts. I don't think he's present for me. This is not about sex or the adrenaline rush anymore.

I try to pull my arms away, but he has a firm grip on them. His fingers tear at my skin and I think he might break my wrist at any moment.

Something tells me that I'm in trouble. "Hey! Stop! You're not wearing a condom." I wriggle my hips around, trying to get him out. Will that stop him?

Through his grunts, he says, "I'm fixed. I can't have kids." He doesn't stop thrusting into me.

"Hey! That's great, but I don't even know you." I push at his chest. I have to get his attention, he's not present anymore. This is not about pleasure or making love.

He stops moving and looks at me. "I'm married and haven't had sex in years. I don't have any diseases." He starts pumping harder.

I'm shocked. I squirm underneath him, trying to get him to stop. "Stop!" I finally yell.

"What's wrong?"

"You're married?"

He grumbles, "I'm separated. Does that make it better?"

"I'd feel better if you were wearing a condom."

"Fuck!" He gives me a couple more pumps and pulls out, but it doesn't stop his forceful approach. He quickly slides down my body and opens my legs, pushing my thighs up off the couch. He buries his face in my sex, lapping it quickly. His fingers squeeze the flesh of my hamstrings.

I don't know what to do. I'm attracted to Zack, but I don't believe him. Is he married or separated? I'm not sure if I even trust him. He scared me just now, but at least he pulled out.

I feel him do this thing with his tongue and my body convulses. I let out a moan. What was that? He does it again and I feel my legs quiver. I try to close them, but Zack forces them apart. I can't let this go on. Oh, but the feeling is overwhelming. He does it over and over again. It's so aggressive and relentless. He doesn't stop. My insides start to tremble and I lift my hips to meet his mouth.

I can't help myself. I explode moaning loudly. I can't catch my breath. That was incredible. What was he doing with his tongue?

There's no time to analyze it or ask him, he crawls back up my body and tries to get inside me again. I quickly regain my composure and push him up, closing my legs slightly, but stiffly, so he can't go any further.

"Come on, Colleen. I did you, now I need a release."

"Find a condom."

"Give me a blow job." He lets up a little and I push him further.

"That's not nice. Don't order me around."

"It's just a blowjob. I'm sure you know how to do it. It won't take long. I promise."

I'm offended by his vulgarity. I shake my head. "I'm sorry, but I'm not going to do that."

"You're such a fucking tease." His eyes are fierce when he tries to open my legs. It feels like he's crushing the muscles in my thigh and I don't know if I have the strength to keep them closed. He collapses onto my body with all of his weight and forces himself further between my legs. My legs shake, getting weaker.

He has to see the terror in my eyes. This is not a nice man. He's like Mr. Baker, in my dream. I need to get away from him. My heart beats wildly, fearfully. I need to fight.

He releases slightly to steer himself into me and that's when I wrap my hand around his neck and push him away, squeezing his throat.

"Get off of me." He's so much stronger.

"Come on, baby." I feel him try to push into me.

I need to do more damage. I squeeze his throat harder and I feel him give a little. It has to hurt. I dig my nails into his skin. He backs off even more and he coughs shallowly.

"What the fuck?" He doesn't budge. He just glares at me.

"Get off of me!" I place my other hand against his chest and push with all my strength, while I'm still gripping his throat. He moves just enough for me to use my knees to push him further, and then, I maneuver my feet on his chest, to throw him completely off of me. He falls to the floor.

I pull together the remaining scraps of my blouse and quickly get up, scrambling into my pants, without my underwear. What have I done? I find my shoes, coat and purse and run for the lounge door.

My hands are shaking, as I fumble for the lock. I look back at Zack and he's staring at me from beside the couch, unmoving.

Fucking jerk. I pause long enough to put my shoes on and run out of the hangar, to the ferry dock. My heart's still beating furiously and I try to calm down by breathing long breaths, but it's no use. I have to get off this island. I see the ferry coming, but it's not fast enough. I keep looking back at the hangar, but Zack is nowhere in sight.

When the ferry finally arrives, I jump on it and tap my foot impatiently for it to leave again. The tears start to fall as the ferry departs.

31.

The alarm clock screams at me the next morning and I roll over onto my back, staring at the ceiling. Ugh. I don't want to move. I can't believe what I went through last night.

I cried all the way home in the taxi, mumbling my address to the driver, between sobs. I gave him an extra twenty dollars to watch me walk to my door, unlock the door, get into my house, lock the door and wait for me to wave from the living room window. Those were my exact instructions. The taxi driver must've thought I was crazy, but in Toronto, he's probably seen worse. When the driver waved back at me, I cried even harder.

Sleep didn't come easily. Not only did I stress over what happened with Zack, but I worried about Mr. Baker breaking into my apartment again. The alarm helps tremendously, but isn't it just a false sense of security?

At two in the morning, I turned on all of the lights and made some warm milk. The thought of warm milk has never been pleasant, but I was so distraught and desperate for sleep, I figured I'd give it a try. While it was warming on the stove, I panicked and turned out the lights again, staying away from the windows. Anyone could see right into my house, through the curtains. I didn't know which was worse. Mr. Baker knowing that I was awake or thinking I was asleep. The warm milk was disgusting, but I drank it slowly, back in my bedroom, with the lounger barricaded against the door. I guess I eventually fell asleep.

I throw my legs over the edge of the bed and slowly sit up. I survey the room and see a sweater that I would like to wear today, but it's underneath my sweaty, yoga spandex. I'll have to find something else. I quickly shower, dress in an old pant suit combination and go downstairs to make breakfast.

While my kettle boils and my bread toasts, I retrieve my sex notebook from my office and stick it in my bag to take to work. I don't want to think about last night at the moment, but I'll need to record the experience soon, before I forget.

How could I have misjudged someone so badly? I was so lucky. It could've ended way worse. *Stop!* I'm starting to cry again. *Eat your breakfast!*

I wash down a dry piece of toast with my tea and feel it scratch my throat on the way down. Even with such a bad night, I'm surprisingly calm about being home alone this morning. Mr. Baker has done so much more to me than Zack. I should feel more panicked. The morning light puts me at ease, I suppose. I take another bite. How can I be more upset at Zack, than the whole abduction scenario? Now, I'm rating my levels of anxiety over *two* violent and insane scenarios that I've endured. Scenarios that aren't even fathomable to the average person. How did this happen to me? I throw out the rest of my toast. I can't eat.

My car is at the office, so I consider walking to work. I'm nervous, but it's usually busy in my neighbourhood during the day, so Mr. Baker couldn't attack me outside my home. Or could he? He did throw that brick through my window during the day... Enough already! I can't think about it and be afraid. I have to walk to work. I'm walking!

It's definitely warm for the end of October. I don't remember it being this warm yesterday. I sat in the office all day, while the workers fixed the broken window and it didn't seem to be cold sitting at Margie's desk. However, just the other night, on my date with Kevin, it was cold. Autumn sure can't make up its mind, but I'm not complaining. I'm all for pushing back the winter. For once, it'll be good weather for the kids, when they go begging for candy on Saturday. Halloween came so fast.

The coffee shop on the corner is empty when I walk in and I'm able to order immediately. I wonder how Jack is. I haven't seen him in a couple of days. I always seem to run into him here and there...and at my house... I bet he had his date with Christine. I cringe as I take a sip of my vanilla latte. He's not here and I'm glad. I still don't want to know about their date.

When I get to my office, I see my new car and I'm relieved that it's still there. I've never left my car on the street overnight before, so I was a bit worried. Upon closer inspection, I see a very long scratch that runs from the front end to back bumper on the passenger side. It's deep too. What could've done that? Son of a... It's my new car! It's what? 3 days old? I can't believe this! I touch the scratch lightly and I want to cry.

Don't cry! I stomp up the walkway to my office and look back at my car. Is this another one of Mr. Baker's tricks? I look up and down the street. Is he watching me? The ominous feeling in the pit of my stomach returns and I'm suddenly afraid to go into my office. He could be in there.

Thankfully, Margie walks up to the door, at that moment. "Are you going to open it or just stare at it?" She laughs and unlocks it, holding it open for me.

I half expect Mr. Baker to jump out, so I'm frozen on the spot.

"I know it's nice outside, but you have to work to do. Go on, get in!" She pushes me forward.

"Ok." I try to shake the thoughts. "Thanks, Margie. My hands are full." I show her the latte.

"Where's mine?"

"I'm sorry—

"I'm kidding. Jerry and I had a coffee date early this morning. We had a wonderful day together yesterday." She beams.

"I'm glad." I look at the bathroom door blankly.

"The new window looks good."

I nod and walk into my office. *Pull yourself together, Colleen!*

"Hey!" Margie calls to me from her desk. "Jerry and I are going to a Halloween party tomorrow night. His work is putting it on at the Sheraton Hotel. I have two extra tickets if you would like to come."

Jerry is an accounting manager at a prestigious firm in Scarborough, where they live. I assume there will be an assortment of other straight-laced, no-nonsense accountants at the party. All of the accountants that I've ever met have been boring, socially awkward nerds. "I don't know." I'm glad she can't see my face. I know I wouldn't find a sample for my Sex Project at that party. That thought surprises me. I'm still going forward after last night's disaster?

"You could bring a date?"

Who would I bring? I'd have to find a sample quickly. Just to appease Margie, I could take Christine, but she'd take one look at the selection of men and drag me out by my hair. "I'll think about it. Do I have to dress up?"

"Of course."

I'm out. I'll tell her that something came up later.

"We have a very busy day today. We've squeezed in some appointments and rearranged others. Most are forty minute sessions."

I hear the front door open and after a minute, Margie pokes her head in. "Your first appointment's here. Charlotte. She's new, but her parents aren't here."

"Give me five minutes." I review Charlotte's file that Margie put on my desk. I know I asked her to put it on my door yesterday, but I do like it on my desk. She knows me well.

153

A week ago, Charlotte's parents called for an appointment and explained Charlotte's situation. She's sixteen years old, getting high grades and doing lots of extracurricular activities to build her resume, but she had a total meltdown when she didn't get perfect on her last biology test. The pressure of getting into college is taking both a mental and physical toll on her. She's tired, increasingly irritated with her siblings and often suffers headaches. She needs to relax.

A few minutes later, Charlotte walks into my office and stands at the door with her arms crossed. Her body language is obvious. She doesn't want to be here.

"Hi, Charlotte. I'm Dr. Cousineau." She doesn't blink. "You can sit down over here, on the couch, if you want." I sit down in a chair, with my back to her and wait patiently.

Charlotte takes another minute and finally, slumps down on a chair, looking at the floor.

"I get that you don't want to be here. No one wants to talk to a psychologist. You probably want to get back to your life and friends." She doesn't say anything. "I completely understand. When my parents died, my aunt sent me to a therapist twice a week and I didn't say a word for a month." I quickly disclose personal information to establish a bond.

She looks at me briefly, and then, looks away.

"I had to listen to this man talk and talk and I couldn't leave. He told me about his family, his children and his dead wife, and all I could do was listen. It was annoying. Finally, she told me that if I did talk, I probably wouldn't have to come to so many sessions, and eventually no sessions at all." I tap my pencil on my clipboard. "I was able to get back to my studies and clubs faster."

"What do you want me to say?" Charlotte asks.

That spiel usually gets the right results. "Why do you think you're here?"

"My dad took my phone away to get me to see you. That's why I'm here."

She's definitely high-strung and frustrated. Her parents must be desperate. "I get why they did it. They're concerned about you."

"Why? I'm getting amazing grades, I'll be able to get into the university of my choice and I don't party and get wasted. They should be happy!"

"You had a biology test a couple of weeks ago. What happened?"

Charlotte grunts quietly. "Is that why I'm here?"

I shrug my shoulders. "You tell me? What happened?"

"I had five exams in three days, and in the meantime, I formed and managed a weekly foreign student peer group and I was organizing a Big Sister function for the GTA. Sure, I was stressed, but I was handling everything the best way that I could and when I got my biology test back...I didn't do as well as I thought."

"And..."

"I trashed the women's lavatory."

"Oh?"

"Yeah, it was stupid. I just threw paper towels everywhere. It wasn't as awful as the school said it was. I cleaned it up and I got detention for an entire week, which I thought was unnecessary. I missed some important meetings, but at least, it won't go on my record."

"Charlotte, it's very important to find a healthy balance. Universities and employers are looking for happy, healthy and confident people who have a genuine joy of learning and independent spirit. High school is a great time to explore different interests."

"I'm in a ton of clubs."

"Universities neither expect nor want only students who take tons of classes and participate in a dozen sports and hobbies."

"What else is there?"

"You need unstructured time, to hang out by yourself and with your friends. It's a fact that we all function better when we have adequate rest and recreation.

"I don't want to do that. I'm fine. I like being busy."

"What do you do for fun, besides your academic clubs?"

She thinks for a minute. "Everything I do is fun. I volunteer at Big Sisters and take a nine-year old out every week. We also hang out with other big sisters at functions. I'm in a languages club after school and love talking with the other members. I'm at social events all the time."

"Do you see these other volunteers or members outside of an organized setting?"

"Well, no... not really, but I don't have time for going to movies or having a coffee, if that's what you mean."

"What if you had a party outside of school, like for Hallowe'en, and you invited people from all of your clubs."

"Oh, I'm on the event committee for the Hallowe'en dance at school. I'll be busy making sure that the activities go as planned."

"So, you won't be enjoying the dance, you'll be working it."

"I'll....I'll like it."

"Could you have a party at your house? A party that you could actually enjoy?"

"I'm too busy to organize another one."

She doesn't understand what I mean. "You need to set reasonable limits on your commitments. You have too many. Your parents and I fear that you don't spend enough time on yourself. When is the time that you allocate for you?"

"What do you mean?"

"Do you spend time on your health or fitness?"

"The physical education credit is an elective. My career path doesn't include it or need it."

"Do you believe that good health is important?"

"Of course."

"What do you do to stay in good health?"

She looks at her hands.

"Do you exercise or walk to school or do yoga?"

"I don't have time for those things."

"You need to make time for it. Aerobic exercise has positive effects on brain function on multiple fronts, ranging from the molecular to behavioral level." I have her interest. "Even briefly exercising for twenty minutes facilitates information processing and memory functions."

"Just twenty minutes?"

"Absolutely. Exercise also helps deplete stress hormones and releases mood-enhancing chemicals, which help us cope with stress better, which your parents and I think you need."

Charlotte rolls her eyes.

"For our next visit, I'd like you to research the gyms or fitness centres in your area. Find some sort of class that you'd like to participate in. I want you to fit two exercise classes a week, into your busy schedule."

"Two?"

"Yes, two. You could try yoga or Zumba…do you like to dance?"

"I can't believe this is happening."

"I'm not punishing you, Charlotte. You'll discover that exercise will result in higher energy levels and greater optimism, that can help you feel clearer and calmer."

"I *have to* do this."

This girl is going to explode. I see a little of me in her and it scares me. I had gone down the same road Charlotte is, and my Aunt Anna got me into sports. In ninth grade, she had told me to choose a sport and I researched it thoroughly, watching TV and reading up on it. I had wanted to do soccer, but it wasn't the right season, so I started volleyball house leagues. It had helped my studies and frame of mind, incredibly.

"No, Charlotte, you don't have to do this, but you do have to see me again and I would like to tell your parents that we're making progress. You probably want your phone back, too. Would it help if you thought of it as a compulsory credit?"

"Fine. I'll do it." She stands up. "Are we done, now?"

We say goodbye and she leaves to book her next appointment with Margie. She'll be thankful that her parents intervened and I'm sure that exercise will be a good fit for her. I'm thankful that Aunt Anna cared enough about my state of mind, but she never came to any of my games and didn't even come to the banquet, when I won the Ontario University Athletics Award.

    Why didn't I see this before? My aunt was emotionally unavailable! She always made something else a higher priority than me. She thought of me just as a family obligation, or as a pupil to mentor or simply, a project. She failed to provide me with sufficient structure, recognition and understanding. All of those things are indicative of someone who is emotionally unavailable. Oh my God! Her reserved and distant personality, lead me to grow up avoiding any close, emotional connections. My aunt didn't show or teach me how to build healthy, attuned relationships. That's why I never had friends in high school. That's why it took so long to get a boyfriend. And that's why I scheduled sex! I was insensitive to Steve's needs and I was distant. I was critical. I am a by-product of a failed attachment bond. This explains so much.

32.

Throughout the rest of the day, my spirit remains low. Feelings of sadness and hopelessness sit deep inside me, but I know I can't let them come to the surface.

I wistfully say goodbye to my last patient and close my door with a sigh. What can I do to feel better?

After saying goodbye to Margie, I bypass my car and start walking downtown toward Dundas Square. Exercise is good. The sun is still shining and I can feel the warmth of it on my face. Vitamin D is good. I don't want to go home to my stuffy, lonely house. Dundas Square is always busy and I'll probably end up at my favourite deli for dinner, for a salad and to people watch. Social interaction is good.

The longer route to the Square, leads me around what is known as the theatre block. Among the theatres, recital halls, movie houses and restaurants that dominate the area, classically-inspired banks are recognized for their heritage values. The Bank of Toronto building stands as a distinctive and prominent visual landmark within one of Canada's most popular retail environments. I stare at the gargoyles on the upper levels of the building as I walk by. Their eyes seem to follow me.

In this district, people are buzzing around me with shopping bags, but I try to take in more of the architecture of the historical buildings. I've admired the fine lines and beautiful detailing before, but it never gets old. I still think that the richly carved sandstone of the Old Toronto City Hall and York County Court House looks like a giant gingerbread house.

The sky starts to darken, just as I get to the deli. I order a chickpea and kale salad. The deli is jammed with people, but I find and one lonely stool in the corner, beside a man who is totally absorbed by what looks like a pastrami on rye. I quickly claim it.

My seat also faces the outside window and as I take my first bite, a man wearing an aviator hat walks by and I almost choke on a chickpea. It's not Zack. How did I get involved with Zack? I remember that I brought my Sex Project notebook, so I pull it out and open it to a fresh page.

Data Collection

Sample #10:

Seek persons who understand study & are willing to express inner feelings & experiences
- Man, aged? (in his mid-40's), CEO
- Handsome, slightly graying hair.
- Fit for his age, not that he's old.

Describe experiences of phenomenon
- I met him a couple weeks earlier, when I signed up for flying lessons. He offered to take me up.
- I called him and made a date, confidently.
- He took me up in a Cessna and the adrenaline rush led me to make out aggressively with him back at the hangar..
- He entered me, without a condom, and I asked him to stop, which he did after much pleading.
- He made me climax via oral stimulation (He did something amazing with his tongue).
- Aggression turned to violence, on his part quickly. He was angered that I wouldn't let him have sex with me without a condom.
- I had to physically kick him off of me, squeezing his throat.
- I ran away quickly, scared for my safety.

Direct observation
- He was a nice, sweet, flirtatious man.
- His violence came out of nowhere and was unprovoked.

- *Future goals: I couldn't really predict the outcome of this sample. I could take a self-defense course.*

Audio or videotape? n/a

Data analysis

Classify & rank data
- *0 out of 5*

Sense of wholeness
- *I feel empty and lonely.*

Examine experiences beyond human awareness/ or cannot be communicated
- *I didn't get a 'flip flop' (again????).*
- *Examining my abundant failures is emotionally unpleasant and it's starting to chip away at my self-esteem.*
- *I can't keep having negative experiences.*
- *Perhaps I should quit.*
- *This task of finding experience is too difficult to be executed reliably every time.*

"Hi, Colleen."

I stop writing and look up. It's Jack. Flip flop. I flip the notebook closed. "Hi, Jack."

"I'm not going to lie, I really want to see what you write in that notebook." His eyes sparkle as he smiles, reaching for it.

The notebook crinkles under my fingers, when I press it to my chest. "It's just my patient notes. It's nothing, just the whole confidentiality issue." I'm speaking quickly. Too quickly. I take a deep breath. "I can't show anyone my patients' notes."

"You used to leave all your files on your living room table and I never peeked once."

Did I do that? Yes, I guess I did. I don't know what to say. How does he remember that?

"It's ok. You can have your secrets. I have some too."

Is he talking about his date with Christine? My stomach lurches.

"I was going to take my sandwich to go, but now that you're here, would you mind if I sit with you?"

I'm surprised to see the stool beside me is now empty. "Have a seat." I stash my notebook away and bring my salad closer to me, to give him some room.

"Thank you."

When he takes his coat off, I get a whiff of his cologne. It's the same scent he always wears. I smelled it that night, in my kitchen, when he made me dinner…and then, we kissed. Flip flop. Oh, for God's sake! I look at him and try to remember him as Steve's friend. He's dressed in khakis and a light blue button down shirt. He looks really good. Dammit!

Jack catches my eyes. "How are you?" He takes a huge bite of his sandwich, with a smile on his face.

I quickly look away and stab at my salad. "Oh, I'm fine."

"Nothing new?"

"No, not really." I could tell him about Mr. Baker's shenanigans, but it's too exhausting. I'm sure he wouldn't find humor in my use of the word shenanigan. He'd flip out.

"How's your new car?"

"How'd you know I got one?"

"I saw it parked in your spot, outside your office yesterday. "It's an Infiniti, right"

"Yes, I love it."

We eat in silence for a few minutes and then I feel someone tap me on the shoulder. I turn around on my stool and I see Chris from cooking class. I'm instantly embarrassed and I glance at Jack, who is frowning at Chris. Here we go again.

"Hi, Chris. How are you?"

"You remember me, Colleen?" He looks surprised.

"Of course I do." *Please don't say anything stupid, Chris.* I stand up and take a step toward him, so that he has to take a step backward. I need to get him away from Jack.

"Who's this?" He gestures toward Jack.

Shit. "This is my friend, Jack." I look at Jack. He stands up and shakes Chris' hand. "Jack, this is Chris." A random guy I seduced.

"Nice to meet you. How do you know Colleen?" Jack asks.

My eyes widen. Are you kidding me? "We met at cooking class." I quickly say, before Chris says anything.

"Yes, we did." Chris smiles at me and winks.

I look at Jack and his eyes darken.

"Well, it was nice to see you, Chris," I turn my head away, hoping he'll take the hint.

"I'm glad I ran into you. I'm happy to tell you that I reconciled with my wife."

I feel relief. He doesn't want to humiliate me. "That's great, Chris," I say. I look at Jack and see that he went back to his sandwich. Phew.

"After our...our date," he laughs, "I felt more confident and alive. I went to my wife and demanded that we get back together."

Uh oh. There goes my stomach again. Date? I don't even look at Jack. "I'm happy for you, Chris."

"Yeah, my wife loves the change in me."

Please leave now. I smile and nod.

"Thank you." He hugs me and whispers in my ear, "We love whipped cream."

I think I may be sick. I peek at Jack. I hope he didn't hear that. He's staring out the window.

"Will you be going back to cooking class?"

"No, probably not."

"Good. I want to take my wife, but if you were there, it would be awkward."

I smile faintly.

"It was nice seeing you, Colleen. See you later." He looks at Jack, but Jack doesn't even move.

"Goodbye, Chris."

I sit back down and start poking at my salad again. Out of the corner of my eye, I see Jack slowly turn toward me.

"What the hell was that?"

"What do you mean?"

"You tell me that you won't date me, even though it's obvious you have feelings for me, but you date *that* guy?"

"It was nothing. This was a while ago. We met at cooking class and went out for dessert after." Wait. I don't have to justify anything to him. "It's really none of your business." I wish I didn't say that.

"None of my business," he repeats slowly, while he glares at me. "You know what? I've been putting off going on a date with Christine because of you, but fuck that. I'm calling her." He stands up and puts his coat on.

"I don't know why you're getting so mad. I never said that I had feelings for you."

He leans in close. I feel his breath in my ear. Flip flop. I close my eyes. He smells so good.

His lips are on my ear when he says, "I can feel how much you want me."

I lose my breath, but then he quickly stands up.

"See you later, Colleen." He throws the rest of his sandwich in the trash and walks out of the deli.

What just happened? How does he make me feel like that? I shake my head. No, I just fell under his spell. He's so good at seducing women. I'm just another one of those doe-eyed women, falling for his good looks and charm. He's so egotistical!

I pack up my stuff, throw out the rest of my salad and head for the office to get my car. I'm not going to spend another minute thinking about Jack.

33.

The next morning, I'm out the door at eight-thirty and driving to the self-defense course that begins at nine. I didn't sleep very well. I analyzed Jack all night and scrutinized myself, too. Every time I cursed and swore that I wouldn't keep thinking about him, I'd find myself remembering when we kissed. In the car now, I'm doing the same thing. I curse loudly and blast the radio.

As I pull up to the building, there's a gaggle of women walking inside. Are they all going to the same course? The building is pretty large, but can it hold this many of us?

Inside, the registration desk is surrounded by women and I only see one female employee helping all of them. I'm glad I came early. I can't even tell if there's a line. I join in the crowd and wait for my turn, while listening to the women chat around me.

"My friend came to this course a month ago and she said that the instructors are incredible."

"I hear that it's really hands-on."

"I just want to be able to defend myself at work."

"The owner is super hot."

It's finally my turn to confirm my spot and she hands me a consent form. I normally look these things over carefully, but the impatient mob behind me makes me sign it quickly.

"Take your shoes and socks off in the change room. Take off all jewelry and place all valuables in your locker." She hands me a key with the number 48 on it. "You need to return the key to me immediately after class or fifty dollars will be charged to your credit card. Next!"

I guess my turn is over. I find locker 48 in the change room and stuff everything into it. I'm glad my pedicure still looks good from four weeks ago. Now what do I do with the key? The key has an elastic-type bracelet attached. Doesn't that defeat the purpose of taking off all jewelry? I look at two women walk by and notice the keys dangling from their ankles. I do the same and follow them out through another set of doors, labeled "Studio".

The studio is quite large. It can definitely hold about one hundred women. There are pull-out stands, like a stadium, and the women are starting to crowd them. I squish in an empty spot on the outer edge, two rows up from the bottom. The lady beside me doesn't look too happy that I sat down beside her and only moves over an inch. She's very petite, wearing head to toe pink spandex. I look at my baggy sweat pants and tee shirt. Oh well.

The floor in the middle of the studio is covered with thick, blue mats. Everything looks brand new and clean. I wonder when this place opened. It even smells new. The gym at the university is raunchy compared to this and I bet there isn't any gum stuck under my seat.

There are only a couple of minutes until we start. There's a lot of talking and laughing. Everyone seems to have brought a friend. Even pink spandex lady is chatting to the woman beside her.

I study my nails and shrug. I'm serious about this. If I brought Christine, we'd be laughing too much and we wouldn't pay attention. I cringe when I think about Christine. Did Jack call her last night like he said? I wonder if they went out. Oh God. I wonder if they had sex!

I'm happy to see a man in a black karate outfit walk barefoot to the middle of the studio. I look at the clock and it's exactly nine o'clock. He's very handsome with light brown, wavy hair. He looks like he'd be solid muscle. He has broad shoulders and his waist tapers to that vee, with help from the belt that cinches his waist. I notice the room is silent.

"Welcome. My name is Darren Wright. Thank you for coming to the Women's Self-Defense Program. We'll be focusing on rape prevention techniques, how to spot danger signs and how to defend yourself when no danger signs are present."

I immediately think of Zack. I had no warning signs of his aggressiveness or of the imminent danger that I was in. That's why it wasn't my fault. I handled it pretty well, but I could stand to know more.

"I will teach you how to defend yourself against common chokes, grabs, bear-hugs and other attacks."

What about knife attacks? I'm thinking about Mr. Baker now.

I see a hand go up in front of me.

"Yes?" Darren points to her.

"Will you show us how to defend ourselves against attackers with weapons?"

I guess I'm not the only one with issues.

"Yes. Definitely. I will show you scenarios with knives and guns. You'll be working with stress and reality-based groups that will emulate dangerous encounters specific to women."

Another woman raises her hand and Darren points to her.

"What if you're not very strong?"

"You're stronger than you think. These training methods will build your fighting spirit and train you to respond both mentally and physically in a time of need, eliminating the danger of freezing or shutting down in confrontation."

That was me. I froze. I didn't know what to do with Mr. Baker.

"Women are not helpless."

I take a sharp intake of breath and almost burst out crying.

"Say it with me. I am not helpless."

The whole room repeats it. I whisper it with them, too embarrassed to let anyone hear.

"Louder," Darren encourages.

"I am not helpless!" I look around and say it with more feeling.

"Louder!"

The room roars, "I am not helpless!" I yell it at the top of my lungs.

"Great job! Here are your attackers." He points to the door at the opposite end of the studio and a man dressed in full protective padding walks out, followed by others. I count ten.

The room starts humming and Darren hold his hands up, waiting for silence. "These men are self-defense instructors, like me. We all have various degrees of black belts and vast street experience. Let's split you up into ten groups."

The sumo attackers walk toward us and start pointing at women, instructing them to get up. One sumo points to me and I follow him, with nine other women to the far corner of the studio. I see the stands closing up, so that there is more floor area to work on.

"My name is Jim and I'll be teaching you how to fend off an attacker with punches, elbows, knees and kicks." Jim is young, barely twenty, I think. He has a brush cut and cute dimples.

"First of all, as soon as the attacker touches you or its clear that escape isn't possible, you have to shout loudly, 'Back off' and push back at him."

Darren comes walking up and listens to Jim. I stare at Darren, instead of paying attention. He has chocolate brown eyes and long eyelashes. His jawline and cheekbones are strong and chiseled. Those ladies were right. He *is* hot.

"By yelling, it does two things. It signals for help and lets the attacker know that you're not an easy target."

Darren interrupts, "The empowerment philosophy assumes that even when physical defense isn't called for, you can also learn to set clear boundaries." He turns to me and takes a hold of my arms. "Use your hands and push my arms off of you."

I do it, but weakly.

"Harder!"

I do it harder.

"Come on! Throw them off of you!"

I do it as hard as I can.

"Great! Now do it again and yell, 'Back off!'"

"Back off!" I throw his hands off of me.

"Excellent!" He smiles at me.

Jim starts doing the same drill with everyone else in my group. "Back off!" can be heard all around the studio.

"You'll get the hang of it soon." Darren says to me. "You did great."

"Thank you." Is he flirting? Or is he just being friendly. I did pay five hundred dollars for his two-hour course.

Darren looks back at me one more time as he walks away. I think he's checking me out. He has his choice of women, why is he looking at me? I wish I wore spandex.

Jim brings us all back together in a small circle. "Effective strikes can be made with the outer edge of your hand, a palm strike or a knuckle blow." He demonstrates each and asks us to try a few lightly on each other.

"Never step in closer. Aim for the parts of the body where you can do the most damage easily. Go for the nose, eyes, ears, groin, knee and legs. They cause the most pain."

Jim grabs a hold of our arms and we pretend to do eye-gouging and scratching. He also shows us how to do palm strikes up under his nose.

When it's my turn, he makes me do it again. "Throw the whole weight of your body into the move to cause the most pain."

"I don't want to hurt you." Even though he's young, he has the body of a giant. I laugh at myself. "Not that I can hurt you."

"You won't hurt me. I promise." He winks.

The heel of my palm lands lightly under his nose.

"That's better."

I didn't notice Daren come back. "That was great. Try it again on me."

I take aim and hit his nose harder than I mean to. He flinches and holds his nose. "I am so sorry," I cry. I'm such an idiot.

"That was perfect. Don't worry about me." He let's go of his nose and squeezes my shoulder. "I knew you'd get the hang of it."

"Are you sure you're ok?"

"I'm fine. Really. What's your name?"

"Colleen."

"Nice to meet you, Colleen." He shakes my hand and walks away, but he does it again. He glances back at me, but smiles this time. When he turns away, I check out his bum. I'm only doing what he did.

Jim starts talking about defending attackers with everyday objects, like a pen or car keys, and he shows us how to hold an object between our middle and ring fingers. The idea is to be prepared when we have to walk anywhere in the dark. I jab and strike the air, knowing that the key could really do some damage.

Then he moves onto instructing elbow strikes and kicks. They're really easy and we partner up with group members to practice. My confidence increases greatly and I begin helping the other participants. The time flies by.

"Please come over and join me around the mats." Darren calls out to all of us.

We make our way over, talking with excitement and energy, and form a large circle around Darren. I think we all feel empowered with strength that we never knew we had.

The sumo instructors have moved off the mats and are leaving the studio.

"Our final exercise today will be how to defend yourself against a knife attack."

I feel anxious, but very alert. I need to learn this.

"First thing you need to do is remain calm. If you panic, you're giving the attacker an advantage. You have to breathe deeply. If you know the attacker, ask yourself if he would use the knife or just threaten you."

Mr. Baker would use the knife, I'm sure.

"Decide to fight or defend. If you go for him, he has a chance to defend himself, but you have the element of surprise. If you wait for him to lunge, it removes most of the ability of defense on his part. You must be ready for anything."

I recognize Jim, without his sumo costume on, walking into the middle of the circle with a knife in his hand.

"Jim is going to help me demonstrate." Darren grabs Jim's wrist, the one with the knife in it. "Choose the hand that's clutching the knife and go for the wrist. It removes the danger of the knife, but be ready for a punch or a blow."

They go through a couple of scenarios and make it look easy.

"Colleen! Could you please come here?"

Me? I look around and point to my own chest.

"Yes, Colleen." Darren laughs. "Come help me demonstrate."

I walk towards him, blushing. "I won't be good at this," I whisper.

"You'll be fine," he whispers back.

He stands behind me, with one arm around the front of my shoulders and his other hand holds the knife, down at my side. "Colleen has learned some major defense moves today. She is ready for this." He brings the knife up to my neck. "What would you do?"

I panic. Mr. Baker comes to mind and I don't know what to do. I can't do this.

"Come on, Colleen. It's a fake knife," Darren whispers. "You can do it."

My next movements are quick. I step forward slightly and tilt my head backward to mimic a head butt to his nose and he plays it well. Darren stumbles and I grab his hand at the wrist, the one with the knife, turn quickly and gently knee him in the groin. He pretends to double over and I hit the back of his head with both of my fists at the same time and turn to run away.

The whole class erupts in applause. I hear, "You go, girl!" I smile and curtsy.

"That was amazing!" I feel Darren's hands on my shoulders and he whispers into my ear, "Wait for me at the registration desk after class."

I'm shocked. What does he want? Is he going to ask me out?

Suddenly, I'm bombarded by women, but they don't want me, they want to talk to Darren. I step out of the way and look back at Darren. He's so busy with the women, that he doesn't notice me leave. Maybe I'm reading him wrong. Maybe he just wants to offer me another class because I need more work.

I take my time getting my belongings out of my locker. I tie up my running shoes and put on my blue hoodie. I look like a gym rat. There's no way that he could be interested in me. That petite woman in pink is more his style, I think. I try to smooth down my hair and pick some lint off my pants. It must be another class offer. That's all.

The registration desk is empty and I see women throwing their locks all over the desk. I start to drop mine into the pile when Darren walks into the room. A couple of women are following him, but stop when they see him walk to me.

"Hey! You waited."

"Yes. I wanted to see what other classes I should do. I know I was pretty bad."

"What? Do you want to sign up for more classes? You're pretty solid with self-defense, but if you want to participate in more, I'd be happy to see you again in that sense too."

"Isn't that what you wanted?"

He laughs loudly. "No. I wanted to ask you out."

I blush and smile. "Oh." I didn't expect this at all. Can I really go through with another sample after my night with Zack?

"So will you?"

"Will I what?"

"Go out with me tonight."

"Oh. Yes. Sure." What happened to thinking it through?

"Are you sure?"

"Yes. Definitely," I laugh.

We exchange numbers and he takes my hand. "I have to do some administrative work, so I'll call you later. We can decide what we want to do."

"Sounds great."

Darren squeezes my hand and walks away. Women swarm him immediately. He's definitely a prime choice for a sample. Why not?

34.

    Darren told me that he had the perfect Halloween costume for me and he'd bring it, when he picked me up. I suggested the Halloween party at the Sheraton Hotel, and he thought it was a great idea. I called Margie and she secured two tickets for us at the hotel's reception.
    The doorbell rings and I hear, "Trick or treat!" behind the closed door. I give a cowboy and a cute angel some mini chocolate bars. I look down the street and the amount of kids coming around seems to be decreasing now, which is good news. I barely have any candy left.
    I hope the costume Darren brings is not a naughty nurse or some other inappropriately sexy profession. He said that I would like it, but how does he know what I would like? I have an old Cat in the Hat costume that I took out of storage, just in case.
    The doorbell rings at eight and I take my bowl of candy with me. I laugh when I open the door and see Darren. "Really? Not much thought put into your costume." He's wearing his black karate uniform.
    "I did change, if you believe it. This one is more comfortable."
    "Sure you did. You probably wear it to bed too"
    'No, I wear my ninja jammies to bed."
    "It figures. Now where's my costume?"
    He holds out a bag. "I'm sure it'll fit. Go try it on."
    "Make yourself at home. There's beer in the fridge and please hand out candy, if any kids come to the door."
    "Sure."
    I run upstairs and empty the bag onto my bed. I start laughing to myself. It's a white karate outfit. What are we yin and yang? At least I'll be comfortable. I put it on and it fits nicely. I stuff some cash in the tiny pocket in the waistband and put the top on, playing with it. I'm sure there's a proper way to tie it up. I just don't know how, so I go downstairs, with the belt in hand.

Darren meets me at the bottom and I say, "Thanks for the karate costume."

"It's called a gi. I knew it would fit."

I hold the ends of the belt in my hands. "What do I do with this?"

"That's an obi. Hold my beer."

I take it and he slides the obi off of me. He places it around his neck and opens one side of the wraparound jacket, pausing to look at me. Part of my white lacy bra is showing. If he opens the other side fully, he'll be seeing me in my bra and I think he knows that. I shrug my shoulders and smile. He takes that as confirmation and opens the other side, but quickly pulls it tight to my body. He barely sees anything. He wraps me up tight and takes the obi around my waist. It's somewhat of a turn on. He smells soapy and clean. I watch him tie it up effortlessly.

"Thank you. It looks good."

"Yes, you do." He eyes me up and down, appreciatively.

"Ready to go?" I look at his beer.

"Sure." He empties the rest down the sink and heads toward the door.

"Let me put the rest of the candy on the porch." I grab the bowl, key in the alarm code, turn off my lights and close the door behind us.

"So, you were all alone today?"

"What do you mean?" I question him, as I put the bowl on the porch. I hope a single kid doesn't take the entire bowl. I hate it when they do that.

"You didn't bring a friend to the workshop today?"

"Oh no, I didn't. Why?"

"I wonder what your friends would've thought about me." He unlocks his car and walks around to the driver's side. I guess he's not going to open the door for me.

When I get inside his car I say, "You're amazing. What you do for women and their self-esteem is just amazing." I gush. "I learned so much today, especially when you taught us that—

"You should see how many women hit on me during these workshops."

What? That's an oddly rude thing to say. "I bet." He starts driving and I get an uneasy feeling.

"I get hit on so much that I had to devise a plan. I pick one woman out of the crowd and focus on her for the rest of the workshop. It usually calms the other women down."

So, I am the chosen one. What sort of egotistical male have I found?

"It really works. They don't flirt as much, or touch me. I still got three phone numbers today, though. They each slipped the papers into my hand when they thanked me for the workshop."

"Wow. Really." So impressive. Assuming that I'm supposed to learn from my mistakes, I should really figure out how I can ditch Darren.

We pull up to the valet station at the Sheraton Hotel and we both get out of the car. I head toward the concierge and ask the lady at the desk for my tickets. Unfortunately, she finds them and wishes us a pleasant evening. I scoff.

"The ballroom is this way." I point and start to walk away, but he grabs my hand to hold while we walk.

"Like I was saying, I got three numbers, but that's a slow day for me."

Are you kidding me? He was eloquent and impressive during the workshop. What happened?

"Some women are crazy. They try to feel me up during the scenarios. I have to peel their fingers off of my gi."

"Oh, hey! There are my friends." I see Margie and Jerry in the hallway ahead. "Margie!"

"Colleen! Hi!" She hugs me. "Nice costumes." Margie is dressed as Fiona from Shrek and when I see Jerry, I'm not shocked. He's Shrek and to be honest, it's not much of a stretch for him. He already has a big, bald head and he's big in the belly. He just needs to be painted green.

I introduce them to Darren and while Darren and Jerry chat, Margie whispers, "He's gorgeous. Where did you meet him?"

"He taught my self-defense course today."

"Self-defense? Good for you. I should've come with you." She jabs me with her elbow.

"You can have him. I'm not sure—

"Shall we go in and party?" Darren comes up and tickles my waist. Internally, I groan, but smile at Margie. "Absolutely."

We walk into the ballroom together and it's decorated with the typical Halloween paraphernalia. Inflated pumpkins and ghosts hang from the ceiling and orange and black streamers are thrown everywhere. It's quite dark, too, but someone hands me a couple of fluorescent glow necklaces. I put one on and hand the other to Darren.

"You can wear it." He puts it over my head. "So, I was talking about the women feeling me up and I can totally understand why they can't help themselves. Besides being good looking, I'm the best self-defense instructor in the city. I have the most credentials and experience."

Where's the bar?

"That joke instructor on King Street thinks he's better than me, but he's not. I make way more money than him and I just opened the biggest studio in the GTA. He can't pull a hundred people into a workshop every weekend."

Oh Lord. I don't need another egotistical sample. "Let's get a beer." I start heading toward the bar and flag down the bartender, as soon as I get the chance. He's dressed as a pirate and I'm not sure if he's looking at me, with the patch over his eye, but I ask him for a couple of beers.

"I pull in way more participants than him and it's all word of mouth. Those women tell their friends and those friends tell other friends. It's amazing how it works."

I nod. Where's my beer? On my toes, I see the pirate making his way back. I grab a beer out of his hand and start chugging as I pay him.

"I got the next one," Darren says.

Beer has never tasted so good. With half of it gone, I start walking through the crowd, ignoring Darren, who is still chattering on about himself. I begin to notice the costumes around me and I can't believe how many Shrek costumes there are. Really though, I can't believe how many accountants look like Shrek, when they're painted green. You'd think they'd talk to each other about their costumes, before the party. There's so many of them. The wives, at least, have a little variation. There's Fiona as an ogre and Fiona as a human, even a few donkeys. Oh, I see a gingerbread cookie, too.

"Do you know what really draws the ladies in?"

Right. Darren is still here. I shake my head. I'm pretty sure he's going to tell me something ridiculous.

"Women want to work with hot instructors. I only hire good looking assistants. Did you notice how hot they are? Women don't want ugly dudes touching them. You had Jim, right?"

I nod, playing along.

"He was pretty hot, eh?"

I nod again. I wonder if he hires instructors based on their egos too.

"Yeah, but he's not as hot as me, right?

I smile and finish off my beer. I shake it in his face.

"You want another? Stay here. I'll get you one and find you."

When he leaves, a waitress carrying bar shots walks by. I stop her and point at two shot glasses with an amber liquid in them.

"You want two Snake Bites?"

"Please." I'm not too sure what's in them, but I don't care. I down the first one, as she's getting my change. It's awful, but I choke it down. I put the empty glass back on her tray.

"You must be having fun." The waitress says as she takes her tip from me.

"Nope. Bad date." I down the second shot and gag. I feel warm immediately.

"Oh, I feel for you." She makes a sad face. "This one's on me." She hands me a shot glass with a yellowish liquid in it. "It's a Melon Ball. It tastes better."

"Thanks." I swallow it easily and she takes the glass from me.

"I hope your night starts to get better."

I look around the ballroom and it doesn't seem like a party. I know that these are all accountants, but you'd think that they'd let loose. They're just standing around, talking. The music is fine, but no one is dancing. What's wrong with everybody? Oh, I think I'm feeling the liquor.

"Hey, here's your beer." Darren is back. "I was talking about Jim. He wanted to get your digits, but I told him that I had dibs. I'm his boss, right? You're too old for him anyway."

I glare at him. He didn't just say that, did he?

"No offense. He's like twenty-one and you're like...what?"

"I'm young enough to date Jim, if I wanted to."

"You're better suited for me, anyway. You're a lucky girl. Any woman would give a million dollars to be in your shoes tonight."

So fucking lucky.

"Now, what about you? What do you do? You must be a hair stylist or something, right?"

"Actually, I'm a child psychologist." Take that, Darren.

"You go to school for that for a lot of years, right?"

"Right."

"So, you're smart?"

"Very."

He pauses, looking upset by this. "Can I show you something?"

"Sure."

He pulls out his phone. "I want to get a haircut. This is a picture of how my hair used to be." I look at his phone and I see a half-naked selfie of Darren in his bathroom, I presume. "What do you think? Should I cut it like that again?"

I look at Darren and then back to the picture on his phone. I can't see any difference. At all. "Yes, definitely. Get it cut again. It's hot." It's fun to egg him on? I'm drunk.

"That's what I thought." He puts his phone away and looks at me. "You are smart."

He suddenly grabs me and kisses me. His lips are warm. I don't like his ego or his personality at all, but at least this is keeping him quiet and he kisses half decently.

When he pulls away, he says, "That girl over there was checking me out. I had to show her that I was taken."

I look over to where he pointed and I don't see anyone staring. An older lady with grey hair is looking around and her eyes stop on me. When I smile at her, she looks away. Was it her?

"I get that all the time. I'll be on a date and women will hit on me. I'm sorry about that."

I roll my eyes and chug my beer again.

"So, a psychologist must make some good quid, right?"

"Yes, I do well for myself."

"I do own my business, so I make all of the profits. I'm swimming in money. I'm the smartest guy you'll ever meet. I'm so savvy with business. I won an entrepreneur of the year award last year."

"Buy me a shot."

"Sure." He waves down the waitress. It's the one from before.

"I'll take a Melon Ball," I tell her, handing her four dollars.

She hands me the shot. "Is your night getting any better?"

I look toward Darren, shake my head and quickly down the liquor.

"What's wrong with him? He's hot," she whispers in my ear.

"He definitely is hot, but…" I roll my eyes. "Trust me."

"I believe you. Have another, on me." She says loudly and hands me another shot.

"Man! Women usually buy me shots." Darren turns to the waitress. "No sugar for me?" The waitress gives him a Snake Bite and he smiles. "See, I get free shots too."

The waitress holds out her hand to Darren. "That'll be four dollars."

He looks angry, but hands her a ten. "Keep the change." He downs the shot, making a face and places the glass back on her tray.

I laugh and smile at the waitress. That was perfect. I walk away, carefully holding my shot. I'm not sure I can do another.

"Wow, you can drink. I don't like to drink alcohol. I try to keep my body in shape. It's a temple—"

"Oh, don't be a pussy," I interrupt. "Drink this one." I shove it in his face. Egoists don't like to be pressured or to be called names.

He looks at me and does the shot quickly.

"See, it's not so bad. Let's go dance." I grab his hand and pull him toward the dance floor.

"I'm a great dancer."

"I'm sure you are." I just want him to stop talking.

The alcohol has numbed me and I don't want to think, I just want to get lost in the music. I sway my hips and put my hands in the air, watching the flashing disco lights and feeling the bass pump through my body. I twirl around and mix in with the dancing accountants and their spouses. They're doing their old school dance moves, mostly staying in one spot, trying to keep the beat. Darren is a good dancer, except for when he does the occasional pelvic thrust. Christine used to call that move, 'rock the cock'. I start laughing out loud. I miss those days.

Darren starts to dance behind me and I feel his hips grinding against my bottom. He holds on to my hips and it reminds me of my Latin stranger at Sangria. I'm instantly turned on. I turn around and reach for his neck with both hands, lacing my fingers in his hair. He looks a little surprised, but doesn't hesitate to pull me closer and rest his hands on my bottom. My upper thighs are on either side of his one leg and he's has me so close that my sex is rubbing against his thigh. I'm very aroused. I pull his head down and kiss him hard.

He pulls away and gestures toward the door. I don't know what he's trying to say, but I don't want to listen to him talk anymore. I pull his lips back down to mine and push my tongue into his mouth. He kisses me back, but only for a few seconds. He pulls away again.

I drop my arms and take a step back. "What?" I yell over the music, frustrated.

"I have to hit the head."

Oh.

He grabs my hand and leads me out of the ballroom. I wave at Margie and Jerry. Jerry's staring at me, with his hand covering his mouth, like he's whispering to Margie about me. I guess I shouldn't be making out at her husband's work party anyway. Who cares? Shut up, Shrek.

The restrooms are in the lobby of the hotel and when we get to them I stop, but Darren pulls me away from them. I stumble a little, but get my footing and follow him. I can't see very clearly. I close one eye and can see a bit better. I drank too much.

I don't ask him where we're going. I don't want him to talk. I trust him enough, I suppose. I think about Zack and get anxious. I don't think a self-defense instructor would do that to women. Would he? It would be a great cover up for a rapist. My heart starts beating faster and I slow my pace. Darren is basically dragging me down the hallway.

"We're almost there." He smiles and tugs on my hand. "Too much to drink?"

Should I be worried?

Darren stops in front of *Ballroom B* and opens the doors. It's a smaller room, but it has a stage at the front with red curtains. The room is empty. The door closes loudly behind us.

"I don't have to use the bathroom. I just wanted a little privacy to talk."

To talk? No more talking! I let go of his hand and head toward the stage. There's a set of stairs to the right, so I stumble up them quickly to get away from him. I notice that he follows me closely.

I walk right up on the stage, behind the curtains, and see brightly painted backdrops that might be from a play about a farm. There's a wooden stand-up pig and a cow and near the back and a tall, green silo. An inviting brown leather loveseat off stage calls to me, so I stumble over to it and sit down, with my head back. When I look up, I see a wooden sun hanging from the ceiling, among the spotlights and it's slowly spinning. I'm drunk.

35.

Darren sits down beside me. "I was the lead in a few plays during high school. I should've pursued it and became an actor. I also did some modelling in college, but I thought it would be better to do something with karate. I was always the best in my class."

I'm going to hit him. Instead, I get up and straddle him on the couch, kissing him hard. Jack suddenly comes to mind and my kiss becomes more passionate.

"Oh, Jack."

Darren undoes the belt of my gi and opens it up, revealing my bra. He pulls the gi off my shoulders and the touch of his cool hands gives me chills. I press closer to him and push my breasts against his chest. He pushes me back enough to caress my breasts over the bra. My nipples strain against his touch and I moan loudly. The thin material of our gis makes it easy to recognize that he is excited. I reach for his hardness and paw at his waistband.

"You want to do it here?"

"Mmhmm," I mumble and stand up, pulling my pants down and kicking off my running shoes. I stand in front of him, posing with the gi half-off my shoulders and in my white satin panties. "You want me?" I touch my sex softly. The alcohol is really making me brave.

"Oh yeah, I do." He stands up and rips the rest of the jacket off my body and pulls the bra straps off my shoulders. He bends over and takes a nipple gently in his mouth. I reach for his waistband and start pulling his pants down. When they get over his hips, the pants fall to the floor and he steps out of them.

He has the body of a Calvin Klein underwear model. He's so hot. "Hello, Marky Mark! What do you have in your briefs?"

I push him back roughly and he falls onto the couch. I take off my bra and toss it to the floor. He doesn't take his eyes off of me. I turn around, with my back facing him and I slowly, daringly, put my thumbs in my panties and pull them down over my hips. I look over my shoulder and he's staring at my bottom. I keep pulling them down and when I get them over my hips, I bend over slowly and bring them down to my ankles. I'm not sure what I look like doing that, but I've seen porn magazines with women doing that same pose. I'm sure it's an eyeful.

He whistles, "Babe, get that tight ass over here."

That's the reaction I wanted. I stand up straight and kick my panties off, turning to him. He takes off his jacket and pulls down his underwear. Now I understand why he has a large ego. I stare at his package. It's so big. I should really research the correlation between egos and penis size.

I start to straddle him, but he stops me. "Hey, listen. I can never get a condom to go on, but I'm really good at the withdrawal method. Trust me."

Are you kidding me? I stand up in front of him. "You don't have a condom?" I'm ready to strangle him.

"I do have one. I just hate wearing them. As you can see, I'm too big for them." He's dead serious.

"Put the condom on, Jack."

"Right." He reaches for his pants and in the small pocket, he finds a condom. I could barely fit a few bucks in my pocket, so it's funny that he actually fit a condom in his. He must've been confident.

I watch him roll the condom on with ease and I quickly straddle him again. I think I got air, like a gymnast would to get on a balance beam. I slowly maneuver him inside me, with some difficulty. Either I'm not wet enough or he's just too thick. He's not budging. I'm frustrated. I don't want any more foreplay. I don't need foreplay. I just want it inside me, but I don't think he'll fit. When I don't think I can put anymore of him in me, I stop moving. I close my eyes and revel in how full he makes me feel.

All of a sudden, he takes a hold of my hips and pulls me further onto him. Oh my God. I'm going to burst open. I need time to adjust.

"Let me please you. I know--

I cover up his mouth with my hand. I don't want to hear him talk anymore. I slowly move my hips back and forth and close my eyes. It's starting to feel more comfortable, in a very sensual way. I really don't need to move much to feel pleasure, but I bring my feet up on the couch anyway, so I can lift up higher and then bring myself down slowly onto him. I repeat this over and over.

"Bite my nipples," I demand.

Darren obliges and squeezes my breasts together. I watch him pinch my nipples and lick them tenderly and then I involuntarily throw my head back, closing my eyes. I love having this control over a man. He's doing everything right and I feel so sexual. I am a sexual being!

I have to stop moving. I'm going to orgasm, but I don't want to. I want to prolong the feeling. It's all about me today. I need this. I lift up one more time and come slowly down on him.

"Lift me up."

He stands up with me in his arms, still attached at the hips. I knew he was strong enough. I hold onto his shoulders and he bounces me on his hips, fast and steady. My breasts bounce and my nipples rub against his chest. His fingers dig into the flesh of my bottom and I watch his arm muscles strain and become vascular. Jack wants my body. Jack wants to please me. This is Darren! I lose my momentum and my mindset. Fuck, Jack! Get out of my thoughts! I wrap my legs around him, so he can't move me anymore.

"Lay me down." I'm barking these orders like I'm some diva, but I know Darren will do anything I say. I'm desperate to get the feeling back.

Darren withdraws and places me on the couch. I lie back, waiting for him to come to me. I watch his muscles bulge as he crawls between my legs. He's so hot. Stupid, but hot.

He watches me, as he penetrates me again and I close my eyes. My sex screams with both desire and angst. I try to relax, but I feel every inch of him forcing me open.

"Go slowly." I open my legs as wide as they can go and push my hips up to meet his. I adjust to his size immediately when he gives an extra push against my apex. It sends me reeling. His movements are excruciatingly slow and my entire body shudders beneath him.

"Faster!"

But Darren doesn't go faster. He deliberately keeps a nice slow pace and then, slams up and into me at the very last second each time. The sheer size of him maintains constant friction against my clitoris and it sends me over the edge quickly. I start moaning loudly and squeezing his back tightly. I pull his bottom into me. My core tightens and my body loses the battle. It's an endless spiraling sensation and I can't catch my breath.

Darren starts pumping faster. His one leg slides off the couch and with his foot on the floor, he uses leverage to drive into me. I hear his breathing quicken and he grunts quietly. He thrusts into me hard and I try to catch his eye, but his are closed, his forehead furrowed. I almost ask him to stop him, when I start to feel a sensuous build-up again, or maybe it never ended.

"Jack!" I moan and the unrelenting ache overwhelms me again.

Darren lies on top of me, unmoving, until I release the grip on his bum. He pulls out of me and gets up, but I lay there with my eyes closed. I'm tired and dizzy. I bring my arms up over my head and stretch my legs out. I don't want to move. The alcohol has finally hit me and I don't feel very good all of a sudden.

"You keep lying there like that and I'm going to jump you again."

I peek out of one eye and the first thing I see is Darren's penis. It's looming over me and even though it's limp, it's still monstrous. I shut my eyes tightly.

"No! I'm getting up." I push myself up to sitting position and steady myself. He throws me my bra. "I can't handle you again."

"That's what they all say."

"I bet." I roll my eyes and put my bra on. "Where's my karate outfit? Gi...whatever."

Darren hands me the gi jacket and then the pants. "I really like you. You're different. You listen to me and you don't talk about yourself, like most women. You're really in tune with my needs."

I smile and pull up the karate pants, stuffing my panties into the small pocket. Oh, Darren, I used you.

"Who is Jack, by the way? I don't have to fight anyone, do I?"

"Jack?" How does he know Jack?

"You called me Jack."

I did? Did I say his name? "I...It's....It's just my nickname for you." I can't believe that I did that.

"Cool. Do you want to go out again?" He stands in front of me and ties my belt.

Oh God. "Darren, this was a one night stand. I don't want a relationship." That was really easy to say.

"Really?"

"Yes. You can understand that, right?" You big dummy.

"Oh yeah. For sure. You're great."

"Perfect. Can you take me home now?"

Thankfully, the ride home is quiet. My head is throbbing. I close my eyes and I feel like I'm spinning. This is not good.

"We're here, Colleen."

I slowly open my eyes. "I can change quickly and give you your gi back or I can drop it off another day."

"No. You keep it. I own a lot of those."

"Oh. Ok. Thank you."

"If you ever want to go out again, you have my number. I had a great time."

"I had fun. Thanks for everything." I put my hand on the door handle. "Can you wait until I get into my house before you leave?"

"Sure."

"Goodbye."

I quickly stumble up the walk and kick the empty candy bowl into the door. I bend over to pick it up and almost fall, but catch myself. I crawl up the door and unlock it, tripping inside. I type in the alarm code and wave to Darren as I close the door, locking it. I put the alarm back on and rush to the bathroom to throw up.

36.

I'm in a session with a patient and I keep yelling at Margie to answer the phone. The phone keeps ringing and ringing and I'm getting angrier and angrier. Why isn't she answering it? Where is she?

Then, I wake up.

It seemed so real. It's my cell phone and it's all the way in the kitchen, I think. I don't remember where I put it. I was too busy aiming for the toilet to worry about it. Ugh.

Too much alcohol. When was the last time I drank that much? Christine and I had gone on a bender one night after exams in university. We had ended up at a Chinese Food place, at four in the morning with total strangers. When the eggrolls had been served, the smell nauseated me and I had to excuse myself to throw up in the bathroom. I think we had been drinking rum that night. I wonder what's in a Melon Ball. The thought makes my stomach churn. I take a deep breath and exhale softly through my mouth.

I miss Christine. I've been ignoring her texts and haven't returned any of her calls. I'm surprised she hasn't showed up on my doorstep. I know she's had her date with Jack by now. I can wait a few days to call her. I'll let the excitement of her conquest wear off before she tells me specifics. Maybe she'll forget the specifics. That'd be nice.

The room is still spinning when I open my eyes. I close them again, but peek to see the time. 7:00 a.m. It's so early! Why am I awake so early on a Sunday? I roll over onto my stomach and put a pillow over my aching head.

Oh, I really need to use the washroom. I crawl out of bed, trip over some shoes and almost fall into the bathroom door. I sit on the toilet a little longer, thinking that I may have to vomit again, but the feeling passes.

Before I leave the bathroom, I brush my teeth and splash water on my face. I dry off and stare at myself. Was that an all new low? Darren was a complete idiot and I got drunk and had sex with him anyway. Why am I doing this? I think I have enough data now for my research project. I don't have to do this anymore. At least it was good sex.

Oh my god! I can call Steve today! It's been two weeks! I bypass my bed and stumble down the stairs excited, but not too steady. I pause on the last stair. Oh, I don't feel good. There's no way I can call him now. I'll wait to figure out what I'm going to say to him.

I grab my phone off the counter and flop down onto a dining room chair, putting my forehead down on the table. I tilt my head to the side and look at my phone with one eye open. Darren texted me. Twice. One is a photo. Oh Lord. I hesitantly open up the photo. It's the picture that he showed me last night of the haircut that he wants to get. Gee thanks. Now the text: *Am I the best you ever slept with or what?* Or what? I delete both texts immediately.

Just as I put my phone down, it beeps again. I groan. I might have to change my number. I look and it's a reminder: *Psychology Symposium Monday 6:00 pm.* I groan again.

I was excited to register for the one lecture by Psychologist, Elizabeth Phillips, called, 'Changing Fear', as it's based upon memory, consciousness and emotion. I thought it could give me different strategies about how to help my patients deal with their fears and anxieties, but I'm really not looking forward to it now. It could be this hangover. Perhaps I'll feel better about going to it tomorrow.

I slide the phone across the table. Shower first. Call Steve later. That's a good plan. I just have to get my body moving again.

With my forehead still on the table, I can see my purse, with the Sex Project notebook sticking out of it. I reach out with my foot and drag my purse to me. I'll get moving soon. I should write about last night, so I can quickly forget about it.

Data Collection

Sample #11:

Seek persons who understand study & are willing to express inner feelings & experiences
- *Man, aged? (in his mid-30's), Karate/Self-Defense instructor*

185

- *Light brown, wavy hair*
- *Solid muscles, strong. Hot body. (Marky Mark comes to mind for some reason).*

Describe experiences of phenomenon

- *I went to a self-defense class at his studio and he asked me out.*
- *We went to a Halloween party at Margie's husband's work.*
- *Conversation was all about him; very egotistical and stupid.*
- *I drank heavily to get through the night, instead of ditching him.*
- *Had sex on a couch, on a stage, behind the curtain.*
- *I was too drunk to really enjoy it. That's a lie. I enjoyed it.*

Direct observation

- *He seemed like a normal, sweet man, until we started talking on our date.*
- *Why didn't I just leave??*
- *If I don't like the inside package, I'm not going to like the outside package (even if the 'package' looks ideal!)—This remains true from the last couple of Samples.*
- *Why am I not learning?*
- *I was very confident. I performed a small striptease and did order him around.*
- *I knew what I wanted to get out of the experience and claimed it.*

Audio or videotape?

- *I received a selfie of him the next day. "Aren't I the best you ever had?"*

Data analysis

<u>*Classify & rank data*</u>
- *2 out of 5*

<u>*Sense of wholeness*</u>
- *It was great sex, but no connection whatsoever.*

<u>*Examine experiences beyond human awareness/ or cannot be communicated*</u>
- *I didn't get a 'flip flop' (again).*
- *I'm becoming sloppy. I need to listen to my instincts. I need to walk away when I don't like the guy.*
- *This project is supposed to be for good experiences, not just to have good sex.*
- *I should have gone out with the twenty-something instructor instead.*

    I can't say that I didn't learn a thing. I was incredibly confident. The alcohol certainly lowered my inhibitions and I may not have performed that strip tease or got him to do what I wanted. In the same sense, I was utterly drunk, so my confidence may not have come across that way to Darren. My strip tease may have been a hot mess and I could've looked like a demanding nympho, but Darren didn't complain and he wanted another date. I think it was a mediocre experience. I did learn never to do shots ever again.
    If Darren and I had made an intellectual connection, would it have been a better experience? It still would've been great sex and great sex *is* what I'm looking for. I should be happy that I got it. What more was I expecting from this research? Ugh. I toss the notebook back into my purse and head upstairs to take a shower.
    The shower feels wonderful and I stay under the hot spray of water for an extra twenty minutes. Leisurely showers are beginning to be a bad habit, but today is a new day. I'm washing the last of my experiences away, but holding onto what I've learned from each of them. I want to show Steve that I'm a new woman. I can please him. I know I can. He needs to see.
    I towel off quickly and sprint downstairs to my phone.
    His voicemail picks up immediately. He must be screening his calls. "Hi, Steve. It's Colleen. I've been thinking about what you said and you were right. I was a robot. I did treat you badly. You're perfect and I

was wrong to make you feel any less. I want to make it up to you in any way that I can. And I mean that. I will do anything. Please call me." I hang up the phone and cross my fingers that he calls me back.

I feel excited and nervous. I don't know what I'm going to do with myself today. I start to put the kettle on for tea, but my doorbell rings. I pause mid-step and try to see the door. My heart drops to my stomach with fear. I shake my head. I'm so stupid. Mr. Baker wouldn't ring the doorbell!

I walk to door and peek through the window. It's Jack. Flip flop. What's he doing here? It's so early. I'm barely dressed for company. I look down at my towel.

I open the door a crack. "Hey, Jack. How are--"

"Why didn't you tell me about the brick through your office window and the phone calls?" He barges through my door and my alarm starts beeping. "And what about your back door! When were you going to tell me that he broke into your house? Look at that half-assed board on there! You need to fix that!"

I know I should key in the code, but I ignore it and yell back, "I don't have to tell you anything! I don't know where you get off telling me what to do all the time!"

"Don't you get it? You're in danger. Mr. Baker is a criminal. He's violent and he could potentially hurt you."

Frustrated, I walk away from him, but I turn around and start yelling again, "You don't think I know that, Jack?"

My alarm suddenly starts to screech loudly. I've never heard the sound before. It's deafening. I panic and start hitting buttons.

"Calm down." He puts his arms around me and holds my hands. I shiver. He's cold. "Take a breath."

I do and I can smell his familiar cologne. Slowly, I key in the right code and my house goes silent. I wiggle out of his grasp and walk to the middle of the kitchen.

He follows me, lightly grabs my elbow to turn me around and whispers, "You should've told me what Mr. Baker's been doing. I could've helped you." I watch his eyes scan my body.

"It's no big deal. I can handle it." I fold my arms across my chest. I'm sure he can see my rigid nipples through my towel. "Look, I'm not really dressed—"

"I specifically asked you to tell me if something happens."

"Jack, that's what the police are for."

He runs his fingers through his hair. "Colleen, I still worry about you."

I don't know what to say. I like that he cares about me, but I keep pushing him out of my thoughts and my life for a reason. He's not on my agenda. He's made it very clear how he feels about me and I can't lead him on. We keep staring at each other.

"I'm going to go change."

"I think you look great."

"Well, I should--

He interrupts me, "I went out with Christine last night."

I back up and clench my towel together. "That's nice."

He takes a step closer to me and he eyes my body. "Do you want to hear about it?"

"Not really." I shake my head vigourously. "No."

"Are you sure?" He puts his hands on my shoulders and slides them down my arms. I get goose bumps and shiver under his touch. Flip flop. I'm very much aware that I'm naked under this towel. I think he realizes it too.

"Do you want to go for a run? I say it louder than I wanted. "You have your workout gear on. Let's go for a run." I start heading towards the stairs. "I'll get changed and we'll go for a short run."

"Ok," I hear him say, but I'm already in my bedroom.

37.

Running along the water makes me feel better. A good run has always cured a hangover and clears my mind. It's very cool outside, but the fresh air invigorates me. It's nice to see that Jack has improved his pace enormously, but it could be that I also haven't run in a few weeks. I bet I could still out run him though.

"Christine and I went out to the Blue Iguana for drinks," Jack says suddenly.

Why does he want to talk about it? I pick up the pace, but he easily stays with me. I don't want to hear about their date.

"She's a great woman. She's really smart and beautiful."

Fantastic. I'm pretty sure that I've started running a seven minute mile, but I know I can't maintain it for very long. Jack has stopped talking, but he's pacing me stride for stride.

"Why didn't... you ever.... set me up with her.... before?" He can barely speak. His words come out sharply between breaths.

I sprint my fastest and when Jack starts lagging behind, I keep going for another thirty seconds. When I slow down to walk and look behind me, I see him walking towards me. I stop and put my hands on my knees and try to catch my breath.

A couple of minutes later, I hear Jack, "You're jealous that I went out with Christine. Don't you see, Colleen? You have feelings for me." He stands over me.

"Jack, that's crazy." I'm not sure if I believe myself anymore. I keep my head down.

"Why don't you tell me why you're so upset then?"

I don't know why. "It's not about me. I know how you are with women and I didn't want you to hurt Christine." Where did that come from? That's a lie. Christine never gets hurt.

"She doesn't want a relationship. She told me that straight out. So, if what you believe to be true about me is actually true, then Christine and I are perfect for each other."

I stand up straight, with my mouth in surprise.

"We could fuck all night and never have to worry about feelings or anything."

"Stop! I don't want to hear about it." Or picture it. Why am I getting so upset?

"Actually, now that I think about it, it's a pretty good deal. Maybe she'll be my booty call."

"You're disgusting." I start to jog away.

Jack grabs my arm. "Christine and I didn't do anything. We talked at the bar for the entire date and afterwards, we shook hands and went our separate ways."

I look at him in disbelief.

He holds up three fingers like a boy scout. "I swear I wouldn't lie to you."

He looks cute, with his boyish grin, but I turn and start walking down the pathway. I feel relieved, but I don't understand why I was so worked up. I shouldn't care that they went out.

"We talked about you all night."

"Me?" I stop and glare at him. How dare they.

"Yup."

I feel the anger stirring up inside. "I'm fine. Ok? You can stop worrying about what happened with Mr. Baker. You guys—"

"Colleen, we didn't even hit that topic. I learned about your university days and your wild nights. When Christine and I started talking, I realized that she was your number one fan. She's like your best friend in the entire world." He laughs. "She truly is your BFF."

I start smiling. "Yes, she is."

"When I figured that out, I couldn't see beyond that. I couldn't date her. And once she knew how I felt about…"

"What?"

"Nothing. There just wasn't any spark between us."

"Are you blind? Listen, don't use me as an excuse. I told Christine that it didn't bother me to date you."

"Well, that was nice of you, but I'm not interested in her."

I don't think any man has ever said that.

"She's not my type. I prefer brunettes."

"Sure you do." I wonder what happened. He must not be a Grade A specimen. He seems like he'd be Christine's type. He's got that killer smile and I loved feeling his scruffy facial hair on my face when we kissed. I shake my head.

"You ok?"

"Yes. Sure."

"Don't be upset. Christine's a nice girl. We left on good terms."

"I'm fine. Really."

"Colleen, do you want to go to dinner with me tomorrow night? I also have two tickets to a Leaf's hockey game."

I can hear my phone ringing.

"You brought your phone? Where did you put it?" Jack laughs.

I fish it out of the small pocket in the waistband of my spandex pants. "Sorry. One second," I say to Jack. "Hello?"

"Hi Colleen. It's Steve."

"Hi Steve." I avoid Jack's eyes and turn my back to him."

"I got your message. It's very intriguing."

"Is that a good thing?"

"Yes. Do you want to come to my apartment on Wednesday?"

Nothing sooner? "Wednesday? Oh, ok. That sounds good. What time?"

"How about eight."

"That'll work. I'm looking forward to it."

"Me too. I can't wait to see how you'll make it up to me."

I giggle. I'm ready to show you. "See you Wednesday, Steve." I hang up the phone and put it back in my pocket. I turn around and see Jack glaring at me now.

"You're seeing Steve?

"Yes, I called him earlier and he agreed to meet me at his apartment."

He holds his hands out, palms to me and shakes his head with confusion. "Why do you want to see him? And at his apartment?"

I exhale sharply. "Jack, you know why. Nothing's changed. You know about my plan."

"What plan?"

"I still want him back. We've been over this."

"You want to go to his apartment and seduce him?"

I blush, "I'll do whatever it takes to get him back." I turn to walk away.

He pulls at my elbow. "Why?" He looks stunned. "Wait! Forget it. I don't want to know." He starts to walk away. "I can't do this anymore."

I go after him. "Jack!" I follow him down the path. "Come on, Jack! Stop!"

He turns around quickly and walks back to me, stopping sharply in front of me. "I can't do this thing with you anymore." He points to me and back to him repeatedly.

"Do what *thing?*"

"I can't be your friend, go running with you or...talk to you."

"Why not?"

He grabs me by my shoulders and looks into my eyes. "I'm in love with you." He bends down and kisses me hard. His tongue invades my mouth harshly and I feel his fingers pulling at my hair.

I am shocked at his declaration and at the passion of his kiss, but I don't stop him. I put my hands on his chest, pulling on his sweaty shirt. I pull him closer. I don't know why I feel so comfortable and excited kissing him. This is what lovers feel. I don't want to think about him this way, but I can't pull away from his embrace.

Jack stops and looks at me. His blue eyes are fierce. "I want to be with you." He kisses me gently. "I wanted you since the first time I came to your house for dinner. You made lasagna and Caesar salad and you juggled everything so perfectly. You had everyone's drinks refilled before they were empty. You were smart and playful and I really enjoyed getting to know you." I look down, but he tilts my chin back up with his fingertips. "But that's not what did it for me. Every time you leaned forward, a curl would escape from behind your ear and you would quickly secure it back." He takes one of my curls that escaped from my ponytail and plays with it. "It would keep falling and you always put it back. It was adorable."

I look at him. I want to push him away, but I'm mesmerized by his blue eyes and his words.

"Just let that curl fall, Colleen."

He's distracting me from Steve, but his words make my heart melt.

"You're not the problem, Colleen. You didn't end your marriage! Steve's an asshole, but I couldn't tell you. I just had to wait. I knew your marriage wouldn't last long. Perhaps that's harsh to say, but Steve didn't deserve you. You were in love with an immature, idiotic adulterer."

I shake my head in defense, the curl flouncing in my face. I try to step back, but Jack's still holding me tightly.

"I think you realize now that you made a mistake. He wasn't the right guy for you, but you're too proud to admit it."

"No, you don't know Steve. You don't know..." Do I even know anymore?

"You're a smart woman, Colleen. Deep down you know that there were signs. Steve's always been a pathetic cheater. He's a little boy and he couldn't deal with your success and your strength. God, your strength! I love that about you. He could never be the man you deserve."

I break out of his arms. "I'm seeing Steve tomorrow." I have to. I have to see if it was my fault all along.

Jack's arm fall heavily to his sides. "You're smarter than this, Colleen."

"Jack, I care about you, but I can't even think about you when all along I've been working towards this goal. I have to see it through."

"Change your goal. You're wrong."

"You can't tell me that. I need to find out for myself."

"You're right. You do." He looks down the street.

"Why are you so angry?"

"You're so naïve, Colleen!" He yells and pulls at his hair with both hands. He cups my face in his hands. "God, you're so beautiful and so fucking naïve. All the signs are there. It's over for the right reasons. Move on."

I don't know what to say. I pull my face away and stare at him, watching his arms drop down heavily to his sides.

"Good luck." Jack starts to walk away.

I grab the sleeve of his shirt. "That's it?"

"What do you want from me?" His eyes are searching.

I don't want him to leave. I want him in my life. That's so selfish. I can't have both. "Nothing."

He looks like I tore his heart out. Without another word, he walks away.

38.

I'm so unbelievably stressed out. I'd go for a run to feel better, but I don't have any energy left. I walk to the nearest bench and slump down on it, burying my head in my hands. I've never been so stressed out before. Sure, I lost it in university, when I was overwhelmed by all of my exams, assignments and extracurricular activities, but that was intellectual stress. Ok, yeah, I was a mess when Mr. Baker abducted me, but that was traumatic stress. And who can forget the stress of Steve leaving me? That was undue stress. I'm not confident with my hasty, half-assed analysis, but go with it.

This is emotional stress and it's a brand new type of stress for me. Love, feelings, doing the right thing, following my heart... I feel awful that I'm hurting Jack, but he was never my priority. I'm not sure how I feel about him, but I'm confident that I'm still in love with Steve. I married him, didn't I? I wouldn't have made such a disastrous mistake. I followed a clear life path and made decisions based on solid convictions. I'm too intelligent to make a mistake, like marrying the wrong type of man. Right?

I walk home and draw a bath. As soon as I get out of my sweaty clothes, the doorbell rings. I start to grab a towel, but run to find some clothes to put on instead. I'm not making that mistake again.

The man at the door is unfamiliar, so I leave the door closed to talk, "What can I do for you?"

He bends down and tries to look through the curtain. "I'm... I'm a friend of Jack's. Jack Frasier? He asked me to come over to fix your back door window."

I hesitate and stare at him through the light cotton curtain.

"My name is Curtis Boone?" He says it more like a question. He's probably annoyed. I slowly open the door. "Jack didn't tell you that I was coming?"

"No, he didn't."

"Jack says that your house was broken into and that there's a flimsy board covering up the window on the back door. He asked me to come fix it."

"Yes, please, come in. I'm sorry."

He picks up a box of tools and steps inside. "I'm going to have to go buy a window pane, but I need to take measurements first." He holds up a measuring tape.

"Sure. Anything. Thanks for coming."

Curtis quickly assesses the door and leaves to go to the hardware store. I text Jack: *Thank you for sending Curtis. I appreciate it."*

I take my cell with me upstairs and pull the plug on my bath. I watch the wasted water empty down the drain. I don't know when Curtis is coming back and it wouldn't be appropriate to get in while he's here. I'll have to take it later.

My phone starts to ring and I almost drop it into the bath water. "Hello?"

"Nice new car. Too bad about the scratch."

It's definitely Mr. Baker. How did he get my cell number? My heart drops and starts beating rapidly. I don't know how to respond.

"You have so many men in your life, shrink. Which one is your boyfriend?"

He's been watching me all this time. Does he mean Curtis, the window guy? Or did he see others? Who cares? I'm not scared! "Oh, you're so tough hiding behind a telephone. Just come get me already."

Click.

He had nothing to say about that. Does that mean he's coming for me now?

Back downstairs, I quickly turn on the alarm and wait on the couch for Curtis to return. I hope he's quick. I put my phone on the table in front of me and stare at it. I want it to ring. I want it to be Jack. But I don't want it to ring and be Mr. Baker again. I really need Jack right now.

Instead, I root around in my purse for Officer Nicholl's card and call dispatch, leaving a message for him. Within minutes, my cell phone rings and I answer.

"Dr. Cousineau?"

"Yes, is this Officer Nicholl's?"

"Yes, it is. What can I do for you?"

"Mr. Baker just called. I recognized his voice right away. He made a comment about the scratch on my new car and he…" How do I tell him about the men?

"And he…what?"

"Sorry, I was distracted. He made a comment about the men that have come to my house recently. I think he means the man who fixed my door and I had another labourer here," I lie, "He asked which one was my boyfriend."

"Ok. Anything else?"

"Well…I may have egged him on. I told him to come get me already."

"You did?"

"Yes, I know it was stupid."

"No, it wasn't stupid at all. Ballsy. Very ballsy." He laughs. "Listen, don't worry. We'll patrol your neighbourhood tonight. Make sure you set your alarm and take down my personal cell number."

He recites it and I take it down. "Thanks, I appreciate this."

"Stay safe."

I hang up my phone and pull a blanket over me. I don't need Jack. I have cops that'll take care of me. I let my head drop back on the couch. I'm so pathetic.

39.

During lunch the next day, Margie turns on the radio, at her desk and we listen to music, while we eat tabbouleh salads from *Taza's*.

"Are you going to the Psychology Symposium tonight?"

"It's crazy how you know my schedule. You're just as organized as I am and you make fun of me for it." I laugh and shake my fist at her.

"Don't give me that much credit, your Google calendar is open on my computer. You never logged out last week." She smiles, sheepishly. "I swear I'm not checking up on you."

"That's ok. I don't mind at all. I've got nothing to hide." I take another bite of the bulgur mixture. "Yes, I'm going. I'm not sure if I'm looking forward to it, but I did pay for it, so I should go."

"You were so excited about it when the information came in the mail. Why aren't you—"

"Shhhh!" I wave my hands at her and point to the radio. I heard Kevin MacLean's name.

"Four women told Toronto police they had sexual contact with MacLean while they were seeing him for therapy. According to court records, the alleged incidents took place at his Toronto office on Charles Street. MacLean has been a sex therapist for four years. A sex therapist or sexologist offers sex therapy and sexuality counselling, consultation, skills and strategies to individuals and families. MacLean's attorney, Gerald P. Boyle, said his client denies anything sexual happened while he was treating the women. Boyle said they intend to fight the allegations. MacLean was arrested Friday night by investigators with the Special Victims Unit and is facing four counts of sexual assault. He's scheduled to appear at a Brampton courthouse on November 15th."

"Colleen! You're so white. What's wrong?"

"I had a date with him last week."

"Who? The sex therapist?"

"Yes."

"Oh my God."

"He was so weird and his office looked like a sadomasochist's playroom, but I didn't think he was like *that*!"

"Did you like him?"

"No. He was very controlling and it didn't end well."

Margie sits beside me and puts her arm around me. "That's awful, Colleen."

I've really been choosing the wrong men. Should I call the police to and tell them what I know? His office? That's a dumb idea. I'm sure they saw his office. I shouldn't associate my name with him at all.

"How did your date with the hot karate instructor end?"

That was another mistake. "Not very good. I went home early."

"It looked like you were getting along on the dance floor. You made that stiff party pretty exciting."

Oh no. I quickly excuse myself and lay my head on my desk. I've dated so many men. Any of them could tarnish my reputation. I never even thought about that. I was immature to just worry about Steve finding out about my promiscuity. What type of consequences would there have been if Zack had raped me or gave me a STD? What if the doctor I saw to treat the STD was Dr. Mark? There are so many scenarios that could still happen. I'm getting sicker and sicker thinking about them.

The rest of the day is a blur. I try to focus on my patients, but I'm kicking myself for such bad judgement. Unfortunately, my bad mood carries into my sessions.

I'm too harsh with Bryan when he tells me he wants to play the poker chip game, but I can't figure out which one. He has ADHD and needs to practice self-control, so I think it's the 'Slow Motion Game' and give him an activity to complete in slow motion.

Bryan instantly complains that it's not the right game, but can't explain or remember the rules to the game he wants to play. He keeps repeating, "I get a prize! I get a prize!"

I get so irritated, that I slam my hand down on the table, but immediately apologize to him. After a little more dialogue, I realize he wants to play 'Beat the Clock' and instruct him to build a tower out of blocks in two minutes. The goal is for him to complete the task without any distractions.

When he's successful, I give him poker chips, which can be cashed in for a prize at the end of our session. We do a few more simple tasks and I try to calm down. I'm appalled at my impatience and stupidity. I could've just checked his file, as I make note of all the games we play. I give him extra chips to make up for my behaviour.

Next, I criticize Mary's drawing ability. She's seven! I ask Mary to draw something that makes her happy and when she's done, I can't decipher the blue square on the page. I guess a house or a pool, but she just shakes her head and won't tell me.

I'm maddened by her stubbornness and act like a child myself, crossing my arms. Finally, she tells me that it's a book and talk about how she likes to read.

Then, I ask her draw something that frightens her. I already know that she's a timid, little girl who's afraid of the dark, strangers and other typical juvenile fears, but again, the drawing is unclear. When she tells me that it's a picture of her bedroom, I snatch the crayon out of her hands and draw pillows on her bed, muttering under my breath. I warily instruct her to make her bedroom less frightening, by adding something fun. She won't take the crayon, so I add balloons and stars, but I get the feeling that I might end up as a drawing next time, and not in the happy picture.

Brittany becomes infuriated when I use the Power Animal Technique to essentially, help her develop better relationships with her peers. At first, I show her pictures of different animals and a horse seems to appeal to her most, so we cut out a horse mask, adding great detail, especially to its mane. I think she's having fun, but she's very hesitant.

When I suggest that she imagine what the animal might do in certain situations and how it might solve a specific problem, she gets irate and offended. It's supposed to be imaginative and enjoyable, but she states that she's old to play with animal masks. She leaves early and I notice in her file that she was supposed to get therapy for her anger issues.

At five, when my last patient leaves, I lay down on the couch with my arm across my face. I've never had a bad day with patients. I've always remained professional and attune to their needs. How have I let my personal life affect my work?

I hear Margie walk in. "I was able to re-book Brittany for next week. Her parents saw how mad she was and were adamant about getting her another appointment."

"Great," I mumble.

"I'm sure it wasn't that bad."

I just groan.

"You have your symposium tonight to look forward to"

I growl loudly and throw my arm down. I forgot about the symposium. "What time is it?"

"You should be leaving now, to make it in time."

Slowly, I stand up and wish that I could go home to bed, but collect my things and follow Margie out.

The downtown traffic is slow-moving and I notice how tense my body is at a red light. I try to stretch my neck while I wait. My samples for the project have been pitiful, Jack's pissed off at me because I didn't tell him about crazy Mr. Baker's behavior *and* because I don't want to date him, and I unknowingly slept with a sex-crazed sexologist! I had such a simple life before. How do I get back to normal?

I park underground, near the convention centre and lock my car door. I stop to run my finger along the scratch on my car, swearing to myself. When will the nightmare end? Could my life get any worse?

The registration desk is on the first floor, but I frown when I see the massive line-up. I try to wait patiently by checking out everyone is line. Men and women, dressed in business attire and carrying briefcases, fill the area. They all seem so serious. These are the kind of people I should be mingling with. I need to get back into my groove. Psychology is the epitome of me. It defines me as a person and I've worked so hard to get where I am. I start to look forward to the lecture.

The woman behind the registration booth finds my name and hands me a name badge and a file folder filled with convention information. The symposium runs three full days, but at the time, none of the other lectures interested me. I rifle through the file and feel a pang of regret. The three days would've helped me get out of my funk.

I find the lecture hall on the floor below and stand in line with the other participants. I'm the only woman so far.

"Is this the stand-by line?" A deep voice interrupts my thoughts.

"No, this is for registered participants."

"Oh. That's too bad." He scans my body and winks. He looks young and very cute. His pale purple button down shirt compliments his tanned complexion. He looks like a GQ model.

I smile at him and point to the stand-by line. "You're over there."

"Thanks." He winks again and walks away.

A couple minutes before six o'clock, an attendant allows us inside the lecture hall. I make my way to the front and sit in the first row out of habit and no one sits beside me.

At six, Elizabeth Phelps walks down the middle aisle toward the podium. "Some of the most important things we can learn in life are what situations and events represent danger or threat." She stands at the front of the room, pacing. "In humans, this type of information is often communicated through social interaction."

Someone comes down my row and sits down beside me. I look to my left and recognize GQ man. He knocks my knees, as he sits down.

"I'm sorry."

"It's ok."

He whispers in my ear, "You're such a keener, sitting in the front row."

I don't look at him. I just hold my finger up to my lips to tell him to be quiet.

"Fear can be learned through direct experience with a threat, but it can also be learned via social means, such as verbal warnings or observing others."

On the big screen, at the front of the room, she shows us a video about fear conditioning with rats. Researchers use a tone as a neutral stimulus and pair it with an electrical shock. After a few trials, the rats exhibit an emotional response to the tone, but when the amygdala is damaged, the rats no longer exhibit a fear response to the tone.

"I wouldn't want to be those rats," GQ man says.

I'm annoyed at his immaturity. This is interesting to me. I turn my head and give him a polite nod, but I'm stunned by his smile. It's gorgeous. I slowly turn back to the lecturer.

Dr. Phelps continues, "Cognitive psychology research on emotion and memory has focused primarily on explicit or episodic memory. We know that episodic memory is enhanced with mild arousal."

"I'll show you arousal."

I smile at him this time. It's hard to be irritated by him when he's so hot.

"Emotion may alter the characteristics of memory, so that memories for emotional events seem more detailed and vivid, even when they're not more accurate. We have extended these studies to behavioral and imaging studies of real-life emotional events, specifically memory for the terrorist attacks of 9/11."

"I can't get into this. Have fun." GQ man touches my knee briefly and then, gets up and leaves the lecture hall.

I'm disappointed, but now I can concentrate. I'm here to learn.

Dr. Phelps starts to explain Post Traumatic Stress Disorder, which I'm all too familiar with, both in my career and my recent abduction.

"After a traumatic experience, a personal sense of safety and trust are shattered. It's normal to feel crazy, disconnected or numb."

I nod in agreement.

"It's common to have bad dreams, feel fearful and find it difficult to stop thinking about what happened. These are all normal reactions."

Thank God.

Her PowerPoint delves into symptoms of PTSD and I check off at least ten points that I have been feeling or experiencing myself. *Jumpy.* Check. *Easily startled.* Check. *Difficulty falling asleep or staying asleep.* Check. *Increased anxiety and emotional arousal.* Check. *Re-experiencing the traumatic event.* Check. And I thought I was fine.

"Most of these symptoms will disappear in time for most people, who have experienced a trauma, but with PTSD, the symptoms get worse and some remain in psychological shock during their lifetime."

I'll be fine.

"It takes effort to think about situations differently. For instance, a person who develops anxiety in social situations might be asked to change the way they think about parties, so that they see them in a different light and have a different emotional response to them."

I know this. How do you think I got out of the house and went back to work after Mr. Baker destroyed my peace of mind? I had to change my mentality. How could I live in fear? I wouldn't be satisfied in life, knowing that I'm holding back in some area. I can't live in fear. Fear is a weakness. It's just not normal.

Dr. Phelps continues speaking and I make notes. She's an amazing lecturer and researcher. When she concludes, I applaud respectfully and fight my way out the door. Everyone wants to talk to Dr. Phillips and I just want to go home.

Outside the lecture hall, I put my notebook into my purse and look around. Everyone is on break now and the foyer is filled with people. I'm tired and I don't want to fight this crowd.

I walk with about a hundred people, toward the escalator and notice GQ man leaning against the wall, but I ignore him and walk past him.

"Hey!" He tugs on my arm as I walk by.

I step out of the crowd and almost bump into him. "Sorry." We're so close that our chests almost touch, but the crowd behind me won't let me step back. He smells good.

"You stomached that whole session?"

I maneuver myself beside him. "I didn't stomach it at all. I found it very interesting."

"Bullshit." He smiles when he says it. God, he has perfect teeth.

"I don't know why you wouldn't believe me. I'm assuming you're here because you have an interest in psychology. That's why I'm here and what she said wasn't new or clever, it's basic psychology."

"Is it now?" He shakes his head and pulls my arm gently. "Let's go have a drink."

That's bold. "No, I have to get home."

"No you don't. It's only eight o'clock. No one has to get home at eight o'clock."

"I do, and I don't even know you."

"I'm Michael Fields." He shakes my hand. "And you are?"

"Colleen Cousineau."

"Now we know each other. Are you married?"

That's a loaded question. "No."

"Then you don't have to be anywhere. Come on, just one drink."

Is this another egotistical male? "I don't think so."

"We can discuss why habituation or extinction procedures do not reduce or diminish fear because personal stress won't allow it."

I cock my head to the side. He may be egotistical, but he's an intelligent, egotistical male. However, I'd love to debate his statement. I'd crush his argument. A good argument would release a lot of stress.

"I have your interest now, don't I? We can continue this at the hotel bar."

"Ok." I must be crazy, but he's adorable and I'm intrigued by him.

The Intercontinental Hotel lounge is a modern urban space. The windows span from the floor to the ceiling and meet a gorgeous glass canopy, allowing us to look out onto the cityscape and up to the stars. It's a full house, but we find two stools at the bar. Stunning blue glass artwork from Stuart Reid floats above my head.

"Red or white?"

"Red, please."

He signals to the waiter. "Could I have a glass of house red and a rye and ginger ale please?"

"Ok, Colleen. Here's my argument. There was a study done in the sixtie--"

"In the sixties?" I interrupt, dumbfounded that he would use research that old. He's like twenty-five, if that. How would he know about that study?

"Let me finish." Michael places his hand on mine.

Wow, he's gorgeous, but so young. My Sex Project quickly comes to mind, but I push the thought back down. I couldn't possibly add him as a sample. This is just an intellectually stimulating conversation.

"Using medical students as subjects, researchers paired a simple stimulus, a light, with a common drug used in surgery. The drug stopped muscle action for about one minute," he pauses for effect.

I remember this study. "Go on," I urge, wanting to hear his logic.

"A person's reaction to temporary paralysis is panic. What do you think happened during the experiment?"

I know what happened, but I'll play along. "I don't know." The bartender drops off our drinks and I take a sip of wine.

"The panic reaction occurred every time the light came on, even though there was no rational connection between a light and being paralyzed."

"It makes sense."

"My point is that researchers couldn't remove the fear. They tried the extinction procedure of presenting the light without the drug, but the fear response did not diminish." He takes a drink and I watch his full lips rest on his glass. Super sexy. "The conclusion was that the fears may never go away." He looks satisfied with himself.

Time to school him. "Well, if the subject had been told that they could overcome the fear reaction to the light and were given training for doing so, like if the light was left on while they talked themselves down, their response to the light would've been less intense."

"True…" Michael places his chin on his hand and smiles that incredible smile of his. It's distracting.

"Or…or…or if the light had been presented many times before the drug was administered, the reaction to the light may have been easier to extinguish." This is my life. I know this stuff like the back of my hand. Why is he making it difficult to recall?

"Good point." He grabs both of my hands and stares into my eyes.

I don't stop talking. "Some fears are unreasonable and harmful, but some are reasonable and helpful." I'm nervous.

He releases my hands. "What about all those people with Post Traumatic Stress Disorder? They remain that way for a reason. You know, like that American Sniper guy. What was his name? Chris Kyle. No one could help him." He points at me, like it's a challenge.

That movie just came out and I guess he didn't see it. "Chris Kyle didn't have PTSD. He helped people living with it."

"Whatever. Anyway, I just don't believe that fears can ever go away."

Michael is grasping now. His lack of available knowledge confirms his age. In psychology, there are many studies that prove fear can be diminished. I think about Mr. Baker and I'm absolutely terrified by him. If I had repeated exposure to him, I'm sure that I'd still be afraid of him. If he was behind bars, it'd be different. "I've seen people overcome fears." Not my own, though.

"So, if you witness someone being attacked by a shark and you become deathly afraid of sharks, you think that the fear can disappear?"

Mr. Baker seems more vicious than a shark. What are the odds I'm going to see a shark in Toronto? "Personal recollections of the trauma can change over time." I'm not sure if I believe this. "Dr. Phelps was just talking about all of this in her lecture. You should've stayed." I try to brush the topic aside. It hits too close to home right now.

"I like hearing about it from you. You're way hotter than Dr. Phelps."

His comment surprises me and I get nervous again. "Fear is a special type of learning and memory. Any traumatic memory can eventually be manipulated or removed."

He brushes a curl away from my face. Jack told me to just let it fall. I tense up and roll my eyes. Why do I think about men that I don't want to think about? I was really enjoying our debate. "You don't have anything to add?"

"I have a bottle of red wine upstairs. Would you like to come to my room?"

"You're so young. No, thank you." I can't do it.

"Colleen, you're a beautiful woman. We're both adults. If you find me attractive, then where's the harm in a little fun?" His fingertips brush my thigh.

40.

Standing at the elevator with Michael, I feel more anxious. I don't know why? I should be used to being alone with men by now. It must be his age. Or it could be that I keep having bad luck with men. I thought I closed the book on my research anyway? Why am I pursuing this? I'd like to think that there's more than one good man out there and Michael seems to fit the profile. He's intelligent and sexy. I think I could definitely learn something and break my unlucky streak.

We get off on the twentieth floor and he leads me down the hall. As he opens the door to his room, I stop at the threshold. I haven't even kissed him yet. What if he is horrible? What if there's no sexual connection?

Michael is waiting for me to go in. "You haven't changed your mind, have you?" He takes my hand and pulls me to him. His lips touch mine softly and his tongue lightly brushes my upper lip.

That's good. I reach up and take his face in my hands and probe my tongue deeper into his mouth. His face is so smooth. Oh my God. How young is he?

He whips me around and the door closes. He pushes me backwards and my back is against the wall. We continue kissing and he slides his hands up my sides, his thumbs dragging up my sweater. I drop my coat and purse on the ground.

We momentarily stop kissing, as he pulls my sweater off over my head. He tosses it on the floor and we begin kissing again. His tongue barely touches mine, so I delve my own deeper into his mouth. He responds by mimicking my every action. He learns fast.

He lifts one of my legs up and slides his hand up my thigh, under my skirt. I feel his warm hand on my bottom, caressing it. His other hand fondles one of my breasts over the bra. I push my hips into his and pull him closer to me. I'm so turned on. I knew I was right. I told Jack that I could have the same response with any man.

The kissing is incredible, but I need more and he doesn't seem to want to move on. I push him away and start undoing his fly. He seems shocked, but doesn't stop me. When I have the zipper down, I pull his pants down over his hips and let them fall to the ground. He steps out of them and tries to figure out my skirt. I undo the side zipper for him and let it drop.

We're still in the hallway and I'd like to maybe lie down and enjoy this. When Michael starts kissing me again, I push him towards the room. I may have to lead the way in this experience. I know he's right and we're both adults, but how much more of an adult am I?

After more kissing, I finally decide that I'm going to continue and take his hand to lead him to the bed. I sit on it and slowly scoot my way back, to rest my head on the pillows. He watches me and I can see that he's thinking. What's there to think about? Then, he quickly takes his shirt off and scampers on top of me. He figured it out.

His hands are all over me, caressing my skin, feeling over my panties and bra. They don't stop and either does the kissing. I still haven't had a flip flop yet. I really need to figure out that secret. I had a couple of flip flops for Jack. Why?

I need to focus! I sit up suddenly and undo my bra, letting it slide down my arms. Michael stares at my breasts and then attacks them. He pushes them up and together with both hands and bites and licks at the nipples. His head goes back and forth and maniacally indulges in them. He has seen breasts before, right? I brush that thought aside and relish the sensation. I'm not going to complain. He is extremely absorbed in my breasts. It feels amazing.

I reach for his hardness and am pleasantly surprised at the size of it. I rub the length through his underwear and move my hips toward him.

Michael stops and watches what I'm doing. I take his hand and place it on my sex. He immediately starts rubbing it hard. It's not nice. I quickly wriggle out of my panties and replace his hand. "Be gentle," I whisper.

He listens and I can barely feel his fingers touch me down there. I push into his hand and moan. He begins to manipulate me a little harder, in a gentle rhythm.

I put my hand in his underwear and grope his erection, rubbing up and down at the same pace. His rhythm gets faster and I can feel his fingers dip into me. I moan louder and copy his rhythm. His fingers are so deep inside me now. With every release he delivers a hard thrust. It's a sensual pace. I can feel an orgasm building up.

"Wait," I whisper. "Do you have a condom?"

He abruptly sits up straight and jumps off the bed. "Yeah! One sec." He goes over to a suitcase and rifles through it.

It's then that I notice the messiness of the room. Clothes and empty, crushed beer cans are everywhere. I see a bottle of red wine on the dresser. He wasn't lying about that. There's also a large bottle of rye and another full case of beer. Is there someone else staying here? It looks like there could be more than two people staying here. It's like a dorm room.

Michael is back in a flash and he starts tearing open the condom with his teeth.

"Let me help." I take the condom from him and he lies down. I get on my knees and pull down his underwear. I almost go down to put him in my mouth, but I feel selfish today. Plus, it might make this over too quick.

I'm surprised that he's still firm when I roll the condom on him. When I finish, I straddle him, putting him inside me immediately. He lets out a loud moan, but doesn't do anything else. I grab his hands, put them on my breasts and begin to rock my hips slowly. It feels incredible.

Michael lets out a moan and I lift my hips and push down harder, at a quicker pace. I even lean forward to bump my breasts on his mouth. He figures it out and starts biting at them again. That's what I want.

I pick up the pace and feel all of the delicious sensations accumulating deep inside me. I start pumping harder and all of a sudden, he makes a weird grunt and goes rigid. His eyes are closed and I stop moving. What just happened? It's over? That's it? I knew it might be over quick, but that was too quick. How old *is* he?

His eyes slowly open. "Fucking unreal! You're so fucking hot!"

I crawl off of him, confused. Was that it? I can't believe I just did this. He's just a baby. Should I leave?

"Hey! Don't worry. I'll be good to go again, in a minute." He tweaks my nipple and his smile melts me. "I want to get you off too."

He'll be ready in a minute? I don't believe he has that kind of sex drive, but I could technically wait to see if it's true. I put my arms over my head and stretch. We are both adults, right? I can wait for more.

The door suddenly opens and I sit up, with the sheet tightly around me. I can hear talking and laughing and then I watch two males enter the hotel room. One is drinking from a beer can and the other has a bottle in a paper bag that he's drinking from. They poke each other when they see us in the bed.

"So, this is where you've been!" One guy exclaims.

"Woohoo! Mike!"

Mike? It's not Michael?

"You finally got some."

Finally? What does that mean? I watch Michael slap five and bump knuckles with the guys. Was Michael a virgin? No! No! He can't be.

"Can you please ask them to leave, Michael?" I whisper.

"Michael? Since when have you been Michael?" They all laugh loudly.

Michael talks over there laughter, "Guys, come on. Can you leave? We're not done."

Oh, yes we are. I clutch the blanket tightly in my hands and start to scan the room for my clothes

"Bro! Round two?"

Michael smiles, but it doesn't have the same effect on me anymore. I'm appalled and ashamed.

"Yeah. Yeah. We'll leave, unless you want some company?" He touches my foot overtop of the blankets.

I pull it away quickly and my heart jumps. This isn't good. I shake my head. "No. Please leave."

Michael looks at me. "Yeah, just go, guys."

"We gotta get a picture first!" One man pulls out a phone and aims it towards us.

"No!" I throw the blanket over my head.

They start laughing and I hear a beer can tossed into the pile of other beer cans.

"We're leaving."

I hear them open the door and their voices get quieter as door clicks shut. I come out from under the blanket.

"All right. Alone at last. Ready to go again?"

"No. I really have to go now." I scurry to collect my clothes.

"Come on. Don't let them ruin our fun."

"How old are you?"

"I thought we covered that. We're both adults."

"When do you graduate?"

"One more year."

Fuck. I hurry and pull on my clothes. "Good luck and goodbye." I rush out the door, to the elevator, tripping into my shoes, as I walk. When the elevator door opens and I see that no one is inside, I start crying.

41.

The hotel and the convention centre are deserted now and I easily make my way down the hallways. No one is on the ground floor either and I take the stairwell down to the parking garage. I've always hated underground parking and today it seems darker than usual. I feel like someone is watching me.

The clicking of my heels echoes through the cavernous garage and I hear some laughing somewhere, but I don't see anyone. I'm a bit relieved to hear other people. I know that if I have to scream, someone will hear me.

I rush to my car and get inside quickly, locking the doors. I look in the backseat, just in case someone is there. I should have done that prior to getting in the car, but I forgot. I take a few breaths and start the car.

That's it! No more samples! I don't need any more experience. I've had enough! I'm going to see Steve in two days and I'm ready for him. I've never been more ready. He'll stimulate me both physically and intellectually. There's an amazing connection between us that I haven't been able to replicate, not that I've been trying to, but none of the men I've met have even come close. Steve will satisfy me and we'll get back together.

I put the car in reverse and I'm startled by a loud honk. I slam on my brakes and look behind me. A gray van is right behind me.

"Sorry!" I say aloud, but to myself. I didn't look before I started backing out. I look down at my steering wheel. *Get a grip, Colleen!*

I wait a few seconds and turn to see if the van is gone. It's still there, unmoving.

"What is this guy doing?" I mutter to myself. I'm getting impatient now. I want to go home.

I put my car in park and open my window. I look out to see if I can see the driver, but I can't. The van still hasn't moved. I don't have a good feeling about this.

The lights in the garage suddenly turn off and, except for the glow of my headlights, I'm in the dark. My heart leaps out of my throat. I blink my eyes a few times to adjust and quickly roll up my window, looking behind me again. I can make out the van and I can see its red taillights glowing. Why isn't it moving?

Is it Mr. Baker? I can't let him get me again. I honk my horn couple of times and then press it down, long and loud. I keep pressing it over and over again. What else can I do? I'm panicking and I feel like I'm going to throw up. I put my car in reverse and back up a foot. I'm not going to smash my new car. I press my horn again repeatedly. The van still doesn't move.

My phone! I get out my phone and try calling the police, but I don't have any service. "Fuck!"

Maybe I can squeeze my way out. I put my car in reverse and turn my wheel as much as I can, slowly backing up until I touch the van. There's not enough room. I give it a bit more gas and I hear my tires squeal. I stop immediately. I thought I could push it out of the way. I shake my head at my stupidity and pull back into my spot.

I lay on the horn again and try to wait patiently. Maybe someone is coming. Maybe they ran out of gas. Maybe there's a reasonable explanation. I will wait here a little longer. Someone will hear me honking. I put my head back against the rest and close my eyes, with my hand still on the horn. I'm safe in my car for now.

A knock at my window scares me to the core. I jump and quickly shift to the middle of the car, with my bottom on the middle console, and look out the window. I can't see the person's face. The tint is too dark. I see a large figure. He's not doing anything, just looking at me.

I'm frozen and the pounding of my heart is deafening. Is it Mr. Baker? It could be his friend, the creepy guy. I'm not going to wait around to find out. I need to do something. I slowly move to my seat and start honking the horn again, not taking my eyes off the figure. He doesn't do anything. He's not there to help me. This guy wants to hurt me.

Move, Colleen! I almost can't control my hands, they're shaking so badly, but I put my car in drive and slowly pull forward. I watch the man, and he doesn't move, except for his head. He's watching me.

I put my car in reverse, brace myself and put the gas pedal to the floor. I slam into the gray van and my body thrusts violently forward. It shocks me. I yelp and my body goes stiff. The impact echoes like thunder and my tires screech loudly, but I don't take my foot off the gas. I'm at a standstill and look around out all of the windows. I don't see the figure any more.

The van suddenly speeds off and I have to take my foot off the gas quickly. I almost hit the car on the other side of the lot. The lights in the garage turn back on and I look at them dumbfounded. Why would he do that to me?

I don't want to stay in this dungeon anymore. I pull forward slowly and hear glass crunching under my tires. I speed down the twisting drive, with my back is completely off the seat, breathing quickly out of my mouth. The van is nowhere to be seen and I almost bust through the vehicle barrier gate, forgetting to brake. I fumble in my purse for my ticket and look in my rearview mirror. No one is behind me either. I can barely get the ticket in the slot. My hands are shaking horribly, but using both hands, I get the ticket in the right place.

I leave the garage, but pull over under a street light and completely break down. My body heaves as the sobs control me. I hold onto the steering wheel tightly and look straight ahead through my tears, but as they continue, I collapse, putting my head down.

After a while, my nose gets too stuffy to breathe, so I rummage through my bag to find a tissue. I blow my nose and then get my phone out. I'm dreading having to call the police again. I take a few deep breaths to regain my composure. Being hysterical on the phone won't get me anywhere.

Dispatch assures me that a cruiser's on the way, so I sit in my car to wait. I'm not calm, nor patient. I repeatedly lock the doors every few minutes and look out the windows erratically. Mr. Baker is certainly doing a number on my mental state.

42.

Officers Ackerman and Lavoie pull up behind me on the street and I take a deep breath, trying to appear composed, but my puffy, red eyes give away my true condition. These officers must be sick of me and I hate to think that they find me weak and fragile. I pull my shoulders back and meet them on the sidewalk.

"Hello, Dr. Cousineau. How are you tonight?" Officer Lavoie asks.

I roll my eyes and speak slowly, controlling my emotions. "I'm sorry to keep on contacting you, but I'm sure the parking garage that I was in, has cameras, so I had to report this." We survey the damage of my car. There's a large dent in the bumper and the tail light is broken, even the license plate is slightly mangled.

"You told dispatch that you were trapped in the parking garage?"

I nod, disheartened at the sight of my brand new car. "It was at the Convention Centre." I continue telling them the story and again, Lavoie writes everything down in his little notepad. I wonder how many notepads he fills in a week. My information alone should fill my very own notepad, I think.

"Did you get a license plate number?"

"No, it was too dark and I only saw the side of the van, never the back."

"And you didn't recognize the man in your window?"

I pause, feeling useless. "No. Again, it was too dark."

"You were right to call us, don't feel stupid. There are cameras in that parking garage and we might be able to pull a plate or get an ID of the person who did this to you."

"It has to be Mr. Baker again. I don't know why anyone else would go to all that trouble."

"Did you go to the courthouse to apply for the peace bond?" Officer Ackerman pipes up.

"No, I didn't get a chance."

He shakes his head. "You should've done it last week. They issue them every Friday." He walks back to the cruiser.

"I didn't know… I didn't think…" I'm going to fall apart again.

Officer Lavoie touches my arm gently. "Apply for one as soon as you can, but know that the warrant out for Mr. Baker's arrest supersedes the restraining order. He'll be arrested no matter what."

I nod, clutching my arms and staring down the street. If he doesn't do anything further to me, he'll be arrested for what they have on him back in Windsor. I'm trying to believe him, but it's difficult. He's eluded the police, thus far.

"Come on. Let's get you back in your car and get you home." He walks me to my car and points to the passenger side. "Did you get this scratch just now?"

"Oh. No, that was there the morning after you saw me for the brick incident. I had parked my car overnight, in front of my office and I noticed it first thing."

He opens the door for me and I sit inside my car. "Has that ever happened before? Any damage to your car or vandalism?" I see him eye my legs.

"No. Never."

"Why did you leave your car overnight?"

What do I say? I went flying? I had sex? I was almost raped? "I had a date and took a cab home."

He looks at me, but has no reaction. "I'll make a note of that, too. It may or may not be related, but we could add another mischief charge to Mr. Baker's list of offenses, if needed."

I nod. There are too many to count.

"We'll follow you to make sure you get inside your house safely."

"Thank you." I'm not going to debate the escort at all. "I appreciate your kindness."

"No problem, Doctor." He smiles and I notice a dimple, up near his eye.

I start the car and look in my rearview mirror. I see Officer Lavoie get into the driver side of the cruiser and talk to his partner. Officer Ackerman shakes his head and Officer Lavoie looks angry, saying something exaggerated, but within seconds, he starts the car.

Hesitantly, I pull out and the cruiser follows. I follow the rules of the road as I drive home. I don't think they'd give me a ticket if I waited at a stop sign for one second, instead of three, but I don't chance it.

My house is dark when I pull up and I park in my driveway. The officers pull up in front of my house and I wave to them when I get out of my car.

Officer Lavoie shouts to me from his cruiser, "You'll need to get your tail light fixed immediately."

I nod and hurry to my house. I quickly unlock my door, key in the alarm and close the door. From the living room window, I wave again and Officer Lavoie waves, but they stay put. This gives me great relief. I enter the code once more and make my way to bed.

43.

Knowing that the police were outside my house last night, helped me sleep comfortably. I convinced myself that they were staying all night, even though I assume they must've left at some point. It was better to believe. It eased my racing mind.

Dressed and ready for work, I eat oatmeal and open my Sex Project notebook.

Data Collection

Sample #12:

Seek persons who understand study & are willing to express inner feelings & experiences
- *Man, aged? (in his 20's). Student!*
- *Gorgeous, great smile, killer teeth.*

Describe experiences of phenomenon
- *I met him at the Psychology Symposium.*
- *We went for a drink at the hotel bar and talked psychology. He seemed very intelligent.*
- *Went to his hotel room.*
- *I felt that I was leading the foreplay and the actual act of intercourse.*

- *He climaxed almost immediately, apologized, but said he would be ready again in a couple of minutes. Incredible stamina!*
- *However, his roommates entered the room before we could try it again. I left.*
- *I did not climax.*

<u>Direct observation</u>
- *I was attracted to him sexually.*
- *I was attracted to him intellectually, at first.*
- *He was a very nice guy, sweet and attentive.*
- *He was very confident in the bar/downstairs.*
- *I think he was very inexperienced, maybe even a virgin.*

<u>Audio or videotape</u>
- *Almost! His roommates almost took a picture.*

<u>Data analysis</u>

<u>Classify & rank data</u>
- *1 out of 5*

<u>Sense of wholeness</u>
- *I pursued this sample out of the need to end my research on a positive note.*
- *The past samples weren't positive and I believed this sample was intellectually and physically stimulating.*
- *During the experience, I realized that I wanted to have sex just for the release, to feel better, for companionship.*

<u>Examine experiences beyond human awareness/ or cannot be communicated</u>
- *I felt stupid and unfulfilled.*
- *Repeated from past samples:*

- *I didn't get a 'flip flop' (again).*
- *I may be looking for experiences that I can't get with a one night stand.*

    I complete this entry quickly and don't dwell on the facts or the emotions that were involved. I just want to forget it ever happened. That was the final entry and the data collection is now complete for my Sex Project.
    "No more samples!" I state loudly, to cement the finality of it. I'm so relieved. I've accomplished so much these last few weeks, despite the fact that Mr. Baker came into my life. The most important step in the qualitative research process is the analysis of data. I really should summarize and interpret it, but I don't know if I have time to complete that process before tomorrow.
    Tomorrow! I'm so excited...and nervous about seeing Steve. What should I wear? Should I put my hair up or leave it down? I should wear the perfume he bought me. I wonder what his condo looks like. How am I going to seduce him?
    Random thoughts cheerfully fill my head, as I collect my things and head out the door, stopping only to reset the alarm. I'm light on my feet and almost skip to the car, but the sight of it instantly ends the thoughts and my stomach plunges.
    What a mess! The night comes back to me vividly and I feel nauseated. Why is Mr. Baker trying to scare me? Why doesn't he just attack me and get it over with? Why all the games? He's such a sadistic bastard. Poor Mrs. Baker. How did she end up marrying him and manage to be with him for so long?
    I drive to work and park in my usual spot, but walk to the corner coffee shop. The caffeine will really make the thoughts race, both positive and negative, but I need consolation, even if it's in a paper cup.
    In line, I see the back of a head that looks like Jack's. I go on tip-toe and step out of line in both directions. I think it's him. Flip flop. I exhale sharply. I'm giddy all of a sudden. *Relax!* I'm happy to see him, but I don't have to be thrilled about it. We left on bad terms the other day and I hope we can still be friends. I'm so glad I parked at the office, so he doesn't see my car.
    Jack orders and I keep my head down, thinking about whether I should say anything. He grabs his coffee and smiles at the barista, making a beeline for the door. His hair falls in his eyes, when he turns and he runs his fingers through it. He looks so handsome.
    When he's about to walk past me, I open my mouth to say something, but shut it when he finally notices me. He doesn't look pleased

to see me. His eyes turn down and his brows furrow. He just nods and keeps walking.

I feel dejected. My heart hurts. Why would he treat me that way? I've been so honest with him about Steve. I haven't led him on...I cringe. He kissed me first! All of those times! He can't hate me for that.

The barista looks at me blankly, "Can I help you?"

I step out of line and shake my head. I don't need a latte. I need to get back on track. Where's that excitement that I had this morning? I walk to work and dig deep, unable to replicate my earlier feelings.

44.

My last appointment of the day is Connie Baker. I haven't seen her since the whole incident. I'm nervous, but I also feel guilty. I haven't called to see if she was dealing with everything appropriately. Professionally, that would've been the right thing to do. It's been two weeks and she might've needed me. Then again, she's six. She probably hasn't even thought twice about me. I guess I'll see in a minute.

I'm sure Mrs. Baker is in the waiting room and I'm ashamed that I didn't even reach out to her. She was stuck in *my* bathroom in *my* office... But it was *her* husband that put her there. I quickly adjust my attitude. There's no blame involved. I'm not angry at her and I don't resent her. It's not her fault. I'm just feeling uncomfortable about the situation. I could've done so much more.

"Good morning, Mrs. Baker." I smile at her.

She stands up and puts her arms around me, holding onto me for what seems like a full minute. Connie stands beside us, watching.

"Hi, Dr. Cousineau. How are you?" Mrs. Baker asks when she releases me.

"I'm great. You?" I look at her and Connie.

She tilts her head from side to side. "We're ok." There's something behind her words and expression that says otherwise.

I wonder if Mr. Baker is bothering them too, but I can't ask that in front of Connie. "Well, let's get Connie in my office now, and the adults will talk after."

Mrs. Baker nods and I escort Connie into my office. She runs to the bookshelf and grabs *Snakes and Ladders*, looking at me for permission.

I close the door. "I like that game. Let's play."

Connie spreads the game board and the pieces on the table and I sit beside her.

"I'm blue and you can be red." She places them in the starting position.

"How's school?"

"Good." She rolls the dice and moves her game piece four spaces. She's goes up the ladder.

I look at her and smirk, "You're so far ahead of me! Who's your best friend?"

She looks at me and smiles. "You are."

I'm surprised by her response. "I am?" I roll and move five spaces.

"Yeah! We always play games when I'm here and we took that trip with my dad." She stops smiling and frowns.

A trip? I should talk to her mom to find out what she told Connie. "Have you seen your dad?

"He came to our house once. He broke the front window and he was yelling really loud. He hit my neighbour and I saw the blood. It was gross. The police came and I got to sit in the police car. It was neat."

"I bet." So, Mr. Baker has been troubling them, but Connie seems really happy and unaffected by everything that happened and keeps happening. "Do you miss your dad?"

She shakes her head. "No. He wasn't nice to me. He always yelled at me and..." She looks down at the dice in her hands.

"What's wrong?"

Connie whispers, "He used to spank me."

I nod and whisper back, "That wasn't very nice, was it?"

"No!" She hands me the dice. "It's your turn to roll."

We continue to play and chat about her life and when she finally wins the game, I give her a brand new colouring book and crayons to keep her busy while I talk to her mom.

"Connie is wonderful. She really seems to be adapting to change and getting over the incident." I take Mrs. Baker's hand and squeeze it. "You don't have anything to worry about. You're doing a great job."

"She's my everything. I don't have any complaints about her. Her dad, on the other hand, has been dreadful." She pulls her hand away and pulls a tissue from her purse, dabbing her eyes. "We moved into my mom's, after the incident and he showed up and broke a window, caused a commotion and broke our neighbour's nose. The cops came too late, of course." She blows her nose. "I can't make Connie move again. She's just made new friends and loves it at her new school. I don't know what to do."

"Did you file that restraining order or apply for a peace bond?"

"Yes, but what good does it do when the police don't come as soon as you call?"

I nod, empathetically. "The police have told me that the warrant is for parental abduction, which is a major priority for them to find Martin." It's weird calling Mr. Baker by his first name. "His information is on the CPIC database, which runs across Canada. They will find him," I repeat the words of Constable Lavoie, with much less conviction.

"I think he's been spying on me, too. I get these vibes…it's eerie. I'm scared, Dr. Cousineau."

I know the feeling. "Lock your doors, don't go out at night, and call the police immediately, if you have any concerns." I'm not dissipating her fears at all, but how can I?

"Thanks. I'm so sorry that you have deal with this."

"It's ok. The good news is that Connie doesn't need to see me anymore."

"Oh no! I couldn't do that to her. She loves her visits with you. My work pays for everything, so I'd really like to continue."

"That's great," I say, half-heartedly. The more they come here, the more chance that Mr. Baker may be lurking around. I feel awful for being so selfish, but the Baker's bring up horrible memories, too. What can I say? *No, you can't come here anymore!* "You can make your next appointment with Margie," I manage.

I peek my head into my office, "Come on, Connie. It's time to go."

Connie runs toward me and hugs my hips. "Thank you, Dr. C!"

I sigh and hug her back. This is why I do what I do. She's so little and helpless. It's the least I can do. I wave goodbye and trudge back into my office.

I travelled the whole spectrum of moods today. I'm so disappointed in myself. I can't even keep my emotions in check anymore. Happy. Excited. Scared. Sad. Dammit! Tomorrow is such an important day! I need to calm my mind. Obviously, I'm going to be a mess of nerves, but I feel I need some kind of support or help.

I look up Dr. Wylie in my address book. He was the therapist that helped me deal with my stress throughout university. Aunt Anna made the appointment, since she obviously couldn't handle my crying or couldn't console me, but Dr. Wylie showed me the tactics to calm me down and prepare me for stress.

Luckily, he still practices and when his receptionist offers me an appointment tomorrow at 5:00 p.m., I jump on it. I hesitate, realizing that the appointment is right before my date with Steve, but I confirm the appointment anyway. I'm positive that Dr. Wylie will help me sort some things out, but when our hour is over, will I be a pathetic mess or ready to take on the challenge? I enter the appointment into my schedule and sit back in my chair.

What about now? I can't go home and dwell on this by myself. I can't call Christine or Jack. God! There's no way I want to get into it with them. I scribble on a pad of paper, writing Steve's name in big, 3D letters.

Wait! Today's Tuesday. I could go to volleyball…I wince at the thought. It'd make me feel better, but what if Ryan's there? I draw a volleyball bouncing on the letter V. Do I chance it? What's the worst that could happen? Fuck Ryan! I'll ignore him and I'll be fine.

I say goodbye to Margie, who is finishing up some paperwork, and I drive home to grab some workout clothes and running shoes. I reset the alarm and head out the door. I'll have enough time to bang out some practice serves, if I hurry.

45.

After changing in the locker room, I head out to the gym, sign up on a team and grab a volley ball. There are a few people starting to gather, but I don't look too closely. I just start hammering the ball against the wall. The noise echoes across the gym, but I keep slamming it, serve after serve. I lose myself in the movement and the technique. It calms me and I begin to feel at peace.

I don't hear the whistle for the start of the game. I feel a hand on my arm, just as I'm about to serve again. It surprises and angers me at the same time.

"What?" I turn to see a woman staring at me. She pulls her hand away.

"The whistle blew and you're on my team."

I nod. Great. I have another female on my team. I hope she can at least bump a ball.

"I'm Gretchen."

I shake her hand silently and walk out to the court. Why introduce myself? I don't care to know these people. They just better be good.

I walk to the back, but turn abruptly and take position two on the front court. I really want to serve, but I don't want to control the game too early. It wouldn't be fair. My calves seem tight, so I hop up and down, trying to loosen up.

The guy who takes the position to serve seems athletic enough. He's long and lean, and his bright yellow Mizuno shoes stand out. So, he owns cutting-edge volleyball shoes, let's see if he can deliver.

He serves underhand and it sails over the net. It was mediocre. I used to serve like that when I was twelve. The other team scrambles to return the ball, but fail. They weren't ready.

"Point," I say to myself. Fuck. I don't want to win because the other team sucks. I want to earn it.

The ball rolls back to the Mizuno man and he serves it to the exact same spot on the other side. I could've predicted that.

This time, I hear a guy on the other team call, "Mine!" and he volleys it over the net.

I'm on it and bump it to another guy in our back court. He stumbles a bit, but is solid when he volleys it in the air.

"Mine!" I yell and step forward, but a female teammate gets in my way. I don't let her break my stride. We bump hips, but I steadily let the ball land on my forearms, perfectly re-bounding the ball up and over the net.

A girl on the other team shanks my return out of bounds.

"Point," I say to no one in particular and jump up and down with excitement.

Gretchen is helping the girl I bumped into, off the floor. They're both eyeing me disgustedly. I shrug and get ready for the next play. I just got us a point. It's the game, bitches.

The game goes on and I dominate the plays, racking up major points. My teammates are weak. They're amateurs, at best. I don't think they even played in high school. There should be rules for who plays in these house leagues. Seriously, if you're going to return the ball, do it, don't just stand there! Thankfully I'm here. They need me to win the game.

At one point, I spike the ball so perfectly, that the other team looks hopeless and inept. I think everyone is in awe. Steve would've been impressed by that spike. I smile and walk proudly to my position to wait for our next serve.

During the next play, I rush to the middle to bump a ball, without calling it, and my whole body knocks into Gretchen. She goes flying and lands on the floor, but I make contact and the ball returns to the other side.

"It's just a fucking game. Calm down," Gretchen says.

Her attitude angers me, but before I respond, I wait to make sure that the ball isn't in play. It's not. The other team misses it. Again. Then I glare at the Gretchen. "What's your problem?"

"You don't have to be so aggressive."

"You don't want to win?" Who says that? Volleyball is all about aggressiveness.

"This is supposed to be fun. Cool it."

I give her a dirty look and turn my back on her, getting into position. What a whiner!

Gretchen executes a half-assed serve, barely getting the ball over the net, and it's returned quickly. I jump and powerfully swat it back. The other team thinks it's out of bounds, so they don't rush to get it. It's in.

"We win." I say and turn around to high five my teammates, but they're already walking off the court. I shrug and sit down on a bench, sipping from my water bottle. It was a great game, even if I did all the work.

Volleyball is such great therapy for me. I feel so much better. Still, I keep my head down, hoping that if Ryan is here, he won't see me. I'll get worked up again if he approaches me. I don't need that hassle right now. I need to keep positive, with Steve and my goals on my mind. I really should play volleyball tomorrow before my date with him. What a great idea.

"Colleen."

Nervously, I look up and breathe a sigh of relief. It's just the volleyball convener. "Hey, James. How are you?" I've known him for years. He's been organizing the games since university and Steve and I used to go for a beer with him on occasion.

"I'm great. Did you have a good game?"

"The best. I'm solid."

"Um..." he coughs. "Your teammates think you're being too aggressive."

My temper flares up and I stand in front of him. "What?"

James takes a step back. "I know. I know. I'm sorry."

"Was it Gretchen who said something? Or that other girl? I didn't mean to knock her on her—

"It doesn't matter who said it." He rubs his balding head. "I know you're tough. You're a great player, but these players are here for fun. It's house leagues."

I stare blankly at James with my hands on my hips. I don't know what to say. I'm furious, but I can't take it out on him.

"Do you think you can go easy on them?"

I want to scream. I grip my hands so tightly that my nails dig into my palms and look to the courts and then, back at James. I start shaking my head and bend down to pick up my water bottle and towel. "I'm done." I walk toward the locker room.

"Come on, Colleen. You don't have to go."

"Fuck this, James." I'm acting like Steve.

I turn abruptly to go into the women's change room and bump into someone. I don't look to see who it is, I just try to get around the person, but the person grasps my arm.

"Let me go!" I use a self-defense technique I learned and break the person's grip.

"Ow! Hey! Colleen!"

It's Ryan. He looks incredible and I blush, remembering his extremely muscular, naked body.

"Dammit! I'm sorry. I have to go." I look at James and start to walk away. I'm so embarrassed.

"What's wrong?" He grabs my hand and stops me.

I throw my arms up in the air. "My teammates think I'm too aggressive! James wants me to go easy on them." I roll my eyes in exasperation.

"Are you kidding me?" He bitterly steps toward James. "Really? Come on, James."

I grab Ryan's arm now. I don't want to start a fight. "Stop. It's ok. I'll just go home."

"No, you're not. You can play on my team."

"No. No, it's ok."

"Come on, Superstar. I dare you not to go easy on me." He smiles and winks.

All I can think about is kissing him in his jacuzzi…and his pool table! I blush again, looking down.

"What's wrong? Don't have it in you?" He dares.

"Fine. Let's play." Anything to get my mind off of that night.

"Be nice out there," James says.

"Fuck that," Ryan says with a smile.

Thankfully, there's no time to reminisce. The game starts immediately and just like our first game together, Ryan and I are a dynamic duo. We know where each other is on the court and he's better on the long passes and I have everything short. We rule the court and the plays and the game is over quickly. It was strenuous and so much fun. Just what I needed.

"We make a good team, Superstar." Ryan walks up to me with both hands held up. I slap them with my hands.

"Yes, we do."

He puts his arm around me and at first, I want to brush it off, but then I relax into it. It feels good. Very comforting.

"Let's go to Hoops for a beer."

Not a good idea. "Nah, I have to go home. I work tomorrow."

"I work tomorrow, too. It's just one beer."

I could potentially go for one beer, but I don't know if my will power will hold out. I know I'm pretty fragile and a warm body would feel so good right now. I want to feel safe and wanted, but, of course, I'm seeing Steve tomorrow! I can't be with Ryan that way! I can't seduce Steve when I have memories and…sexual pains of Ryan from the night before.

"No, I really can't."

"Superstar, you're killing me. I think about you all the time and now, you're right in front of me. I'm begging you to come with me for a beer." He holds up his two-finger Boy Scout salute. "No strings, I promise."

This time, I'm strong. I smile and shake my head, taking his hand down. "I'm sorry, Ryan."

He looks sad. "Ok. Let me walk you out, at least."

"I just have to grab my bag first." I head to the locker room and take my things out of the locker. I pack up and attempt to tidy myself in front of the bathroom mirror. I almost want to go for a beer with Ryan. Almost. He's such a sweet guy, but I can't do it to Steve. My research is over. Done! Finished! I need to see if it was all worth my efforts.

Outside, we walk to my car and I hug my coat tightly around me. The sweat in my hair gets chilled instantly and I shiver.

"My car is across the lot. I'm fine to get there on my own."

"I'm a gentleman. Please let me see you to your car."

He says stuff like that and I swoon, but I just shrug, trying to ignore him and fish the keys out of my bag.

I unlock my door and Ryan opens it for me.

"You're not going anywhere," he says.

I look at him. He's being really pushy. "Ryan, we've been over this. I can't do this—"

"Your tires are slashed." He points to the backend of my car. "And the rest of your car doesn't look too good either."

"What?" I rush to look at the tire, bend down and find a six-inch gash at the top of the tire. My heart races immediately. Mr. Baker. "Oh no…" I lightly touch the outline of the slashed rubber.

"Do you have any enemies, Colleen?"

"My passive volleyball teammates?" I try to make a joke, but I think I might be sick.

"Colleen?"

I exhale loudly. "It's a long story, Ryan."

"Maybe you can fill me in, while I drive you home." He offers me a hand to help me stand up.

I take it and realize that I have to accept his offer. "Ok."

It's a short drive, so I give him directions and present him with the condensed version. "A couple of weeks ago, my patient and I were abducted at knifepoint by the patient's father and we ended up in Windsor. We think he was going to sneak us across the border to Detroit, but he was…stopped." I don't need to tell him about Jack.

"Stopped?"

I pause, trying to think of the easiest answer: "We got away."

"Jesus, Colleen." He reaches over and touches my arm. "That's crazy. Are you ok?"

"Yes, I'm fine…Now." I look out the window. I don't need to be reminded of all of this. "The abductor, Mr. Baker…has been doing stupid things lately."

"You mean he wasn't caught?"

"Nope."

"Do you think he slashed your tires?"

"Yup."

"Fuck. What else has this asshole done?"

"He threw a brick through my office window." I say it like it's an everyday occurrence.

"Holy fuck. Why haven't the police done anything?"

I shrug. "They can't find him."

"And why is he doing all of this to you?"

"I don't know. He's pissed, I guess."

"I guess." He pauses and turns the car down my road. "Are you sure you're ok? You can stay at my house tonight."

Seriously? I look at him with a small smile.

He takes his eyes off the road and looks at me, then quickly glances back at the road and back at me, smiling. "Ha ha. No, seriously. I have a spare room."

"No, it's ok. I have a house alarm."

"Damn, you really are a strong woman. Any other chick would be reeling in fear." He touches my hand. "You're amazing, Colleen."

I'm not so amazing. "This is me." I point. "The gray brick with the short hedges."

"I'm not a criminal lawyer, but I can do the job, if you need my services." He parks in front of my house and turns to me, reaching for my hands. "You still have my number?"

His hands are hot and his touch tingles through my body. I just want to hold him close and put my head on his chest. Instead, I pull my hands back. "Yes, I have your number. Thank you for the ride." I pick up my bag. "I'm glad you were there to drive me home." I avoid his eyes and reach for the door handle.

"Not yet, Superstar. My services are not quite finished." He tugs my coat. "Hold tight. I'll walk you to your door."

"You don't have—"

"Stay there," he commands.

I watch him get out of the car and walk around to my side to open the door. I get out and we walk in silence to the front door. I unlock it, stepping in to shut the alarm off.

"Thanks again—"

"I'm coming in." He has his hand on the door. "I'm going to make sure that no one is in here."

"Ryan..." I'm actually relieved that he's going to do this. I don't say another word.

He disappears and I wait patiently in the kitchen. I can hear his footsteps above me and I know he's in my bedroom. It's strange to have him in my house, especially where I sleep. It's very intimate. I begin to think about Ryan's arms around me. I ache for that kind of affection. Ryan would oblige, I'm sure.

A couple minutes later, I hear him walk downstairs and then, he appears back in the kitchen.

"You didn't strike me as a slob, Superstar."

"Pardon me?" Jack hinted at that before, but never came out and said that I was a slob. Is it really that bad?

"Your bedroom is in desperate need of a deep cleaning." He pulls out my pink lacy bra from behind his back.

I blush and run to grab it from him. He's too quick. He holds it above his head.

"Give it to me!" I squeal. I jump up and barely reach his hands.

"Fine." He hands it to me, but doesn't let go when I reach for it.

I look into his eyes. I forgot that they were brown. I thought they were blue, like Jack's. He releases the bra and I squish it up, hiding it behind my back.

"It's all clear, but I could stay if it would make you feel better. Your bed is big enough for the both of us." He takes a step closer to me.

I think for a half a second, step backwards and force a laugh. "I don't think so, Ryan." I see Steve tomorrow. It wouldn't be right.

"No, really. Your bed's big enough. I laid down in it to make sure. It's very comfy."

"What?" He was in my bed? Why does that sound so alluring?

"I'm kidding." He walks toward the door. "I can't take anymore rejection!" He winks and opens the door. "Call me anytime. I'm here for you, whenever you need me."

"Thank you, Ryan."

He smiles. "Turn your alarm on."

I watch him walk away for a few seconds, then close the door and key in my alarm code. I peek out the window and watch his car pull away from the curb. I'm happy that my mental state has returned to normal and I'm thinking clearly again. That was a close one.

46.

The next morning, I take a cab to work and remember to call roadside assistance when I get into my office. I ask the company to pick up my car, fix the tail light and anything else that needs to be repaired. Finally, I ask them to deliver the car to my office. I should've asked them to detail it, too, but it's still as clean as when I first got it. No need to go overboard. I just want everything to be perfect for tonight.

There's a spring in my step and my mind is clear. I start straightening my desk, placing my pencils in the container, but in no particular direction. Erasers up or erasers down, it doesn't matter. I smile to myself.

"What are you grinning about?" Margie asks when she drops a file onto my desk, stopping to lean on the edge.

"Nothing."

"You're fibbing. What's going on with you?"

"I have a date with Steve tonight." I can barely contain my excitement.

"Steve?" She asks incredulously. "You've been going on dates with other men. I thought you were moving on."

How do I explain my Sex Project to Margie? "They were just casual dates. Nothing developed from them. I was just buying time until Steve was ready to see me." I could never tell her what I've been doing. "We're going to talk about reconciling." I clap my hands together.

"Wow. That's so good," she says slowly. "I'm happy for you."

"Thanks! Carpe diem! Let's get the patients rolling!"

The morning proceeds slowly and I keep watching the clock, willing it to be quicker. At lunch, my cell phone rings, and I see that it's Christine. I answer it immediately.

"Hey!"

"Don't *hey* me! You haven't been returning my calls!" She screeches in my ear.

"I'm so sorry. I'm an awful friend. I was busy with work and life and—Guess what?"

"What?" She laughs, forgiving me easily.

"I have a date with Steve tonight!"

"You do?" She, too, is disbelieving. "I thought you were going to wait?"

"It was two weeks on Sunday. I did what you said and kissed his butt. I didn't like it, but I did it and he called me right back and I'm going to his condo tonight!" I dance around my desk, shaking my hips.

"You're really going to do it? The whole seducing thing?"

"Yes! That's what all the research was for." Why does she sound doubtful? "I'm so ready to get him back."

"Oh."

I stop dancing. "What do you mean 'oh'? I thought you'd be happy for me?"

"I am...I just thought that you were going to move on."

"Why would you think that?"

"It's just that... I don't know... I thought... Jack is totally hot for you!" She finally blurts out.

"What? How do you know that?"

"On our date, all he did was talk about you. He talked about the dinner parties you had and your amazing culinary skills. He gushed about how sweet you are and how he admires your dedication to fitness... He didn't stop. He's got it bad for you, Ci-Ci."

I shake my head, trying not to listen. "I know that he likes me, I just didn't know that you knew."

"Yup, he wasn't interested in me at all. Not one, single bit. It was actually quite the disappointment. He's so hot."

"It doesn't matter. I've already told him that I'm not interested and he knows that I want Steve back." This is killing my happy buzz.

"He told me all that and he also told me that he thinks you're making a big mistake," she says softly. "And so do I."

"What? I don't need this from you, Christine!" I want to hang up the phone.

"Come on, Ci-Ci, Steve is a cheater and a narcissistic prick. You can do so much better."

I feel sick. "Why are you telling me this?"

There's a moment of silence, then she whispers, "Steve hit on me on Saturday."

I'm definitely going to throw up. "What?"

"I was out with my work friends and ran into him at the Blue Iguana. He was very inappropriate," she pauses. "He told me that I was beautiful and that he always wanted to fuck me. When he grabbed my ass and wouldn't take no for an answer, I signaled to Ted, a bouncer I know, to throw Steve out. It was awful."

"No, no, no..." She can't be telling me this now.

"Ci-Ci, you don't need to like Jack, but you need to realize that Steve's not a nice guy. You should move on."

Every time Christine says something more, the anger inside of me increases.

"You can do so much better than Steve. He's—"

"Stop! Just stop it!" I explode, "It's bad enough that you can't take rejection from a guy who likes me, instead of you, but you have to continue to put me down and tell me how awful my husband is?"

"Ci-Ci, no, I wouldn't—"

"I don't want to hear it! Stay out of my life!" I hang up my phone and storm out of the office, out the front door. I ignore Margie's stare and charge to the sidewalk.

I take a few deep inhales and forcefully exhale them out. Christine's jealous. Plain and simple. She can't find happiness with casual sex, so she wants me to be miserable with her. Is it so unbelievable that a hot guy likes me? It probably killed her to find that out. Her poor, precious ego! Wow! She really isn't God's gift to men! I kick at a rock on the sidewalk and it flies onto the road.

And to make up a story like that! Steve would never hit on her. He always called Christine a slut! She basically did all the guys on the volleyball team and the football team! He'd never touch her. Why is she being such a bitch? I walk down to the corner, crossing my arms to keep warm.

After a few more deep breaths, I walk back into the office. "I needed some fresh air," I state plainly to Margie and close the door to my office, not waiting for her reaction.

Can I please have a do-over morning? I wish I didn't take Christine's call. I might not have even come to work today. I place my arms on my desk and drop my forehead down onto them, closing my eyes.

Margie nudges me a few seconds later, "Are you ok?"

"Sure," I say uncertainly, sitting up straight.

"Are you ready for your afternoon?"

No, but I smile and lie, "Absolutely!"

The afternoon is slower than the morning and during my last appointment, I remember that I have an appointment with Dr. Wylie.

"Shit!" I say louder than I should have.

My patient, Sydney looks up at me from her book, 'What It Is to Be Me' and points, covering her mouth.

Ironically, Sydney had Asperger's, and has a tendency to swear, so I fish a toonie out of my purse and throw it on the table. "I'm sorry that I swore. It won't happen again. The toonie goes into your swear jar at home."

She nods her head and goes back to her book.

What happened to my compassion? My practice is suffering because I'm so caught up in my own problems. I know I should see Dr. Wylie, but what if he's negative and questions the reconciliation? I know what I want. I don't need help. No more distractions. No more negativity. I need to focus. But how?

I say goodbye to Sydney, cancel my appointment with Dr. Wylie and send Margie home. I turn off the lights and lie on the floor in corpse pose. I focus on my breathing. I slow it down, constricting the air flowing within my throat and breathe through my nose, making a loud, ocean-like noise. I feel calmer. Now, what do the yoga instructors say?

It's my thoughts that determine whether my words and actions will be positive or negative. Whatever I want in my life, I want it because I love it. Think about what I love. Think about what I love. Think about what I love.

47.

Steve's new condo is near Dufferin and Queen and when I pull up, I'm disappointed with the façade and location. It's shabby, outdated and it looks out of place among the industrial type buildings around it. Listen to me! *Stop criticizing!* He needs to be complimented and praised. I'm a changed woman!

Shoot! I'm also very early. He can't think that I'm the same old practical Colleen! I look around and drive across the street, to park in a convenience store parking lot. I'll sit here for a few minutes to wait. I may even be fashionably late! I giggle and sit back in my seat.

It's a good thing he won't recognize my car. It looks brand new again. I'm so happy that it's fixed. The automobile club did a great job on it. I can't even see the scratch along the side or the dent in the bumper anymore. More memories physically erased. I wish something like that would work with my mind.

My phone suddenly beeps and I see a text from Ryan: *"Hey, Colleen. I had a visit from a strange dude today. He was a large guy, black eyes and reeked of booze. He asked my secretary if I had been to Windsor in the last month. This may be your Mr. Baker. Call me."*

What the hell? I dial Ryan's number immediately.

"Hi, Superstar. How are you?"

No time for formalities. "Hey. What happened?"

"I was in my office and I heard this guy asking my secretary questions about Windsor, so I step out and find this ugly mother fucker. He didn't take my hand, he just sized me up and said, 'You're not him'. He left immediately after, without saying another word."

"That's weird." What does that mean? Did Mr. Baker think that Ryan was Jack? Was he looking for Jack? "Do you really think it was him?"

"Yeah, after I called you, I searched the most wanted list on the Toronto Police Services website and found Martin Baker's mug shot. It was definitely him. I thought you should know. I'm going to report it to the police, to be safe. The police need to know what they're up against. This is bullshit."

"Thanks, Ryan." I'm so worked up now. Did Mr. Baker follow me to Steve's too? I frantically look out my window.

"I also wanted to tell you something else."

"What's that?" Oh no...

"Remember when we talked about our university days and I told you about the douchebag on my volleyball team? The one who had the ego, thought he was a god on the court and cheated on his goddess of a girlfriend."

"Of course. You couldn't remember his name."

"Yeah," he pauses. "I remember it now. I looked at my old volleyball team picture last night after I got home from seeing you."

"Who is it?" My stomach starts turning.

"Steve Bellaccicco."

How did I know he was going to say that? I slam my head back against the headrest a few times. Bad timing, Ryan! Bad, bad timing!

"Are you ok?"

"Of course."

"Colleen, I looked him up and know that he's your husband or your ex-husband," another pause. "It would've been quicker to learn that information, if you had taken his last name," he laughs awkwardly.

I stay quiet, closing my eyes. I will not cry.

"Listen, I know that you're going through some stuff and maybe trying to move on, so I'm sorry if this hurts you. I could've kept it to myself, but if it were me, I'd want to know. Perhaps it will close some doors for you and help you move on."

I take a deep breath. "Thanks for letting me know, Ryan. You're a good guy." My voice wavers a little.

"That's the kiss of death right there. I'm a good guy."

"Come on, you know what I mean."

"Yes, unfortunately I do, but I want to reiterate that I'm here for you, if you need me."

"I appreciate that."

"Stay safe, Superstar. I'm worried about you."

"Goodbye, Ryan."

I drop my phone into the cup holder and bang my head back against the headrest again. Why now? I'm trying to open the door, not close it. I want to work it out with Steve, not go in there with my guard up.

First Jack, then Christine and now Ryan. Who else thinks they know my husband? Should I believe everybody and just give up?

The anxiety is sitting heavy on my chest. The pressure scares me. I feel like I'm going to lose control. I need to calm down. Breathe.

Ok. Ok. This doesn't mean a thing. He sowed his oats in university. So what? Most men do. He ended up marrying me when we were out of school. He knew that I was *the* one. I shake my head at my idiotic thoughts. We exchanged vows and he loved me. I check my face in the rearview mirror and pat my head absentmindedly. You can't fake love. He still loves me. We just lost our way. He needs to be reminded how much he loves me. I'm the perfect woman now. I'm not a workaholic anymore and I'm not even a perfectionist neat freak. I'm a normal woman. He'll love me even more when he realizes this.

My heart's beating faster now, excited to see Steve. Everything I did for research comes down to this moment. I'll be able to please him in the way that he wants and needs. I clap my hands together like a child. I'm sure that his desires are plenty. He's all man and I'm ready to prove that I can be the woman he desires. The entire package. All of this research that I've done has taken me a long way. This is it. The big payoff. I will show him. My confidence is back. I can do this.

I park in a visitor's spot, outside his condo and march into the building with confidence. The door is locked and there's an intercom on the wall. I quickly scan the names on the list and find *S. Bellaccicco*. I punch the digits into the machine and look up into the camera. Is he looking at me? I pull my shoulders back and smile.

After a few seconds, a loud buzzing noise resonates from the door and I tug on the handle and it opens. I guess he could see me.

The elevator takes me up to the seventeenth floor and when the doors open, I take a deep breath and step out to find his apartment.

Before I knock, I take off my coat and put it over my arm. I pull down the vee neck on my dress and try to push my breasts up and together. The bra helps a lot with lift. I finally straighten my dress and pat down my hair. This is it!

48.

After a few knocks, Steve opens the door, with a beer in his hand, and his eyes go directly to my cleavage. "Wow! You look great."
That's a good sign. He's changed a lot though. His hair is receding and seems very thin on top. It looks like he's gained some weight, too. But he's *my* Steve. He looks very handsome in his business shirt and light blue tie.
"Thanks, Steve. You look fantastic too."
He stumbles backwards and walks away from the door. How many drinks has he had already? I watch him walk away and I look at the open door. I shrug, close the door and lock it. See! He already feels comfortable around me. I put my coat and purse on a chair and walk into the condo.
His apartment would be a decent place, if it wasn't a complete mess. Beside the couch, is a pile of clothes, consisting of button down shirts and sweaters. I think they're dirty. Steve suddenly pulls off his tie and his shirt and throws it into the pile. Yup, it's the dirty pile. He untucks his white undershirt and pulls it over his gut.
"Do you want a beer? I don't have any of that girly shit wine."
"Sure. Beer sounds good."
He leaves the room and I look around. Everything looks dirty. The couch has stains and crumbs all over it, the rug has a large, reddish circle under the coffee table, and the walls have been touched up, but not painted. He has a dining table, but it's covered with newspapers and dirty dishes. The rings from wet glasses on the wooden top make my skin crawl. It was beautiful table.
Steve comes back, already chugging his beer and waves mine in front of me.

"Thanks." I twist the cap off and take a sip. He throws his cap onto the floor and makes his way to the dingy couch. I want to chug my beer to get some confidence, but I shake the urge. I don't need that crutch.

"Your message was interesting," he says. "I'd like to hear more. You said something about me being right." Steve takes another gulp of his beer and belches loudly.

"Yes." I sit down beside him and muster up all of my flirting and seducing skills. I let my knee touch his and toss my hair back. "You were right all along. When you left me, you told me that I was too organized and methodical. You were right. I didn't make time for you."

Steve sits back and takes another swig of beer. "I like the sound of this."

I smile and put my beer on the table in front of us. "My focus was on work and that was wrong. I needed to focus my energy on you. You left me because I didn't please you, because I didn't make you happy in the bedroom. I'm here to change all that." It's hard to admit to these things. I'm not convinced that these traits are negative

He tips his bottle upside down. "Hey, are you almost finished your beer? I'm done and I need another?"

"I can go get you one," I say slowly. He didn't say anything about my proclamation.

"It's in the fridge."

"Oh. Ok." That's his reaction?

I walk into the kitchen and am disgusted by the mess. Dirty dishes in the sink, moldy bread on the counter and cases of empty beer bottles piled on the floor. My house is messy, but this is borderline condemned. I shake my head. I can't be critical of him. He's living alone. It's the bachelor's life. He just needs a woman's influence again. My influence.

I grab two more beers and go back to the living room. I'm disappointed to find him watching a football game on television. I'll just have to distract him.

I sit down beside him, a little closer than before, and hand him his beer.

"Cheers," I say.

Without looking, Steve taps my glass and he suddenly explodes, "Interception! Oh my God! Go! Go! Go! Touchdown!"

Should I keep talking? This is so awkward. We've known each other for years, but I feel like a stranger. Doesn't he want to talk about us? Why did he invite me here?

"So... How do you feel about what I've been saying?"

"Unbelievable!" He looks from me, to the television and mutters, "Yeah! Yeah! What you've been saying." He looks back at the game. "That was awesome!!"

He's still watching the game! What's going on here? He doesn't care! Holy fuck. This is falling to pieces.

"Good. It's a commercial. Now, what did you say?"

This is not how I pictured things. I have ninety to one hundred and twenty seconds to state my case. "I'm apologizing for my behavior during our relationship. What do you think about that?" I'm starting to think that my behaviour didn't lead to the demise of our marriage.

"I'm glad you've come to your senses. You were ridiculous. I never felt like I could do anything right around you, even sex."

I can't believe that I did that to him. Poor Steve. "I'm sorry that I made you feel that way." I put my hand on his thigh.

He looks down at my hand. "You're sorry, eh?" He smiles and raises his eyebrows. "How are you going to make it up to me?"

Does he mean sex? I get excited. I can do that. That's why I'm here!

Placing my beer on the coffee table, I smile at him and get on all fours. I don't take my eyes off of him as I crawl between his knees. I unzip his pants and start tugging them down. He lifts his hips to help. Over top of his underwear, I gently rub the length of him.

"Is this a good start?"

"Yes. Absolutely."

I start kissing his stomach and pull his underwear down slightly to lick his hips. I breathe my hot breath onto his growing erection. My hands massage his inner thighs and make their way up to the band of his underwear again. I pull it away from his skin and I lick the tip of his hardness. I rotate my tongue all the way around the head.

"For Christ's sakes!" He yells.

I jump back, letting go of everything.

"Catch the ball, you mother fucker!"

He's watching the game? How can he do that while I'm doing *that*?

"Sorry, babe. What a great play! You can keep going. It's a commercial again." He drinks the rest of his beer in one last swig.

Oh. Ok. Maybe I should do a strip tease instead? That might keep his attention. No, I'll keep going. It's difficult to stay focused, but I'll finish what I started. I lick the length of him, slowly and deliberately and he gets hard immediately. This gives me hope.

"Grab my junk."

What? Junk? Does he mean...? Ok. I hesitantly take my fingers and fondle underneath, while I take the entire length of him into my mouth.

"Squeeze it."

Oh. Ok. I do.

"That's it. Keep doing it. It feels good."

Sex talk. He knows how to sex talk. Why didn't he do it before?

Steve grabs my head and starts pushing me in a rhythm that is too much for me. The entire length of him fills my mouth and hits the back of my throat. I feel like I'm going to gag. I feel my teeth scrape him. I'm going to bite him! I fight the strength of his hands, wrenching my neck, and pull away. I take his hands in mine. "Let's continue this is the bedroom."

He looks at the television. "Yeah, I guess I can record the game." He picks up the controller, presses some buttons and then turns it off.

"Let's go, beautiful." He picks up my full beer and takes me by the hand, leading me down the hall. He releases my hand and I watch him put his hand down the back of his underwear and scratch his bare ass. I keep following him, second-guessing my motivation. If my research taught me anything, I know I should be leaving now.

His bedroom is like the rest of the house. Messy. There's a pizza box and empty beer cans on the floor. It's like a frat house. I wonder when his bed sheets were last cleaned. I shake my head. I can't think like that. Relax. It's not an issue.

"I'll sit here, like on the couch, and you can finish what you were doing." He lies back, resting on his elbows. "You were always good at blowjobs."

I continue standing, confused. "I've never done that to you before."

"What? Come on. You did it all the time."

"No, Steve," I say quietly. "I've never given you a...blowjob."

"My mistake, but don't let that ruin this moment." He stands up and starts kissing my neck. "You want to get back together? I like that idea."

I don't understand how he could not remember that I never gave him a blowjob. How many women has he been with? I feel his breath in my ear and it tickles.

"I've always loved you. Colleen." His hands travel up the sides of my body.

My heart melts. That's all I've ever wanted to hear.

"I love your gorgeous body and your sexy legs. You're so hot."

I take a hold of his shoulders and push my hips into his. "Oh, Steve. You were so sexy in university and such a jock on the court." I grab his ass and squeeze hard. "You were so good. You taught me so much." I kiss his neck.

He pushes me back a little. "Yeah, but you didn't need me. You were so fucking good at everything and such a princess," he snorts. "You even won that award that I was supposed to get." He frowns like a child.

He's pissed. Does he resent me? "Forget that." I slide my hands down to his underwear and run my hand over his package, but he is flaccid.

"I love you. You took care of me and provided for us, while I finished school. That meant everything to me." I start rubbing harder, trying to make him erect.

"Then you fucking started making more money than me, working more hours, and left me alone."

Oh. He's bitter. I take my hand away. "Steve, come on. None of that matters. We can move on from here." He has to remember all the good times.

Steve starts laughing and I back away from him. "Move on? First, you embarrass me in university and get the award *and* the scholarship that I wanted. Then, you have to get a fucking PhD! You're fucking incredible. You just had to keep shooting higher and higher and show me up."

He's jealous of me? I didn't know it was a contest all this time? I'm shocked at how self-centered he actually is and I'm surprised that I never recognized it.

"God, I was too good for you. Do you know how many women wanted me? And I stupidly chose you. Smart, little Colleen. Pretty, little Colleen." He starts slurring his words. "You fucking had it all! The man and the legend, and you gave it away to be a shrink! You couldn't stay at home and pay attention to me. You had to have a fucking career and belittle me."

"Is that why you cheated on me?" I've had enough of his idiotic rant.

He steps back. "I didn't cheat." He puts his hand up in defense.

I roll my eyes. "I know everything, Steve. You don't have to lie." He's so pathetic. "We're past that now."

"Ok. Yeah, I did cheat on you! All the fucking time! I only married you because you were the trophy wife. Gorgeous, smart and high class. I had a reputation to uphold."

I feel like I've been smacked in the face. Deep down, I always knew, but the confession still hurts.

"You're too smart and too fucking good for anyone. I started banging chicks in university, when you were studying. Then I banged my secretary and other women in the office. Fuck, you had no clue. You were too busy being good at everything."

"Did you ever love me?"

He pauses to think. "Maybe... I don't know. I just know that our marriage helped me get where I am. When we had those dinner parties with my bosses, they thought I was the cat's meow. I had a stable marriage with a knockout, psychologist wife. Now that I've moved up in the company, it doesn't matter anymore."

"You didn't leave me because I was horrible in bed?"

"Colleen, I pity fucked you. I was getting laid all the time by different broads. I even fucked your slutty cousin on our wedding night. She was always hot for me."

"You're a bastard!" I storm to the front door and grab my coat and purse.

"What? No blowjob?"

He catches up to me, pulls my arm to stop me and then, pushes me against the wall. I can't move.

"Let me go!"

"You know you want me. You love me. Let's have one more romp for old times." He forces his lips on mine and he grabs my breast.

"Get off of me!" I knee him as hard as I can between his legs.

"Arghh!" He groans and falls to the floor.

"Asshole," I whisper, and when I open the door, it hits him in the head.

He curses, but I ignore him and slam the door shut.

I burst into tears and blindly make my way to the elevator. How could I have been so wrong about him? Why couldn't I see the real Steve?

There were signs all along that I just chose not to see. I'm so stupid! All that research! I was sleeping with all of those men for no reason and I could've been happy with any of them. Well, some of them.

Inside the elevator, I lean against the back wall and wipe my eyes, but the tears keep falling. I challenged my whole morality for Steve. I was promiscuous. All for what? I've got notches on my bedpost and did some pretty explicit things. I groan. That wasn't me!

I hurry to my car and once inside, I close my eyes and try to stop crying. Oh my God! I slap my forehead. Jack! He was so right about Steve! He was only trying to help, to make me see, and he was so sweet. Why didn't I listen to him? I let all of my resistance and ignorance hurt any relationship that we could've had. I've completely burnt that bridge now. My stupid plan! What have I done?

My tears slow down and I start to drive back home. I have to call Christine and apologize. I didn't believe her either! She's been my best friend for years and she's the person that I should've believed. But I know she'll forgive me... She has to! Maybe she'll come stay the night. I need her.

At the last second, I pull into the liquor store parking lot. This is a wine kind of a night. I check out my reflection and see that my eyes are puffy and red, but at least I've stopped crying. I blow my nose and head into the store.

I roam the aisles, looking at all the different varieties of wine. I laugh at the irony, as I choose the *Fat bastard* Chardonnay. Steve really was disgusting. What was I thinking? He's a fat, balding bastard.

I turn to walk to the counter, but spy a *Zandvliet My Best Friend* Sauvignon blanc. I grab it and smile. Two bottles ought to do it for me and Christine.

Back in my car, I don't feel sad or alone anymore. It's strange. I don't even think I'm hurt about Steve. I was hanging onto Steve for whatever reason, but maybe deep down I knew that he wasn't for me. I feel lighter. The weight of the whole absurd plan has been lifted. My mind is suddenly clear and I have true hope for my future. I smile. Good things can only happen from now on.

I drive home quickly and almost dance up the walkway to my front door. I put the wine down on the porch, to unlock the door, and step one foot inside to key in the alarm code. As I pick up the wine, I notice a figure standing on my front lawn. It's dark, but when my eyes adjust, I know that the large, menacing figure is Mr. Baker.

He's staring at me, not moving and my heart starts racing. It's going to jump out of my chest. He's about a hundred feet away from me. I could reach out and touch him. What's he doing here? I need to lock the door, but I can't get my feet to move.

In what seems like slow motion, Mr. Baker takes a sip from his flask, without taking his eyes off of me. That small distinguishing action causes all of the horrific memories to flood back into my mind. It propels me into survival mode.

I bring my foot into the house and with one shaking hand, I slam and lock the door. It's a struggle to punch in the alarm code, to turn it back on. The alarm beeps negatively at me. I try again and again. Finally, I drop the wine and it crashes to the ground, soaking my feet. Fuck! What's the code?

END OF BOOK TWO

Made in the USA
Charleston, SC
20 July 2015